CREDO'S LEGACY

Book Two of the Alex Wolfe Mystery Series

ALISON NAOMI HOLT

Denabi Publishing

CONTENT

CHAPTER 1

I sat across from a man who had a white smile painted on his face. White and red circles surrounded charcoal grey eyes that misted over as he vehemently denied kidnapping his ex-wife's latest boyfriend. As he spoke, he fiddled with the curly orange wig he held in his lap.

We were sitting under the stands of the Pima County Rodeo Grounds in a changing room reserved for the clowns. His eyes shifted between the detective's badge attached to my belt and the Glock holstered next to it. I wasn't surprised when he threw the wig violently against the wall and stood up.

I sat back and crossed one leg over the other. "We're not done, Carl. Sit down."

"Am I under arrest or what?" He glared down at me, his hands resting on his hips, his legs spread apart, ready for a fight. I almost smiled at the grown man in clown paint wearing blue jeans four sizes too big. When I looked up and saw tears in his eyes, I got back to business.

"Carl, listen. I investigate these kinds of cases every day. I realize you and your ex are going through a messy custody battle, and I also know that when children are involved, I have to do a very careful, thorough investigation. I can't do that unless you talk to me. You're free to leave if you want, and like I told you earlier, you're free to talk to a lawyer. I'm not here to railroad anybody, but accusations have been made and I need to look into them." I waited patiently until he pulled his chair back and sat down.

He dug his elbows into his knees and rested his forehead in the palms of his hands. After a few minutes, he raised his head. "Look, Detective Wolfe, you've been asking me questions for an hour. What more could you possibly need to know? My ex made up this whole kidnapping story to paint me as a bad guy because she wants sole custody of our kids. I love my two little girls. No father's ever loved his kids more than I love mine." The tears spilled over and he reached up and wiped them with his sleeve, leaving a long smear in his greasepaint. "I didn't kidnap anyone, and I won't just roll over and let her have my girls without a fight." He rubbed his face again, using the time to compose himself.

I hated this type of case, a divorce where the kids become victims and one or both of the parents are dragged through the dirt. "The girls travel around the country with you going to rodeos every other month, right?"

"Yes Ma'am, and they're with their mother the other months. I'm not sure what we'll do once they get into school, but right now it works okay."

He was right. We'd been talking for almost an hour, and so far, he hadn't told me anything I didn't already know. "When do you plan to leave Tucson for your next rodeo?"

"I'll be here until the middle of next month; then I head up to Montana with the girls." His eyes were sad black dots staring out of his happy clown mask. I offered him my hand. He wiped his sweaty palm on his pants before enveloping my hand in his.

I walked to the door, looked back, and smiled. "Don't worry Carl, I haven't convicted too many innocent people in my career. I'll keep in touch, okay?" I left him in the clown room under the stands and walked through the breezeway where concession stands selling hotdogs loaded with cholesterol lined the walls.

As soon as I stepped out from under the stadium seats, I saw my best friend since forever, Megan O'Reilly, standing outside the gates with a group of protestors holding signs decrying the use of animals in rodeos. "Oh, good grief."

I started toward her but stopped when her friends saw my badge and began chanting louder and waving their signs at me. News cameras turned my way, hoping for some kind of story they could run on the five o'clock edition.

Megan laughed as she caught my eye.

I motioned for her to meet me a little ways down the chain link fence so we could talk away from all of the noise.

She walked over carrying her sign high so the cameras could get a good shot. "Hi, Alex. Long time no see." She said it like we hadn't just eaten ice cream and watched a movie together the night before.

I leaned forward and grabbed a square of chain link. "You didn't tell me you were gonna be here today. You havin' fun?"

"Yup. A bunch of cowboys came through, and one of 'em asked for my phone number. Boy did he have a cute, tight butt!"

"Did you give it to him?"

She tilted her head sideways, then pulled down her sunglasses. "Well duh! Do I look stupid or something?" Her bushy hair stuck out from her head like a carrot-colored tumbleweed and her fair skin glowed beet red everywhere except for the two patches of white hiding under her sunglasses.

"You better put on sunscreen or they're gonna mistake you for a rodeo clown and throw you in with the bulls."

She glanced over my shoulder and barely raised her chin to let me know someone was coming.

I turned and smiled at Sgt. Pete Dougherty, who'd been assigned to keep an eye on the protestors. "Hey, Pete, what's up?"

Pete and Megan had met each other a few months earlier during a birthday party for our 93-year-old friend, Mrs. Highland, while all three of them were laid up in University Medical Center. Pete smiled, shook his head, and looked at Megan. "I thought I recognized that redhead yelling at me from behind the fence. How ya doin', Megan? Alex, good to see you."

"I'm just leaving. I wanted to take a minute to laugh at Meg first."

Megan stuck out her tongue as she shook her sign at us.

Pete nodded in the direction of the Police Command Post. "The lieutenant's afraid you're gonna start some kind of incident, Alex, so he asked me to come over and make sure everything was all right. He's worried sick he'll get some bad press that'll ruin his chances for promotion. What a dweeb." He shook his head, then looked pointedly at Megan. "And that stays right here, or you'll get me in trouble."

I patted him on the shoulder. "Don't worry. Megan may be a nut, but she knows when to keep things to herself." I cocked one eye at her. "Right Gertrude?" Gertrude had been her grandmother's and her mother's middle names, and her mom had saddled Megan with it to carry on the family tradition. She hated it.

Pete raised his eyebrows. "Gertrude?"

Megan picked up her sign and pounded it on the fence. "You are *dog meat*, Frieda!"

Okay, so I hate my middle name too.

The reporters saw her hit the fence with the sign, and once again, all the cameras swung our way.

The three of us looked at the lieutenant, who started toward us.

I turned back to Megan. "Smile pretty for the cameras. We don't want to be the headline news story today, do we?"

She pretended to laugh while I put on a happy face for the press.

When the lieutenant walked up, we were busy comparing notes on the effects of cow manure on tomato plants. He casually leaned against the fence, letting the media know there really wasn't a story here. "Any problems here, Ma'am? I hope Detective Wolfe hasn't said anything offensive."

She innocently batted her eyes. "Oh, I'm sure she'll be glad to take back what she said, won't you, Detective Wolfe?"

I stared at Megan a minute, then shifted my gaze to the lieutenant whose eyes were boring into mine with all kinds of directed meaning. I crossed my arms. "Miss O'Reilly, I am *so* sorry I made fun of your pet cow, Gertrude, dying the way she did. If you'd like to split the cost of butchering her, I'd like to have some fresh meat for my holiday celebrations with my family."

Megan blinked.

I could tell she was having a hard time keeping a straight face. She loved animals, but she definitely loved her steak and hamburgers too.

The lieutenant dropped his hands to his side and stared at me, clearly not believing what he'd just heard.

Feigning shock and outrage, Megan picked up her sign and rejoined her friends in the picket line.

I clapped the lieutenant on the shoulder. "Well L.T., I'm all finished with my clown interview. I'm headin' back to the office. See you around." I winked at Pete behind the lieutenant's back as I walked out to the parking lot to find my car. They were still standing next to the fence when I exited the lot heading North on Sixth Avenue toward our office.

I work in the Special Crimes Division, which is located on the third floor of the main police station. Our unit shares office space with the Child Abuse and Domestic Violence units. Our desks are on the right, with Child Abuse on the left and Domestic Violence in the back. The sergeant's offices are enclosed in see-through cubicles at the front left part of the room, and the secretaries sit in the front right.

I walked into the office and headed back to my area. My partner, Casey Bowman, sat at her desk sorting through mounds of paperwork scattered haphazardly across the desktop. "How'd it go with the clown?"

I threw my canvas briefcase on my desk before flopping into my chair. "I didn't get a confession, if that's what you mean. He actually seems like a pretty nice guy. What'd the kids say?"

"Not much. The three year old can barely talk, and the five year old had a heck of a time trying to remember what she was supposed to say. Unless the mom turns up with a credible eye witness, I don't think we have any kind of case."

Our sergeant, Kate Brannigan, walked up to our desks.

Kate and I have an interesting relationship: I piss her off, she chews me out. Right now, she stood with her arms crossed, eyebrows raised. "Did you have fun at the rodeo?"

I nodded. "You mean when I interviewed the clown?"

She shook her head. "No, that wasn't exactly what I was referring to." She continued to wait, tapping her fingers on her forearm while Casey sat back and grinned.

I put my feet up on the bottom drawer of my desk and tilted back in my chair. "Maybe you mean did I enjoy all the tight hind ends crammed into dusty blue Wranglers? Definitely."

Casey looked from Kate to me and back to Kate again. "What'd she do this time? The suspense is killing me."

Kate leaned against the pillar next to our desks, her blonde hair pulled back into a ponytail with her bangs hanging just above her eyes. She was a beautiful woman who had the ability to comfort or terrify, whichever was needed at the time.

"Well, Lieutenant Caruthers just called. He was sputtering so much I couldn't tell what he was upset about, but I did catch the words 'Wolfe' and 'headlines' and 'rodeo.' Any idea what he's talking about?"

I put my finger to my chin and thought a minute. "I guess it could have something to do with my offer to help one of the animal activists pay to have her pet cow butchered if she'd share the meat with me." I looked at Casey, who covered her eyes with her hands.

Kate straightened up, stared at me, then looked out the window behind my desk. She opened her mouth to say something, then shut it again.

Casey peeked out from under her hand and I winked at her.

Kate nodded as she walked back to her office. "That'd do it all right."

Casey leaned forward and rested her elbows on the desk. "Please tell me Meg was the animal activist."

I nodded as I looked over at the sergeant's desk. "She was, but don't tell Kate."

At that moment, one of our newer detectives, Nate Drewery, came ambling into the unit carrying two puppies that looked to be about six weeks old. One was obviously a full-bred German Shepherd, and the other couldn't have weighed more than two pounds. He put the shepherd on Casey's desk.

The little one jumped out of his arms, slipped around on Casey's paperwork, scampered onto my desk, and pounced on my chest. His oversized ears shot straight up from his head and his merry eyes shone out of a bright, intelligent face. The little guy leaned back, wagged his tail wildly, and then reached up to lick my chin.

Nate looked like a proud papa. "Whaddya think?"

Casey hugged her fur ball, who sat cuddled in her lap leaning against her chest. My guy crawled up between my head and the back of the chair and lay across my shoulders.

Casey asked, "Where did these guys come from? I thought your apartment complex didn't allow pets."

Nate shrugged, a stupid grin on his face. "I'm not keeping 'em. You guys are! Merry Christmas!"

Casey and I looked at each other as I pulled the puppy from behind my head. "Oh no. It ain't Christmas, and you're not Santa Claus. Here, take him." My bundle fit easily in one hand as I held him out for Nate to take him back.

Nate held up his hands and backed away. "I can't keep 'em." He pointed to my puppy. "That one's a PappyWaWa. He's a mix between a Papillion and a Chihuahua. My friend had to leave town unexpectedly, and she couldn't put them in the pound."

"So, you offered to take them?"

The puppy squirmed in my hand, trying to gain his freedom.

I set him on my lap, careful to keep his feet firmly planted on my thighs while I examined his silky, tri-colored coat.

The little guy climbed up onto my desk, wagged his tail, and wriggled again before letting out a playful, shrill bark.

Casey chuckled. "I think he's telling you that you're stuck with him, so you might as well enjoy it. Nate, you've got to stop fixing the problems of every girl you meet. They always see you coming."

Another detective yelled across the room. "Yeah, and he's always well rewarded."

Catcalls sounded around the office.

Nate bowed and accepted the accolades. At six-two, he filled his clothes impressively with wide, muscular shoulders and handsome, Scots-Irish features. Just 25-years-old, he still wore his bachelor status proudly.

The little dog barked at me again. When I reached for him, he scampered out of reach into the dark recesses of my out-basket. He plopped his hind end down, lowering his head impishly and waiting for me to make the next move.

I inched my hand slowly along the desk until he jumped out to pounce on it. I glared at Nate, who'd known exactly which puppy to give me and which one to give Casey, who was currently rubbing her nose in her calm puppy's soft fur. My little scamp was just like me, the only difference being he weighed 132 pounds less than me and had four legs and a tail.

There was no sense arguing with the inevitable so I made a little nest for him in one of my file drawers where he curled up and went to sleep.

Nate wandered triumphantly back to his desk as I began sorting through my in-basket and carefully organizing all the paperwork into the correct folders.

When lunchtime rolled around I gathered up the pup, who awoke primed and ready to play, and headed home to introduce him to my other dog, Tessa, a white, long-haired hunting dog I'd acquired a few months earlier. Tessa loves everyone she meets, so when she bounded out of my front door, I put the puppy on the ground and let the two of them introduce themselves.

The muffled sound of my house phone reminded me I'd lost it earlier in the week when Megan had come over to cook her signature Shrimp Puttanesca. I followed the ringing to an antenna poking out of the cushions on the couch. The phone was tangled in some frayed edging on the cushion and I had to put my head down on the sofa to talk. "Hello?"

"Hi, Alex. It's Gia."

I'd met Gianina Angelino a few months earlier while investigating a homicide. Her father, Tancredo Angelino, had been the head of a mafia crime family who'd moved to Tucson in the early seventies. When he'd retired, Gia had taken over the family business.

I managed to untangle the phone before I spoke. "Gia, I haven't heard from you in a while. What's up?" I walked back to the door so I could keep an eye on Tessa and the puppy.

"What do you know about DNA testing?" I heard her take a puff on her ever-present Cuban Slim cigar.

"You mean the technical stuff? Nothing. What do you need to know?"

She didn't answer right away. After a few moments of silence, she said, "I just received a strange telephone call. Listen, I don't want to discuss this over the phone. Do you think you could come by for dinner? I'll have the cook prepare a light meal."

I didn't particularly want to go out after work, but she'd helped me out on several occasions, and I owed her. "Sure, I'll be there about five."

"Perfect." Not much for small talk, she immediately disconnected.

I began searching for a suitable container to keep the puppy in while I finished my second half of the day at work. I rummaged through the shelves in the laundry, finally settling on an empty paper towel box. I put an old sheet in the bottom, giving him a comfy place to sleep. When I lowered him onto it, he blinked up at me with sleepy puppy eyes and curled up for his second nap of the day.

I headed back to work, anxious to whittle down the number of cases I still had open. For most of them, I'd already done the legwork and all I had left was to write the closing supplement. My main problem was that every time I sat down to write, Kate sent me out to interview someone or to back-up another detective. When I walked into the office, Sharon, our division secretary, was the only person there.

She looked up from her typing and smiled. "Hi, Alex. I heard Nate talked you and Casey into taking those two puppies. I saw the woman who had them. Wow!" She put her cupped hands in front of her chest. "I think Nate would've taken a horse from her if she'd asked. He was following her around like a puppy himself."

"Thank God she didn't have a horse then." I grinned at her as I walked back to my desk where I spent the next several hours writing closing supplements. When I finished, I printed out the paperwork and carried it to the records basket at the front of the office. I dumped it all in, said goodbye to Sharon and drove to Gia's midtown home.

Gia lives in an enclave where older million-dollar homes have been overrun by urban sprawl. Over the last fifty years, the beautiful neighborhood has managed to remain an island, undisturbed by the busy roads, businesses, and slums that now surround it on all sides.

Different colored marigolds lined both sides of the drive. The beautiful flowers always seemed to be in bloom no matter what time of the year I stopped by. A six-foot stucco wall surrounded an inner court-yard, and as I stepped through the gate, I couldn't help but admire how perfectly the gardener kept all the plants. No dead leaves hung on the stems or littered the ground, the flowers were in full bloom, and the gardener always cut away any that had bloomed past their prime.

I rang the doorbell and listened while the distinctive, Middle Eastern gong echoed throughout the home.

After a few minutes, Gia opened the door wearing a tight-fitting red sweater tailored to accentuate every sensual curve of her well-kept, fifty-year-old body. A thin line of smoke drifted into my face from the cigar she held poised between her fingers.

I avoided the cloud as best I could and stepped past her into her marble-tiled foyer. "Why do you smoke those things, anyway?"

A hint of a smile sparkled in her dove-grey eyes, but she ignored the question as she preceded me down a hallway paneled in a light oak that accentuated the priceless artwork hanging on the walls.

Along the way, I bent down to read a signature at the bottom of one of the paintings and was shocked to see "Leonardo" in the bottom righthand corner. I jumped back, afraid I'd somehow destroy a price-less antique just by breathing on it or something.

Gia stopped at the doorway to the library and smiled when she saw me jump. "Alex, that's only a copy; I have the original out on loan to a museum. You don't actually think I'd have it hanging in my hallway do you?"

When I glanced up, she'd disappeared through the doorway. I followed her into her oak-paneled library where thousands of books lined the shelves. A bottle of Glenlivet and two snifters awaited us on the coffee table.

Gia motioned for me to take a seat on the brown leather sofa. Gracefully pouring each of us a glass, she slipped two fingers around the stem of one and held it out to me.

Before I'd met her, I'd never tasted Glenlivet. Gia had introduced me to it a few months earlier and had spoiled me for the ten-dollar a bottle kind I used to order from my local pub. I took the glass and sipped slowly, savoring the now familiar mellow smokiness as the liquid slid down my throat. I absently ran my finger around the rim, wondering why I was sitting in Gia's library sipping scotch at this time of the evening. "You said something about DNA when you called. Like I said, I don't know a lot about it." I leaned back into the overstuffed cushion, flipped off my shoes, and put my feet up on the sofa.

Her gaze shifted to my feet. Once again, amusement flickered and she lowered herself into an armchair. "Alex, you're the only person in the world who would dare do such a thing when visiting me." She reached down, pulled off her Gucci sandals, and rested her feet on the coffee table. She lifted her glass in a toast. "When in Rome...."

I gently tipped my glass against hers, then took another sip. "You said you got a strange phone call. What was it about?"

She set her glass on the coffee table, exchanging it for a photo album. Sticky notes marked various pages, and I guessed she'd been going through it earlier in the day. She pushed my feet off the cushion, clearing a space and sliding in next to me while at the same time opening the album in her lap. "Do you remember I told you about my twin brother, Credo, who was murdered when we were nineteen?"

I remembered all right. A rival mafia family had brought him out and killed him in front of her. I nodded and waited for her to continue.

She pointed to a picture of a darkly handsome young man standing on a beach wearing Hawaiian swim trunks and sunglasses. A generously endowed woman hung on each arm, all three of them laughing at the person holding the camera.

"This is Credo. We'd been visiting relatives in Italy, and he decided we should go show off his body to all the lovely Italian sunbathers. He was playfully conceited and, as you can see, rightfully so. He was the most handsome man on the beach that day." She flipped through page after page of a happy, laughing young man.

We sat for quite a while; her telling stories, me listening intently. When we reached the end of the album, she closed it and held it in her lap. She turned and settled against the sofa's arm.

I copied her movements on my end, watching as she brought her perfectly manicured feet up onto the seat cushions. I did the same, thankful I had socks to cover my uneven toenails, which I was now determined to cut the first chance I got. We sat facing each other while she gathered her thoughts.

Her hands trembled slightly as she lit another cigar.

I had never, ever, seen Gia upset by anything. I wondered what could have shaken her so badly, and I have to admit, this crack in her armor of power and self-control unnerved me a little bit.

She took a long, deep pull on the cigar and absently blew the smoke over her shoulder. "Credo and I were very, very close. You've heard of twins who know what the other is thinking?"

"Yeah."

"Well, we always knew what the other was thinking *and* feeling. If he was in physical pain, sometimes, even if I wasn't in the same building, I'd feel the same pain." Her eyes shifted from the album in her lap up to my face. She caught and held my gaze, daring me to contradict what she'd just said.

When I didn't say anything, she continued. "His given name was Tancredo, but we always called him Credo. He might have been my father's life and namesake, but he was *my* very being. I lost myself for many years after he was murdered." She paused and absently caressed the photo album. "I even thought about suicide, but somehow I knew Credo would be angry at me for throwing away what he couldn't have." She picked up her Scotch and took a small sip.

I did the same while we sat quietly in a room where the only sound was the steady ticking of an ancient grandfather clock standing majestically on the opposite side of the room between two floor-to-ceiling bookcases.

While waiting for her to continue, I watched her face and was shocked to see the hint of tears forming at the corners of her eyes. She angrily swiped at them and then the anger was replaced by something I didn't recognize. Indecision maybe? Confusion? "Gia, what's wrong? How can I help you?"

She stubbed out the cigar in an ashtray. Her brows furrowed as she reached for a newspaper article lying on the coffee table. She handed it to me. "Do you remember reading about an eleven-year-old girl who stabbed her foster father to death two weeks ago?"

I glanced at the article. "Yeah. Homicide's still working the case. Why?"

"Her caseworker called me. She's been trying to locate relatives for the little girl, and she came across a letter from the girl's grandmother addressed to the girl's mother. Apparently they're both dead now. Anyway, the letter apologized for never revealing whom the mother's father was—the little girl's grandfather. Does that make sense or am I confusing you?"

I did a quick recap. "There's a girl in foster care. Her now deceased mother was born out of wedlock, and the also deceased grandmother never told her daughter who her dad was. The dad is also the foster girl's grandfather."

Gia smiled. "It sounds clearer when you say it. The long and the short is, the letter named my brother, Credo, as the woman's father, which would make him the little girl's grandfather."

"Which makes you her Great-Aunt—and you need DNA done to make sure she's really related to you. Wow, talk about a pit of vipers. This kid just killed somebody. What do they want you to do about her?"

"If she is Credo's granddaughter, I'll do anything and everything in my power to clear her name, and I'll raise her as my own child. If she's not—" She lifted a shoulder and left the sentence unfinished.

"So, what do you need me for? It's not my case. Homicide is handling it."

She re-lit her cigar. "After I spoke to you, I realized I needed an attorney working on the DNA aspect, so I called Bill Silverton and got him looking into that."

I was starting to get a little nervous because I couldn't see where I fit into the picture. "Gia, I'm not sure what you want. Another detective has the case. I don't have anything to do with it. That means that legally I can't look up records for you or give you any type of official information. So, if that's what you want, well, you need to talk to the lead detective."

She turned her head and blew smoke out of the side of her mouth, locking suddenly angry eyes onto mine. "You mean you won't, 'take someone out' for me if I ask?"

I studied her a minute to see whether she was kidding and then slowly shook my head. "I know you'd never ask anything like that. I'm just, you know, getting us both on the same page." I could tell I'd pissed her off somehow, and I swirled the ice around in my glass and watched the little waves of Scotch form a tiny whirlpool to give myself time to think.

She put one foot on the floor and sat forward. Her soft grey eyes had turned to steel, a warning sign I'd learned to heed during our short, chaotic friendship. She spoke quietly and punctuated her words by stabbing the cushion between us with her index finger. "Let's get something straight, Detective Wolfe. We are *not* friends because you're a cop. I neither *want* nor *need* you on my payroll. If that's what you're thinking, you can get out of my home *right now*."

I relaxed, feeling more than a little foolish. I shrugged, trying to diffuse her anger. "Yeah, I guess I knew that. After all, you've got plenty of people to do murder and mayhem for you when you need it." I grinned at her, hoping she'd realize I hadn't meant to insult her.

She leaned back and put a thumb up to her temple; the cigar nestled between two fingers, her elbow resting on the back of the sofa. Her body relaxed, and I was relieved when she finally smiled. "I'm not going to touch that one." She brushed a barely discernable scuffmark off one of the cushions. "I'm sorry, Alex. This whole thing has me shaken up more than I realized. I guess I'm a little touchy."

"A touchy Mafia Don. Should I be nervous or something?"

She cocked her head and studied me, the humor back in her eyes. "I thought you'd already learned that lesson, Alex. You should always be a little nervous around me." She was, of course, referring to the time she'd had me kidnapped and brought to her home because I'd refused two invitations to meet with her.

I swirled my Scotch again and kept quiet. Truth be told, she did scare me a little bit, but I wasn't going to let her know that.

"Look Alex, all I'm asking is that you familiarize yourself with the case, get a feel for how it's going. You don't even need to tell me about it. I trust you to make sure everything is done correctly."

I set down my glass, pulled my knees up to my chest, and wrapped my arms around them. "Well, I can talk to whoever has the case, but for the most part, all our detectives are really good. I don't think you have anything to worry about." *I hope.* I reached for the hors d'oeuvre's her butler had just brought in and set on the coffee table.

She sipped her drink. "I could go through Chief Larkin, but I've found if I want to find out what's really going on in an organization, it's better to talk to the people who actually do the work."

"The peons, you mean?"

She chuckled as she reached for a petit four. "Alex, you may be a lot of things to the department, but a peon isn't one of them. A 'P.I.T.A.', yes... a peon, definitely not."

"P.I.T.A.... pain in the ass. Thanks a lot."

We finished eating in silence, and when I thought the time was right, I lowered my feet to the ground and pulled one of my shoes over to put it on. She handed me the other that was somehow sitting just out of reach. "I'm not worried, Alex, but if she is my great-niece, I want everything done exactly the way it should be. No shortcuts."

"I'll see who has the case. If nothing else, I have a friend, Ruthanne, who's a homicide detective I can talk to. But I'm positive they're doing everything right. We have a good group of people up there right now." I pulled on my shoes and double knotted the laces. Gia saw me to the front door, showing me various paintings as we walked through the hall. We said our goodbyes, and as I walked to my car I thought about everything we'd talked about and wondered how Gia would handle raising an eleven-year-old girl who'd apparently just killed a man.

CHAPTER 2

Before I left for the office the next morning, I took Tessa and the new, as yet unnamed, puppy over to visit my agoraphobic neighbor, Newton Goren, who only leaves his home once or twice a day to let Tessa out to exercise. Newt and I have been friends ever since I rescued him from a pushy salesman who refused to stop ringing the doorbell until Newt answered the door. Since he never answers the door, I helped the salesman off the property and received a shy wave from behind a set of curtains.

This morning, I walked up to the window and knocked on the glass.

After a few minutes, the curtain moved a few inches as Newton peeked out.

"Hi, Newt. I wanted to introduce you to my new puppy. He doesn't have a name yet, but he'll be staying in a box in my house. Could you let him out when you let Tessa out?" I held the squirming puppy up in front of the window.

Newton put a tentative finger up to the window and then disappeared behind the curtains again. That was as much of an answer as I ever got from him, but it was enough. I knew he'd take care of the little fellow. I took the dogs back to my house to settle them in for the day.

On my way to work, I received a call from Casey. "Hey, Kate just called. Your rodeo clown went to his girls' daycare this morning and left with them. He's not supposed to have unsupervised visits until this kidnapping case is done. Do you know how to reach him so we can try to get the girls back?"

I pulled off the road and reached into my briefcase. "Hold on a second...I think he gave me some phone numbers." I grabbed my notebook and leafed through the pages. "Yeah, here they are. I'm about five minutes from the station. I'll meet you there and we can make a few calls."

When I walked into the office, the place was deserted except for Casey, who sat rifling through papers at her desk. "Where is everybody?"

She shuffled some more, obviously looking for something. "There's a promotion ceremony in the main lobby. I think they all went to that."

I always worry about promotion ceremonies because you never know what idiot is being promoted to a higher rank than you. Most of the people are usually fine to work for, but there's always that one with a chip on his shoulder or an over-active ego that everyone tries to avoid. "Anybody interesting getting promoted today?"

She shook her head. "Not really. Unless you think Eddie Carlson is interesting."

I whistled quietly. "God, I hope I never have to work for him. All he cares about is looking good and impressing people, and he doesn't care who he steps on to do it."

I reached into my briefcase and took out my notebook to look up Carl the Clown's phone numbers. My extension rang just as I picked up the receiver. Carl's voice surprised me and I covered the handset and mouthed "Clown" to Casey. I pushed the speaker button and hung up. "Hey Carl, what's up?"

"I think my ex-wife's messing with me again. She called me a few minutes ago demanding I return the kids to their daycare. I don't have the girls, Detective Wolfe. She says I took them."

Casey sat forward to make it easier to talk into the speaker. "This is Detective Bowman, Mr. Boyd. I'm working with Detective Wolfe on your case. We received a call a few minutes ago from Child Protective Services saying you picked your girls up from daycare. You're saying you didn't?"

"No Ma'am, I didn't. I'm at the Rodeo grounds. I got here two hours ago and I haven't left since."

Casey and I exchanged disgusted looks. Somebody was playing custody games, which usually meant wasting a whole lot of our time to sort everything out. I told Carl we'd get back to him and hung up. "We need to talk to Kate about this one. I think it just got messy."

Casey paged Kate, who walked into the office a few minutes later. She put some stuff on her desk and walked over to ours. "I was down at the promotion ceremony. What's up?"

We filled her in on recent developments. When we were done, she leaned against the pillar to think a minute. "Has anyone talked to the mother yet? Today, I mean?"

We shook our heads and waited. Kate always worked out a game plan before she did anything, and we knew if we started giving suggestions she'd just walk away for a few minutes so she could collect her thoughts. If we waited, she'd ask whatever questions she had, then make a decision.

"So Casey, your gut feeling when you interviewed the girls who supposedly saw the kidnapping was that someone had coached them on what to say, right?"

Casey nodded.

"And Alex, your gut feeling on the dad was that you didn't think he kidnapped the boyfriend?"

I ran that around in my head a second. "Well, kind of. I'm not one-hundred percent certain, but he didn't confess and he seemed like a genuinely nice guy."

Kate listened and added that to her equation. "Have we spoken to any other relatives, or to people at the daycare?"

Casey shook her head. "You just assigned us the case yesterday. We both interviewed the mother, and then I went and interviewed the kids and Alex interviewed the dad. This just came up this morning."

Kate sighed. "Well, the first thing we need to do is locate those kids. Why don't you two head over to the daycare and I'll call the mother to see if she knows anything else. Call me when you're done."

Casey pushed all the papers on her desk into a stack and stuck the whole mess into her in-basket. Over the years, she'd perfected the scatter system of filing. Throw everything onto your desk and search through it to find what you're looking for. I'd be totally lost, but it seemed to work for her.

I stuck my notebook back into my briefcase as we headed out to the garage. We decided to take one car instead of two since it looked like we'd be working together most of the day.

Casey headed for her car when we stepped out of the elevator.

I headed for mine and jangled my keys. "I'll drive. You drive like an old lady."

"Yeah, and you drive like a bat out of Hell. I'm driving."

We stared at each other, neither wanting to give in. Casey reached into her pocket. "I'll flip you for it; you call." She pulled out a quarter and flicked it into the air.

"Heads."

She caught it and flipped it onto the back of her hand. "Tails. I drive." She quickly stuffed the coin back into her pocket.

"Hey, I need to see it. That's not fair. Do it again." I walked over to where she was standing and pointed at her pocket.

"Nope, I won. Nobody said anything about best two out of three. Get in." She beeped open her doors and got into the driver's seat.

"You cheated." I threw my briefcase into her back seat and climbed into the passenger's side. "You always cheat." I buckled my seat belt and pouted.

"Good God, you're just like a little kid sometimes, you know that?"

"Fine."

Casey chuckled and adjusted the radio as we drove to the daycare. "So where do you think the little girls are? You think the mom has them somewhere?"

"That'd be my bet. I didn't get the impression that Carl was devious enough to kidnap his own daughters, or smart enough to call us to feign innocence."

We parked outside the daycare and walked inside, stopping at the front counter to watch the absolute chaos happening not ten feet away. Thirty or forty kids were running around in the little room while two young women tried to bring some order to the pandemonium.

One harried woman called over to us. "I'll be right with you. We had someone call in sick today and things are a little... uh... busy." One little girl standing next to her dumped a cup of juice onto another kid's head. The woman grabbed the girl and redirected her to a box of Lego's near the corner of the room.

I raised my eyebrows. "And we think *our* job's hard."

"No kidding, you couldn't pay me enough to work in a place like this. Look at that kid." She pointed to a little boy sitting on the ground with his finger up his nose. He wasn't digging; he just rested it there. We watched him for a while, wondering just how long he'd sit like that.

I crossed my arms. "What do you think he's doing?"

"Beats me."

The door behind us opened, admitting a girl in her late teens. She ran her hand through bright, red-spiked hair while surveying the room. "Jeremy, get your finger out of your nose. Heather, stop playing with yourself. Both of you go wash your hands, now." She pulled off her sweater and headed into the battle zone.

The woman who'd originally spoken to us walked up to the counter. When she saw the detective badges on our belts, she hesitated. "Oh, I didn't know you were the police. Sorry you had to wait." She put her hands up as though she wanted to fix her hair, then thought better of it and put them down by her sides. "How can I help you?"

Casey took out her identification and handed it to the woman. "I'm Detective Bowman; this is my partner, Detective Wolfe. We're here about Amanda and Chrissie Boyd. Could we talk to whoever signed them out?"

"Oh, that was me. Their father came in and checked them out about an hour ago."

"Did he show you any identification?" I pulled out my notebook to take notes while Casey continued with her questions.

"No... I mean, yes... yes he did." She brought out the log people had to sign when they checked in their kids or signed them out. "Their mom brought them at seven-thirty, and their dad came and checked them out an hour later."

Casey checked the log and pointed to some writing. "Is this his signature?"

The woman shook her head. "No. He forgot to sign it, so I put his name there so I could remember who took them."

Casey watched her a second. "You said he showed you some I.D.? What type of identification did he use?"

"I think it was a library card. He said he'd left his wallet at home and that was all he could find in his truck. We laughed about it at the time." She hesitated. "Is there some kind of problem?"

"Can you describe the father to me?" I'd been writing down her answers and waited while she thought about the question.

"Jeez, we were really busy with everyone checking in their children right about then... and like I said, we were really short handed, so I didn't pay too much attention."

I continued to wait while she thought.

Casey studied her, taking in every body movement and facial expression that might tell her whether the woman was lying. I'd worked with her long enough to know when something bothered her. Something was bothering me too, but I couldn't put my finger on it.

The lady glanced behind her, probably to make sure none of the kids were killing each other. "He was a cowboy. He wore a cowboy hat. He was about six feet tall I guess. I'm not very good at heights." She shook her head. "That's about all I can remember. Sorry."

Casey slowly nodded, then looked at me to see whether I had anymore questions. I had one more I wanted to ask. "Did the girls seem to know him? Did they call him 'Dad' or anything like that?"

"I honestly don't remember. Eight-thirty is one of our busiest times, but they didn't seem scared or anything. They just left with him."

Casey took out her business card while I grabbed one of mine. Casey smiled. "Sorry, I didn't catch your name. We just need it for the report.

"Hannah Brawley."

We handed her the business cards and asked her to call if she remembered anything else.

As we got back into Casey's car we called Kate, who told us to meet her back at the office. When we walked in, she was on the phone and she motioned for us to take seats next to her desk. She hung up and wrote something on her desk calendar. "So what'd you find?"

I pulled my notebook out of my pocket. "We spoke to the woman who released the girls. She says it was busy, and she wasn't paying close attention. When a man—a cowboy—came in and asked to pick up the girls, she gave them to him."

"Did he show I.D.?"

"A library card."

"Did the girls seem to know him?"

"She couldn't remember."

Kate reached down and pulled out the bottom drawer of the desk. She put one foot on the drawer, crossed one leg over her knee and began tapping a pen on her shoe.

I leaned back and put my feet on her desk too. The tapping stopped and I took my feet off her desk. The tapping started again. I fidgeted in my seat, anxious to get to the work piled on my desk.

Kate stopped tapping and I looked up. "Are we keeping you from something, Alex?"

"No Ma'am." I slid down in the chair and crossed my arms.

"All right, let's recap what we have. First, we have a messy divorce with two small children in the mix. Second, the ex-wife's boyfriend is missing. She thinks he's been kidnapped; the kids supposedly saw the kidnapping but aren't talking. Third, the two kids are taken from daycare, the mother says the father took them, and the father says he didn't."

Casey and I didn't say anything, and Kate started tapping again. "The question is, do we pull out all the stops and treat this like a child abduction, or do we continue on a small scale until we can rule out all the other possibilities?"

Since she hadn't asked our opinions, we didn't give them. "Alex, you have the picture of the boyfriend, right?"

I nodded.

"Take that picture back to the daycare and show it to the woman who released the girls. Ask her if she recognizes him. We might get lucky and solve both problems with one stroke." She reached over and handed Casey a piece of paper. "This is a list of family members who live in Tucson. Go talk to everyone you can and see what you come up with."

I'd left the picture in my briefcase, and my briefcase was in Casey's car. I followed her down to the garage and sighed as I took it from the back seat. "I hate these cases. They're such a waste of time. Why can't people be adults when they get divorced and split amicably? Why do they have to drag the kids into the mess?"

"Let's hope that's all this is. Otherwise we have two little girls missing, and the department will spends thousands of dollars and hundreds of hours trying to find them." She rested her elbow on the roof of the car. "Call me when you're ready for lunch. I think you'll get done way before I do."

The elevator bell dinged, and my friend, Ruthanne Penn stepped out. She didn't see me behind Casey's car so I followed her up the incline to where her car was parked. "Hey, Ruthanne, wait up."

When she turned, her smile stretched from ear to ear. "Alex! I haven't seen you in a while. How have you been since that shooting a couple months ago?"

She was referring to a case I'd been involved in where the suspect had been shot and killed before he could kill a young friend of mine. "Life's good. I'm trying to keep my head down and stay out of trouble." I held out my hand and she shook it. "Hey, are you involved in that case where the little girl killed her foster father?"

"Kind of... it's Eric's case, but I've done a few interviews. Why?"

"Just between you, me and the fence post?" I raised my eyebrows, knowing she'd say yes. We'd been friends since before I'd joined the department, and I trusted her implicitly.

"Okay, but just remember, these fence posts have ears." She nodded toward a pillar next to her car, and I realized she was right.

"You have time for a coffee? I'll buy."

"I always have time for you, Darlin'." She gave me her best come-hither look and I laughed. Ruthanne was famous for her sexual exploits, and she didn't discriminate based on race, sex, religion, or creed.

"You never give up, do you? I'll meet you at Sleepy Time Café and fill you in on all the gory details."

She grinned as she got into her car. "I will never accept defeat, Alex! One day you'll come to your senses! See you there."

I watched her back out of her space and drive away. Ruthanne was a trim 5'5" with shoulder length brown hair and a friendly, round face with a ready smile. She knew about more departmental skeletons in closets than anyone else I knew.

I'd parked my car two aisles away, so I hiked down the ramp, opened my door and threw my briefcase on the passenger seat. I drove to the café and walked in just as the waitress brought two iced teas to Ruthann's table. "Thanks, Marlene. How'd you know?"

Marlene humphed. "How'd I know? Have you ever ordered anything besides iced tea with a bagel and cream cheese?"

Ruthanne slid the container with sweetener my way. I grabbed six packets and poured them into my tea as Marlene headed to another table. Ruthanne put two packets into her tea, then sat back ready to listen. "So why the interest in the Shelley Greer case?"

The sweetener settled to the bottom of the glass, and I used my straw to stir it up again. "Well... I guess... I don't know." I hadn't thought about exactly what I wanted to ask. I'd told Gia I'd keep an eye on the case, but I hadn't sorted out in my own mind exactly what that entailed.

Ruthanne lowered her chin as she looked at me. "Well... you guess... you don't know. That says it all right there, doesn't it?"

I rubbed the bridge of my nose. "Sorry. I'm not even sure what I want to ask. Let me tell you my problem, and maybe you can help sort some things out in my mind." I filled her in on Gia's relationship to the little girl. Ruthanne knew all about my friendship with Gia, except for little details that might compromise certain investigations—like, for example, Gia's involvement in the shooting I'd been in earlier in the year. I'd needed back-up in an extremely fast-moving situation, and Gia had sent her bodyguard without any questions or delays. He'd killed the suspect, but as far as the department knew, the shooter was still a mystery. I intended to keep it that way.

When I finished, Ruthanne put her elbows on the table and rested her chin on her fists. "All right, so what's Gia worried about? That we'll screw up the investigation?"

"No, I don't think so. I got the impression this whole thing has thrown her for a loop, you know? Kinda' knocked her off balance, and she's just not used to feeling that way. I think she's just trying to get her equilibrium back."

"What are the chances this kid is her great-niece?"

"We won't know for sure until the DNA comes back. Does she look at all Italian?"

"Yup."

I held her eyes a minute. "What kind of a kid is she?"

"Stubborn, angry, streetwise—in a lot of ways she's eleven going on twenty. In others, she's a scared little girl. I kinda like her, though. Every now and then, I catch a glimpse of a mischievous elf hiding inside." She sipped her coffee. "She did it, you know. There's really no question about that."

When she said "mischievous elf," I thought of the few times I'd seen the same look in Gia. "What color are her eyes?"

Ruthanne brought her eyebrows down. "What?"

"What color are her eyes?"

She thought a minute. "Well, I'm not sure. I'll have to get back to you on that. I didn't really notice."

"She killed the guy?"

"Yuppers. Slid the knife in slick as you please."

"Why?"

"She claims he came in and tried to molest her, but Eric doesn't believe her. She was real antagonistic when he interviewed her; that's why they wanted me to talk to her. She seems to like women better than men."

I couldn't think of any more questions right at the moment, so I changed the subject. "So how's the new guy in your life? What's his name?"

"Which one?"

I should have remembered she rarely had only one person on the line. "The one you picked up at the U of A basketball game. Remember? You 'accidentally' dropped your popcorn in his lap and you just had to help him scoop it all back into the bag?" I laughed as I remembered the night. "Then you took your napkin and rubbed all the butter off his zipper, remember?"

"Jason! Yeah, I really got a rise out of him, didn't I?" Her laughter filled up the restaurant, and people turned to see who was making all the racket. "He's been over a few times. You should come over sometime when he's there. I'll bet the three of us could have a great time." She raised her eyebrows up and down several times.

"I shouldn't have asked." I picked up the bill. "Look, would you just kind of keep an eye on the Greer case for me? That way I can tell Gia I'm on top of things if she asks."

"Consider it done." We walked out of the restaurant and she patted my hind end as she passed behind me on the way to her car. "See ya, Darlin'."

"Ruthanne!"

She raised her hands as she walked away. "Sorry... sorry, my bad."

I loved her like a sister, but sometimes she drove me absolutely crazy. I wondered whether she was my payback for the way I messed with Kate. I smiled as I got in my car and headed back to the daycare.

CHAPTER 3

"**D**o you recognize this man?" I handed the picture of the mother's boyfriend to Hannah while twenty three-to-five year olds vied for her attention.

"Sorry about the noise. Linda called in sick again this afternoon, and I don't have anybody for back up." She turned and screeched right next to my ear, "Jeffery, Honey, stop running! You'll hurt yourself." Her caterwauling had the same effect as running fingernails down a chalkboard. The hair on the back of my neck stood up and my teeth hurt. Jeffery completely ignored her.

Total chaos filled the room. Four boys chased Jeffery, who was running around grabbing juice cups out of kids' hands only to turn and sling the juice back at the pursuing mob. Two girls sat huddled in a corner crying, and another kid carefully built a house of cards while protecting the building with his body. One boy, the same one we'd seen earlier in the day, had his finger jammed up his nose, and two little girls jumped rope while yelling a song at the top of their lungs. When Jeffery ran up and upended the card table, I'd had enough. I yelled at the top of my lungs, "*Shut up!*"

Absolute silence resounded throughout the room. "*Sit!*" I pointed to the ground, and twenty bottoms hit the floor simultaneously, round eyes staring out at me from shocked faces. "You!" I pointed to the kid with his finger up his nose. "Put that finger anywhere but there!" He slowly took it out, thought for a second, and stuck it in his ear. I raised my eyebrows and stared at him a second. "Well, okay, I guess that works. Now, I don't want anyone to move until I'm done, got it?" Twenty heads nodded at the crazy woman.

I turned back to Hannah, who was staring at me, aghast. "You can't talk to these children that way! They're just babies!"

"Would you just look at the picture?" My nerves were shot. I really needed to get out of there.

Hannah glanced angrily at the picture, then handed it back. "No, I've never seen him before. Now if you'll excuse me, I have to try to repair the mess you've made of my class."

"The mess?" I raised my hands, exasperated. Twenty kids were sitting silently watching my every move, and she called it a mess. "Fine! You!" I pointed to the kid with his ear plugged. "Put that back in your nose! You, you, you, you, and you!" I swept my finger between the five juice kids. "Start running around like maniacs!" Six sets of eyes stared at me.

Hannah glared at me. "I think you need to leave, Detective. You've done enough damage already."

I turned on my heels and stalked out, thanking God my mother had never succeeded in her quest to get me married off and pregnant to any man who'd take me—*pregnant* being the operative word. "Damage?" I muttered the word as I drove back to the main station. I was still muttering as I pushed through the door to our offices.

Kate watched me stalk past her cubicle. "Alex?"

"*What?*" I threw my keys onto my desk as I fell into my chair and put my head in my hands.

Kate walked over and stood close to my desk. "I just received a call from the owner of the daycare. Did you—"

"Yes!" I raised my head and yelled at her. "Yes I damaged a room full of five year olds by telling them to shut up! Yes! I told a kid to get his finger out of his nose! And yes, they were all in one piece when I left!"

Kate cocked her head sideways as she leaned on my desk and said quietly, "You may be pissed off, Alex, but I suggest you remember who you're talking to."

I put my head back in my hands. The screaming kids were one thing, but an angry Kate was quite another. I sat up and put on my happy face. She visibly reined in her temper, then pulled out Casey's chair and sat. "Why don't you tell me what happened so I can head off Internal Affairs when they call. You haven't been in trouble for almost three months, and I'd like to keep it that way. In fact, I think we're working on a personal record for you."

I filled her in on everything, relieved when she started chuckling about the kid sitting obediently with a finger in his ear. When I finished, she asked whether Hannah had recognized the man in the picture.

"No. She barely looked at him, but she said she'd never seen him before."

"That still leaves us with two missing children and a missing boyfriend. I haven't heard from Casey yet." She stood up to stretch. "It's almost lunch time. I hope she comes up with something soon."

My desk phone rang, and I reached over and pushed the speaker button. "Detective Wolfe."

"Alex, it's Megan. You know that cowboy who got my phone number yesterday at the rodeo? He came by last night. What a kick! He brought whipped cream and—" Her voice echoed throughout the office and I jerked up the receiver at the same time I punched the button to take the call off speaker. Covering the receiver with my hands I looked up at Kate, who had a comical expression on her face.

I shrugged. "I think he brought the whipped cream to put on some pie or something... you know, for dessert."

Kate snorted. "I wasn't born yesterday, Alex. Tell her I've found that chocolate body sauce goes well with whipped cream. It adds a little extra flavor." She grinned as my mouth fell open and my eyebrows came down as far as they could possibly go. Kate wasn't supposed to say things like that. She was my sergeant. I watched her walk back to her office, then put the receiver up to my ear.

"...and then we just lay in bed and relaxed for a few hours. Cowboys really are more fun, you know?" She hadn't stopped talking and I'd apparently missed the recap of the previous night, which was actually just fine with me. Why is it that everyone has a fantastic sex life except me?

"Hey, Megs, I've gotta go. Can I get the rest of the details tonight? Casey and I are working a case right now."

"Well, you can't call tonight. Cowboy and I are riding again. I'll call you tomorrow, okay?"

We hung up as Casey walked in. When she sat down, I blurted out, "So, how's your sex life?"

Casey eyed me suspiciously. "It's fine, thanks for asking." She studied me as if waiting to see what I'd come up with next.

"Well mine sucks, thank you very much. It's a sad day when Kate is having better sex than I am."

"Kate?"

"Never mind. Did you find out anything?"

Casey swiveled around to look at Kate, then back at me. "Kate has a better sex life than you?"

"I said never mind."

"That's pitiful, Alex."

Kate chose that moment to walk back to our desks. "What's pitiful?"

I stood up so I could stare down on Casey and said with as much meaning as I could possibly get into my voice, "*Nothing.*"

Kate looked from me to Casey then back to me again. Casey shuffled some papers on her desk, mumbling quietly, "Pitiful."

Kate had about fifteen years on me, but men and women still admired her good looks whenever she walked across a room. She'd been happily married for the last twenty-five years to the same man, and it's a known fact that when you've been married that long, sex is either a birthday or a Christmas gift, and that's about it.

I tried to bring the subject back to the case. "Did you find anything on the girls?"

"No, but all the neighbors think something fishy's going on. All of them had good things to say about the dad. I guess he's great with the girls, goes to birthday parties. He even dressed up like—" She pointed to me. "What's that new kids' cartoon that's so big now?"

"How should I know? I don't do kids."

Some of my earlier agitation must have bled through because she sat up in her chair and chuckled. "Sorry I asked. What's eating you?"

"Apparently I traumatized everyone at the daycare today. Anyway, the dad's a good guy. What else did they say?"

"One lady told me she thought she'd seen the boyfriend go in the house last night, but it was dark and she couldn't be sure. They all described the mother as white trash with little money and even less class. You know that shirt she had on yesterday? The one that looked like it was painted on? Well I guess that was her conservative outfit."

Kate listened, then made a decision. "All right, we're going to ratchet the investigation up a notch. I'm going to brief the lieutenant on what we have so far. You two go back to the rodeo and start talking to people there. See if you can dig up anything on either the mom or the dad. Overtime's authorized; don't go home until you check with me."

I looked longingly at all the backed-up paperwork in my in-basket, then followed Casey down to the garage and rode with her to the rodeo grounds. My phone buzzed on the way there, and when I opened it, Ruthanne asked where I was.

"Casey and I are headed to the rodeo. Why?"

"Well, it's probably nothing, but someone must have seen us talking at the café because Eric asked what we were talking about. I told him you were curious about Shelley's case and he got all pissy, saying the case was none of your business. I thought you guys were friends."

Eric and I were friends; at least we were friendly at crime scenes and such. "What do you mean he got pissy? Can't you discuss a case with another detective? Tell him... oh, never mind. Where is he now? I'll finish what I'm doing here, then find him and try to patch things up, okay?"

"He left a while ago. Said he had to do some interviews. I'll tell him you're looking for him the next time I see him."

"Thanks." I hung up and filled Casey in on what she'd said about Eric. Neither of us could figure out what his problem was, so we decided to wait until I spoke to him before we came to any hasty conclusions. At the front gate of the rodeo grounds, Megan was marching in a circle with her protester friends and I waved as I walked past. She shook her sign at me, yelling at the top of her lungs, "Pigs should support other livestock! Down with rodeos!"

As I turned around and sidled up next to her, I whispered. "Pigs should support other livestock? Did you stay up all night thinking that one up?"

Megan covered her mouth so the other protesters wouldn't see her giggling, then stepped back, shouting, "Animals have rights too!"

A camera flashed as she ferociously growled in my face, and I knew we'd be the next day's Metro headline. Casey grabbed my arm to steer me away from the media just as Lieutenant Caruthers walked up. He leaned over and spoke to Casey, hissing through clenched teeth, "Get that worthless waste of a paycheck out of here, Detective Bowman." Caruthers and I had a long history of him screwing up and me calling him on it. Unfortunately, that type of relationship didn't lead to warm, cozy hugs whenever we were around each other.

Casey almost pulled my arm out of my socket before I could tell him where to shove it. She pushed me in front of her and said over her shoulder, "Yes Sir. Sgt. Brannigan sent us over to talk to some of the rodeo people. We're headed inside now."

I shrugged her hand off my arm and managed to get out the first three letters of "Asshole!" before she grabbed my face and covered my mouth with her hand.

She pulled me toward the stands. "Three months and you haven't been in trouble once, Alex. You starting to get itchy, or what?" We walked under the stands and headed out back where the rodeo personnel kept the livestock. "Look, I'm gonna use the litter box. I'll meet you over by the bull pens if you think you can keep out of trouble without me around."

"Very funny." I began working my way around the green, steaming landmines while talking to various rodeo folks, asking about Carl Boyd and his girls. No one had anything negative to say about Carl and they all loved his girls. The bull riders respected his ability to keep them safe from fifteen hundred pound bulls, and everyone said he was a wizard at team roping. As I made my way deeper into the livestock pens, I ducked under a chained "no access" area, poking around on the off chance that maybe Carl had his girls or the boyfriend secreted away somewhere.

A huffing noise came from behind a portable stall toward the back of the enclosure. Seven-foot-tall reinforced plywood encircled a twenty-foot diameter pen. Since curiosity and intrigue are the icing on my cake, I searched until I found a hole in the plywood big enough to wedge my foot into. I pulled myself to the top and as my eyes cleared the edge, I came face to face with the biggest, meanest looking Brahma bull I have ever seen in my life.

Angry eyes in the middle of a flat, furry head sized me up and apparently found me wanting. Head lowered, he rammed full force into the plywood at the same time someone came up behind me, put their hand on my crotch, and threw me over the enclosure into the pen.

I'm not sure which of us was more surprised, me or the bull. I landed sprawled along his back, legs wrapped around his neck, face splattered into his spine. One spin sent me flying into the wall where I hit my head and slid down just in time to avoid being flattened by his forehead. He swung his head sideways and caught my arm with the side of his horn, sending me hurtling back toward his hind end, where I knew I definitely did not want to be.

I hit the ground running on all fours, leapt for a fingertip grab at the top of the plywood, and looked back just in time to see his head a few feet away from crushing my spine. I wrenched my feet up far enough to clear his head but lost my grip when he crashed into the wood. Twisting around on my way down, I managed to land belly first across his neck. As he swung me around, I had one clear thought in my head and I screamed it frantically. "Casey! Casey! Help me! Casey!"

Centrifugal force sent me flying away from the bull as he spun in a tight circle. As I slammed into the wall I reached up to try once more to pull myself out, only to succeed in making myself a target again. He rammed into the wall inches from where I'd been before I'd pushed off, rolled, and landed on my feet in the center of the ring.

"Alex? Where are you! Alex!"

The bull lowered his head and pawed the dirt, blowing huge waves of air out his nostrils and sending dust billowing up from the ground just beneath his nose. "Casey!" As he charged, I pushed off his head, executing a perfect pirouette into his ribs. He swung in a circle trying to reach me and out of my peripheral vision I saw Casey's head poke above the plywood. I stayed in the middle of his turn, backing up into his body to stay away from his blunted horns.

"Jesus, Alex!" She jumped into the pen, grabbed his tail, and jerked hard enough to really piss him off. He reversed direction and went after her, barely missing her back as she grabbed the top of the plywood and raised her legs.

I grabbed his tail and jerked the other way just as two rodeo clowns vaulted over the walls and took over the job of distracting the bull. I'd hit my head pretty hard on his spine and again on the wall, and I was having a hard time focusing. Casey grabbed my arm, hauled me to the wall, put my foot in her hands, and threw me over the plywood into the arms of a couple of surprised cowboys. They dropped me unceremoniously to the ground so they could reach in to pull her out, then rescued the two clowns, who were apparently doing a heck of a lot better job of staying away from the bull than I had.

Blood trickled into my eyes, my shoulder felt numb and the room spun, but all in all, I felt pretty good considering I'd just gone ten rounds with a ton of enraged steak tartar.

Casey knelt in front of me holding up some fingers. "How many fingers do you see?"

"Five."

She slapped me on the side the head with her five fingers. "What the hell were you doing in that goddamn bull pen?"

"Ow! Knock it off!" I pushed to my feet, only to fall backwards into one of the cowboys.

He set me back down on the ground and awkwardly knelt next to Casey. "What *were* you doin' in there, Ma'am? He's a killer, that one." He shifted, trying to make room for his right leg, which didn't seem to bend too well.

I wiped the blood off my face with my shirtsleeve and listened to the bull bashing up against the walls of the pen. "I climbed up... to look inside." My vision blurred, then came back into focus. "Somebody threw me in." I lay down in the dirt so I could get my bearings.

Casey pulled out her cell phone. "I can't believe you're still alive." She pushed some buttons, then started talking into the phone. "Kate, it's Casey." She was quiet a second, then she looked down at me. "Well, yeah, it is about her. I just pulled her out of a pen where a two-ton Brahma bull was doing a tap dance on her. I need to take her to the hospital to get checked." She paused. "Well, she's not too bad. Luckily she hit her head, and we all know that's her hardest body part."

I struggled to my feet, still pretty dizzy. "I don't need to go to the hospital. I'm fine."

"All right, we'll meet you there."

"No. She doesn't need to... come. Tell her... not to come." I grabbed for the phone just as Casey turned sideways and shut it. Several cowboys watched us, concern written on their faces. Apparently it was just fine for them to come away with concussions and broken bones, but for a woman to get hurt was another matter. One rule I've noticed with cowboys is that chivalry is definitely not dead.

I walked unsteadily out to the parking lot with Casey holding my arm just above the elbow. Megan came running up just as I'd opened the car door and slid into the seat. "What happened to you? Jenny said you had blood all over your—" She stopped mid-sentence as I brought my eyes around to meet hers. Apparently I didn't look so good.

"What?" My hand involuntarily went to my face as Meg reached for the back door, threw her sign on the seat, and climbed in. When I swiveled around, I turned the rear view mirror my way. "Whoa." My eyebrow above my left eye was twice the size of the other one and blood was seeping out of a cut just above the hairline. My left cheek wasn't swollen, but it had turned a strange combination of deep red and black all the way around my jaw line so that I had a multicolored smile running along the bones. The bruise line opened and closed each time I worked my jaw, which gave me a kind of ghoulish, skeletal appearance. I put my head back on the seat as Casey reached across me, pulled the seat belt around my chest, and buckled it.

She put the car into reverse, muttering as she backed out of the parking space, "I leave you for five minutes—*five minutes*—and you decide you want a new career as a bull fighter!" She threw the car into drive, spun out of the parking lot, and gunned it down Sixth Avenue heading for the hospital.

"Somebody... threw me in there, Case... it's not like..." I put my hand up to my head and rubbed my temples. "it's not like... I saw a 1500 pound... bull and said, 'Gee... he looks like he... wants his ears scratched.'" My words sounded strange to me. The adrenaline rush was wearing off, and I began to feel every bone and muscle in my body. My right shoulder still felt—well, actually I couldn't feel it at all, which kinda' worried me. I lifted my arm, sending shooting pains cascading down my back. I moaned as the lights all went dark for a minute.

The car stopped and Casey reached over and touched my leg. "Alex, you still with us?" She sounded worried and I nodded, which caused more muscles to spasm and whatever lights had returned winked out again. She gunned the accelerator and I felt the car lurch forward, "Shit! Five minutes—five *goddamn* minutes—and you jump in with a goddamn bull!" She picked up the microphone, "9David73, Call University Medical Center. Tell them I'm bringing 9David72 in with possible head injuries, ETA five minutes."

The dispatcher's disembodied voice answered, "10-4."

Kate's voice came on, "9David70 to 9David73, how bad is she?"

"73 to 70, she's in and out of consciousness."

"10-4."

In and out of consciousness? No I'm not...

Megan reached over the back of my seat to put her arms around my neck and brought her face close to mine. "Hang in there, Alex. You're okay, just a little shaken up, that's all. Talk to me while we're driving, okay? Tell me what happened."

"I... uh... heard the bull.... Pulled myself up... to look... somebody threw me... over." My thoughts seemed fuzzy, making me want to drift off into a peaceful sleep. I felt Megan's face next to my ear and heard her say in a nearly panicked voice, "Keep talking, Alex. Don't go to sleep, okay? Tell me something... um... tell me about your new puppy."

"What... pup... py?" *I don't remember getting a new puppy. Do I have a new puppy?*

The horn honked and I heard Casey yell, "Get out of my way, Asshole!"

Megan's hands tightened on my chest and I smiled a little. "You mean she's... not driving like...." I had intended to say "an old lady," but something unintelligible came out instead.

B right lights shone in my face, and someone was holding my eyelid open. "Alex, can you hear me?"

I moaned.

"Can you open your eyes?" I slowly opened one eye and saw Kate, Casey, Megan, Maddie, Marcos and an E.R. doc standing around the gurney, all looking extremely worried. Opening my eye brought on an attack of nausea so I closed it and started to drift again.

Quick vignettes raced through my mind: me in a wedding dress with my mom in the front row crying, Casey holding her neck and sliding down a wall, Megan lying bleeding and alone at her K9 academy, Kate yelling at me. *Kate yelling at me?*

"Alex! Open your eyes! That's an order!"

That sounded real. I forced my eye open again and saw Kate standing over me. The doctor put his hand on her back. "Good, if she goes out again, try to bring her back just like that. We need to keep her conscious."

I mumbled, "You... yelled... at me."

Kate gave me a worried but reassuring smile. "I'll do it again if you don't keep your eyes open."

Casey and Megan weren't next to my bed anymore. My tongue felt thick. "Where'd..." I tried to say, "they go?" but nothing came out.

"It was a little crowded in here and the doctor asked them to step out. They're right outside the room. Don't worry; they're not going anywhere. You just worry about you right now."

"My head's... my hardest...." I felt nauseated again and closed my eyes. "I'm sick."

I heard the doctor's voice. "I can't give you anything just yet for the nausea, Alex. Can you tell me what month it is?"

"October."

"Do you know the date?"

"Uh, 12th... 13th... 30th?" I continued answering questions, right on through having to give him the months backwards, which I can't normally do anyway, so I wasn't too concerned when I messed them up. The lights bothered my eyes, so I closed them and tried to drift off to sleep again.

Kate squeezed my arm. "Alex, open your eyes."

I opened them and saw Maddie filling a syringe. I thought she was going to stick it into me, but she reached up and inserted it into a tube that ran down next to my stomach instead. I lifted my arm and was horrified to see an I.V. running into the back of my hand. "Wha...?" I reached over with my other hand to pull it out, but Kate pressed down on my arm again.

"It's okay, Alex. Just leave it, okay?"

My captain and lieutenant chose that second to stick their heads in and Kate nodded to them. She reached up and brushed some hair off my forehead. "I'm going to step out for a minute too, all right? Remember, I gave you an order." She winked at me and I managed to smile back even though my cheek hurt like hell.

I somehow stayed awake long enough to reassure the doctor that I had stabilized. After I suffered through being poked and prodded, shoved into a tube for an MRI, and taken for several x-rays, they eventually admitted me to a private room for overnight observation. The captain and lieutenant came in and talked for a while, then went home. Kate pulled up a chair and sat while Casey went to find two more chairs for her and Megan.

Kate put her foot up on the rail under my bed. "You know, I didn't know it at the time, but my life was pleasantly boring before you transferred into my unit." Her affectionate grin made me feel better somehow.

I smiled back, then winced at the pain in my cheek. "Always glad to oblige, Boss."

Casey brought in two chairs, which she set next to the bed. Megan pulled hers close and sat before reaching over and taking my hand. "Go to sleep, Alex. I won't leave you. I'm right here, okay?"

My eyes felt heavy, and I mumbled, "What about Tessa?"

Casey sat back in her chair. "I'll stop by and pick them up on my way home to feed my critters. I'll keep them until you're back on your feet."

My eyes closed, and I muttered, "Them?"

Casey chuckled. "Don't worry about it, Alex. We've got your back."

All the lights went out and I fell into a deep, dreamless sleep.

CHAPTER 4

Two days later, Casey and a hospital technician brought a wheelchair to my room to take me to the front of the hospital so I could go home. "I'm not riding in that." I stood up to walk to the door, but Casey blocked my way.

"Hospital rules. You gotta ride and he's gotta push, so sit down and shut up." She put a hand to my chest and gently pushed me back.

I sighed while I carefully lowered myself into the chair. "Aren't we in a cheerful mood today?"

She shrugged. "Sorry. I knew you were gonna argue, so I thought I'd cut you off at the pass."

We rolled down the hall and took the elevators to the emergency room. When the door opened, Megan, Maddie and Marcos greeted me with a cake and ice cream. "Surprise!"

Maddie looked *tres chic* with her spiked hair colored to match her purple scrubs. She'd replaced the stud in her nose with a circular ring sporting a silver elephant, and she wore a cobra ring wrapped around her upper arm. "It's chocolate cake with triple fudge macadamia nut ice cream! It doesn't get much better than that!"

Marcos tilted the cake so I could read the inscription: *Never squat with your spurs on.*

I smiled as best I could. I'd been practicing in the mirror so I didn't scare people with my swollen eye and cheek, but the results still left a lot to be desired. I got out of the chair and picked up a plastic knife to cut the cake. "Thanks guys, it looks great." I handed Casey a piece. "Here. You get the first piece since you were stupid enough to jump into the bullpen to rescue me. By the way, did anybody find out who threw me in there in the first place?"

Casey took the plate from me. "No, and I've talked to every cowboy and cowgirl at the rodeo. I've seen enough Skoal sliding around inside men's mouths to last me a lifetime." She raised her eyebrows at me, "And I've met some nice tight wrangler-clad cowgirls too."

I sighed. "Great. Meg gets the cowboys, you get the cowgirls, and Marcos gets the cows. What does that leave me?"

Marcos put his hands on his hips. "Excuse me? Cows?"

Maddie laughed and patted his tush. "Marcos, you'd do the cowboys, cowgirls, cows and goats if they'd let you. Don't play Mr. Innocent with us."

Marcos perked up. "There are goats?"

Everyone in the E.R. chorused, "Yuck!"

Megan kicked him in the shin. "That's not only disgusting, it's illegal and inhumane, and you'd *better* just be kidding."

Marcos jumped away from Megan and laughed. "Of *course* I'm kidding. Maddie's the one who brought it up for Pete's sake."

I tried to glare as best I could, but I don't think my face cooperated. "Yeah, but she was only kidding. With you, we never know." I handed him his cake and ice cream and he winked at me with his incredible, chocolate-brown eyes. If I didn't have to worry about every sexual disease known to man, I'd jump his bones in a second.

Casey took a bite of cake and pointed at me with her fork. "Oh yeah, I forgot to mention, the two little girls are still missing. The mother received photographs of them eating cake the same day you decided to jump in with Gumby."

Memories of the solid muscle that tried to kill me went scurrying around in my brain. "Gumby? The bull's name is Gumby?"

"Yeah. I guess one of the bull rider's daughters got to name him, and her favorite toy is her Gumby."

"Gumby... great. I can see the headlines: Gumby Kills Detective Wolfe During Kidnapping Investigation. Anyway, the girls are still missing?"

Casey finished her cake and dumped her plate into a nearby trashcan. "Yeah, it's the weirdest thing. The mother gets a phone call from them every night, they talk for about thirty seconds, then the line goes dead. We've tapped the lines, obviously, but so far we haven't been able to trace anything."

The icing on the cake made my stomach queasier than the medication I had to take, so I pushed it around to make it seem like I'd eaten more than I had. When I didn't think anyone would notice, I folded the paper plate in half and lowered it into the trash. "Have there been any ransom demands?"

"No, just the picture and the phone calls. And the kids don't sound upset or scared so we're assuming they know whoever has them."

Megan piped up. "A picture of them eating cake? Sounds like my kind of kidnapper." She'd finished with her first slice of cake and put a second one on her plate, topping it with two scoops of ice cream. "Hey, Alex, didn't you tell me somebody's boyfriend was missing too? What happened to him?"

Casey answered for me. "He's still missing too. We're working both cases full time now." Casey pulled out her keys. "I'll go get the car and bring it up to the door."

We finished visiting and I dutifully climbed back into my wheelchair and let Maddie push me out to the sidewalk where Casey was holding the passenger door open for me. "Good grief, Case, I'm not an invalid you know. I can open my own damn door."

Casey shut the door after I climbed in, then moved around to slide into the driver's seat. "You're welcome."

I hated being corrected and muttered, "Well... I'm not an invalid." I also hated it when I acted like a little kid, but sometimes the kid just appeared out of nowhere. I picked up a folder sitting on the seat. "So what's our next step?"

"Your next step is home to bed. The doctor didn't release you back to duty status yet."

Here came the kid again. I slid down in the seat and crossed my arms. "I'm not staying home in bed. I'm fine."

"Well, I can't tie you to the house, but you're not working on the kidnapping case, or any case for that matter. Kate told me to tell you that's an order."

"You can't give me a third-party order. I don't think that works."

Casey took out her phone, hit speed dial and put it on speaker. Kate answered. "Sgt. Brannigan."

"Hi Kate, it's Casey."

Kate didn't hesitate. "That's a direct order, Alex. You will *not* work on any investigation until you're returned to duty status. Do I make myself clear?"

I slumped further down in my seat, frowning.

Kate lowered her voice. "Alex."

I mumbled, "Clear as a bell." I heard her chuckle on the other end.

Casey stopped for a red light. "I'll see you in a little while, Kate. I'll be dropping her at her house in a few minutes." She disconnected and looked over at me with her eyebrows raised into an innocent expression.

I stayed quiet until we pulled up to my house. I got out of the car and growled at her as she came around to my side of the car. "Et tú, Bruté?"

She walked me into the house and settled me on the couch in front of the television. "Don't worry, Alex. At least you can't get into any trouble lying here on the couch."

By the time Casey brought a pillow and a blanket from my room, set a glass of water on the coffee table and put out all my pain medications and muscle relaxants, I wanted to strangle her. When she finally left, I picked up the remote and flipped through the endless reruns of daytime television while I drifted into and out of a dream-filled sleep.

Megan stopped by after her last dog obedience class. The pepperoni pizza she carried through the door smelled wonderful after the can of chicken noodle soup I'd fixed for lunch. By that time, I'd watched about all the T.V. I could handle and was happy for the company. Megan flopped down onto the couch after she set the box on the coffee table. "Oh shoot! I forgot the drinks!" She dashed back outside and returned shortly carrying a six-pack of vegetable juice. Flopping down on the couch again, she pulled a can from the plastic ring and handed it to me.

I gingerly took the can between my thumb and forefinger. "What *is* this?"

"That's what's gonna get you better quicker. You need to eat more fruit and vegetables."

She wore her hair pulled back in a ponytail and I wondered whether she'd put the rubber band in too tight. "Have you gone completely off your gourd? I don't drink this stuff!"

"Tony, my new cowboy, says you'll heal faster by drinking it, and he should know since he rides bulls too." She popped the top on her can and sipped a little bit. Her nose scrunched up and she shivered before grabbing a piece of pizza to wash out the taste. She pointed to my can with the slice of pizza. "Go on. Drink it."

I popped the tab and slowly raised the can to my nose. I took one quick sniff and gagged. "I can't do this, Meg. It smells awful."

"Hold your nose."

My nose was one of the only parts of my face that wasn't bruised so I reached up to pinch it shut and brought the can back to my lips. I took a quick sip and shuddered as the thick liquid made its way down my throat. Megan handed me a slice of pizza, which I greedily shoved in my mouth to cover the aftertaste lingering on my tongue.

Megan picked up her can to read the ingredients. "Pretty disgusting, huh?"

I shoved the pizza into my mouth again and bit off a huge chunk. "Disgusting is too nice a word. I think detestable and repugnant might begin to describe it."

"Yeah, okay... hold on." She ran out the door again and returned with two four packs of wine coolers. "I thought these might help too." Her usual mischievous grin spread across her face, and I laughed as I exchanged the can of vegetable juice for a bottle of Black Cherry Fizz.

"But you do need to eat right, so I'll go shopping for you and get you some stuff."

"Megan, I am not an invalid. I don't need you to shop for me." I groaned when I moved a little too quickly and my back muscles went into a spasm. When the pain went away, I grabbed a second slice of pizza and washed it down with the Fizz just as my cell phone rang.

"Alex? It's Ruthanne. How's the noggin?"

"Its fine. What's up?"

"Well, remember our conversation about Shelley Greer?"

"Yeah."

"She escaped from the detention center today. A, shall we say, slightly overweight deputy took her to a hearing and she ran out an emergency exit and disappeared. The deputy made it to the door before he ran out of breath."

I stayed quiet a minute while I processed the information and thought about what, if anything, that had to do with me. "So how hard are they searching for her?"

"Considering she committed a homicide, pretty hard. She's only eleven years old. How difficult can it be to find her? Eric walked into the hearing five minutes after she'd left. He's been out looking for her ever since, along with three Tucson P.D. officers and five deputies."

I rubbed the top of my forehead where the doctor had given me five stitches. "How long has she been gone?"

"About—" She paused and I guessed she was checking her watch. "Three hours now. I'll let you know if we find her."

"Thanks for the heads up. Come by to visit me. I'm bored stiff."

"Are you in bed?"

"Not when you're around, I'm not. I'll see you later, okay?" We hung up and I wondered whether I should call Gia to let her know what had happened. Knowing her, she probably knew before I did. I called her anyway just to make sure. When she answered, I got right to the point. "Hi, Gia. It's Alex. Have you heard about Shelley?"

I heard her pull in a breath, which meant she had her cigar fired up. "I have."

"Okay, I just wanted to make sure you knew about it." The silence extended well past the point of comfortable conversation. "Gia?"

"I'd rather not speak on the phone, Alex. I understand you have a concussion and some bruised muscles but no broken bones. Are you up to coming to my house if Gabe picks you up?" I'd never seen her without her bodyguard-slash-chauffer, Gabe. I think he'd probably been used as the prototype for the original Italian Stallion. He was tall, rugged, and unflappable, with a cute little dimple that always appeared when something amused him, and I usually amused him.

Her connections and access to classified information always astounded me. "First of all, how do you know what type of injuries I have? And second, I can drive myself if I go anywhere."

Gia chuckled. "You shouldn't even have to ask the first question, and with the medications you're on, you shouldn't be driving."

She even knew what medications I was taking? "Do you even know when I have sex?"

"You haven't had any in a while."

I pictured her grey eyes laughing at me and smiled into the phone. "Why can't you come here?"

"Alex." She sounded a little perturbed. In Gia's world, when she calls, people come running. "Gabe left ten minutes ago. He should be at your door in another ten minutes. I'll see you when you get here."

That put my hackles up and I probably spoke with more pique than necessary. "Gia, I don't come running whenever you summon me. That may work with your brown-nosing politicians and flunkies, but it doesn't work with me. If you want to talk to me right now, you can come here. Period!" I couldn't believe I'd just said that to the most powerful mafia don this side of the Mississippi. My heart felt like it would pound right out of my chest, and having Megan staring at me with her mouth open and a horrified expression on her face didn't help my confidence any.

The line was quiet for at least a minute before I realized Gia had hung up. I returned Megan's stare, than sank back into the cushions. "I am so screwed."

Meg slowly nodded as she swiveled around to check the front window. "Does the mafia do drive-by shootings?"

"Gia wouldn't do that." I got up and pulled the curtains shut on the window anyway. "Maybe we should go get some hamburgers or something?"

"We just had pizza."

"Oh yeah." We sat and waited for Gabe to show up. After fifteen minutes with no shots fired, the two of us let out a shared sigh of relief. After thirty minutes and still no Gabe, we began talking in low voices as though we were afraid someone might overhear.

When the doorbell rang, Meg practically jumped out of her seat. A few seconds ticked by and she sniffed, raising her nose in the air trying to identify the strange odor that suddenly wafted through the house. "Do you smell cigar smoke?"

I breathed in and the paralysis that immediately overcame me when I recognized Gia's brand numbed my brain. I knew that spicy aroma as well as I knew my own brand of perfume. Lord knows she'd blown it in my face enough times. I whispered, "What do I do?"

Megan looked from me to the door then back to me again. "I guess you should answer it."

I nodded and when I stood, I hitched up my pants and took a big breath. "Okay, here goes nothing." When I pulled open the door, Gia stood with one arm crossed over her chest, the elbow of her other arm resting in her palm with her cigar held lazily next to her face. Gabe stood behind her; the dimple in his chin showing as he slowly shook his head and looked up at the sky. I waited stupidly, too scared to say anything.

Gia raised her eyebrows. "If it was raining out here, I'd be soaked by now."

"Oh... um, come in. Come on in. You remember Megan, don't you? Come in. Come on in." I sounded like an idiot, even to myself.

She walked through the door and nodded to Megan. "Good to see you again, Megan." She turned and indicated Gabe who waited on the front stoop. "Megan, you remember my chauffer, Gabe?"

Megan nodded.

"Why don't you step outside and visit with Gabe for a few minutes while Alex and I come to an understanding?"

I shifted nervously, not sure I wanted my only witness to leave.

Megan gave me up in a heartbeat. "Yes Ma'am." She ducked her head and left, pulling the door closed behind her.

I glanced around the room. "Do you want to sit down? I don't have any Scotch, but I've got some wine coolers."

She took a puff on her cigar, turned her head without taking her eyes from mine, and blew a thin line of smoke toward my kitchen. She didn't move to the couch, and I turned and indicated it again with my hand. Her eyes flashed, and I crossed my arms and raised my chin, trying to look calm and unconcerned.

She stepped over and ground out her cigar on the pizza box while she exhaled another cloud of smoke. "Alex, do you now how old I am?"

I shook my head, surprised by the question.

She returned and moved in close to me. "I am 51-years-old. And do you know how many times in those 51 years someone *dared* to speak to me the way you did over the phone?"

I shook my head again.

She reached up to rest her hand on my shoulder. "Take a guess."

I shrugged and concentrated on not pulling away. "You shouldn't have just assumed I'd obediently leap into the car with Gabe when he showed up. I don't jump to your beck and call, Gia. We're friends. I'm not your flunky." I stayed where I was, though it was a struggle not to move. The color rose in her face and I wondered whether I'd pushed her one step too far.

She remained as still as a statue. I flinched when she reached up and grabbed my chin between surprisingly strong fingers. "Zero."

My eyebrows pulled together as I tried to figure out what she meant. Then it dawned on me. No one had ever spoken to her like I had. She must have seen the light bulb turn on in my little pea brain because she cocked her head and repeated angrily through gritted teeth, "*Zero!*"

"I'm sorry, Gia, but—"

"But *nothing*, Alex!" Her intensity surprised me, and I stepped back, only to have her step forward as though we were doing some kind of weird dance. Fire smoldered in her eyes. "There is one fact you always fail to figure into our relationship. *I am Gianina Angelino*, and I have warned you on numerous occasions *never* to forget that. It has nothing to do with my ego or my social status; it has to do with the reality of my position and the rules of the game that *must* be observed in order to stay alive, both for myself *and* for my friends." She squeezed my chin and when I tried to pull away, she brought her other arm around my neck and held my head still. I could have forced her to let go, but I chose not to. "I live in a *very* dangerous world, Alex, and because we've become friends, you live there too." She paused a minute to let that sink in, then let go and stepped back. "You will *never* speak to me like that again."

I understood what she was telling me, and I stared at the ground and nodded, not sure what to say.

She sighed and spoke in a quieter tone. "Alex, we are moving through uncharted waters for both of us. Ever since my brother was murdered, I have neither enjoyed, nor allowed, a relaxed, impertinent, unfettered friendship, and you have never befriended anyone who wields the sort of power I control. I doubt you even realize exactly who I am. I think we both need to tread a little more carefully from now on."

I don't know why, but I really liked this lady and valued her friendship. Her eyes had returned to the beautiful soft grey that I'd first encountered, and on an impulse, I reached around and pulled her into a hug. She stiffened, then put her arms around my shoulders and returned the embrace. When I stepped away, I pointed to the door. "Can I let them back in now?"

She nodded. "Gabe will stay in the car, but I'm sure Megan is dying to get back in to see if you're still in one piece." When Gia pulled open the door, a squatting Megan, who looked like she'd had her ear plastered up against the door, fell across the threshold.

Gia chuckled and held out her hand to help her to her feet. "She's not dead." She looked over her shoulder at me. "Although I did think about it a time or two."

I grinned. "I explained the facts of life to her, and I've got her pretty well cowed."

Gabe snorted as Megan took Gia's hand and pulled herself to her feet.

Gia gracefully moved to the couch and pointed to the pizza. "May I?"

Megan ran over. "Of course! Here, let me take one to Gabe." She grabbed a slice and a napkin and ran back out to Gabe, who looked at Gia.

She raised her eyebrows again and nodded.

He accepted the pizza before heading back to the limo.

I went into the kitchen and brought out three wine coolers.

Gia took hers, but as she sat on the couch she took mine away from me. "Alcohol, pain killers and muscle relaxants don't mix."

I took it back from her and opened it. "Tough." I took a long drink and sank back into the cushions. The medications were wearing off, and I washed down two more pills with the wine to dull the pain.

Gia looked regal sitting on my couch in her dark grey pinstriped business suit, stockings and high heels. She watched me drink the wine cooler as she addressed Megan. "Has she always been so stubborn?"

Megan nodded, "Yup. Once, when we were in kindergarten, we were supposed to be taking a nap, and Alex kept mimicking every move I made. The teacher told her to stop and when she didn't, Mrs. Connors moved Alex's sleeping pad over to the corner away from everyone else. Well, Alex didn't think much of that, so once the teacher sat down again, she snuck into the kitchen, got a gallon of milk, tiptoed back in and poured it all over me."

When Gia started laughing, I pointed my pizza at Megan. "You left out the fact that you'd just pulled my pants down in front of the rest of the school when we were out on the playground."

Gia took a sip of her wine, her wistful expression surprising me. "You know, Credo was the only person with whom I could share the type of friendship you two have. I miss him so much."

My eyes met Megan's, and we knew she was right. We had a friendship that neither time nor distance would ever take away.

Megan scrunched back into the couch. "I love the way you name your horses after him. Credo's Hope, Credo's Dream... that's so cool. Alex has one named after her too." When Gia looked at me and raised her eyebrows, Megan laughed. "His name's Baboon's Backside, and

Credo's Dream beat him." She stuck out her tongue at me and I threw my crust at her, which, unfortunately, had to travel across Gia.

Gia glanced at me the same way Kate does when I need to stop, and I wondered whether the two of them were genetically related somewhere back in the gene pool.

I took off my shoes, put my back up against the armrest, and stretched my legs across Gia until my feet were resting in Megan's lap.

The steel flashed in Gia's eyes before she sighed and put her hands on my legs and rested them there. She slipped off her high heels, relaxed back into the cushions and put her feet up on the coffee table. "You may *never* tell *anyone* I did this."

Mortified—or terrified, I couldn't tell which—Megan let out a breath and took a swig of her wine cooler. The combination of the medicine and the wine had the predictable effect of making me sleepy and I needed to find out what Gia had wanted to tell me before I fell asleep. "So, what couldn't you tell me over the phone."

"It's not that it can't be discussed over the phone. I rarely say anything personal where someone else may be listening in. What I wanted to ask you was, if law enforcement can't find Shelley, would you go out and get her? We won't have the results from the DNA for an indeterminate amount of time, and if she is my grand niece, I don't want her living on the streets."

I thought a second. I really didn't feel up to wandering the streets trying to find a street-wise eleven-year-old who didn't want to be found, so I hedged. "Well, I'm pretty sore today, and probably tomorrow too. How about, if they don't have her by the day after tomorrow, I'll go find her?"

"That's fine, and when you locate her, I'd prefer you'd bring her to my house instead of back to the detention center."

The room was quiet while I processed what she'd just said. I blinked several times, my brain working feverishly to come up with a polite way to tell her that wasn't going to happen. "Well, if you can work it out with Child Protective Services for her to come stay with you, of course I'll bring her there."

"CPS has nothing to do with it. She'll stay in my home with me where Gabe and I can keep an eye on her."

Uh oh. "Well, since the state has custody right now, I'll have to turn her over to them."

The slow smile spreading across her face worried me. "We'll discuss it again once you find her, Alex. For right now, it's enough that you'll agree to find her." She sat forward. "Now, if I could get out from under your legs, I'll have Gabe drive me home." Even with drugs and alcohol in my system, I still remembered my manners. I walked her to the door and waved at Gabe. When they'd driven away I returned to the couch to crawl under the blanket and fall fast asleep.

CHAPTER 5

Two days later, I found myself in the part of town known as the Vistas, not because the neighborhood had a great view, but because all the streets had the word "Vista" in their names. Only a few blocks away from the detention center, the area would be a perfect hiding place for someone who didn't want to be found. Rundown, abandoned houses were the norm, drugs were rampant and the population had an extreme dislike of law enforcement. I parked my Jeep in front of a local convenience store and gave the clerk twenty dollars to make sure it didn't disappear while I was gone.

I still hadn't been released to duty status, so I fervently hoped Kate wouldn't find out what I was up to. The light jacket I wore concealed the Glock semi-automatic handgun stuffed down the back of my pants. I shoved my badge into my front pocket in case I needed to identify myself to some other cops. I slipped my cell phone into the other front pocket in case I needed to call those other cops for help before I could flash my badge at them.

The neighborhood consisted of several streets that wound their way through the area in a mindless pattern reminiscent of a bowl of spaghetti without the marinara sauce. I wound my way around until I came to a home that belonged to a sixty-five-year-old African American woman I'd met several years earlier when I'd kept her grandson from bleeding out from two bullet holes in his chest while we waited for the paramedics to arrive. While we'd waited, I'd tried to distract her with inane conversation, and somehow we'd discovered a mutual interest in 1960's rock and roll. Since that time, she and I have had a shaky truce as far as the "us vs. them" attitude that permeates the Vistas.

As I approached her house, I could see the front door standing open. Many of these older homes don't have a working heater or air conditioner, and the front door is used to regulate the temperature inside the house. It wasn't smart to startle people in this neighborhood, so I stood to the side of the door before calling out, "Trisha, you home? It's Alex."

I smiled when I heard some men cussing inside, objects being pushed across surfaces, and drawers opening and closing. When Trisha's twenty-year-old grandson finally came to the door, he wore the expression of a completely innocent young man. "What you want, Wolfe?"

"I want to talk to your grandma. Is she home?"

"Nope." He pulled up his jeans, which were five sizes too big.

"When will she be back?"

"Don't know."

It was pointless to ask him anything else since apparently saving his life hadn't given me any brownie points in his book. I took a stab at it anyway. "I'm looking for an eleven-year-old white girl who ran away near here. You seen her?"

He snuffled and rubbed his nose with the back of his hand. "Shit, Wolfe. A white girl in this hood? She'd be meat by now." The neighborhood housed predominantly black families, and I knew he was right. Shelley would be toast if she got into the wrong crowd.

There was no sense waiting around for Trisha, so I pointed to the smear of cocaine powdering his nose, "You got some snow stickin' to the end of your nose. You might wanna take care of that before you go anywhere."

He quickly wiped his face with his sleeve before disappearing back into the house.

My cell phone rang, and I answered it while I walked back out to the sidewalk.

Ruthanne spoke quietly, as though she didn't want anyone on her end to hear her. "Alex, I thought you should know. We're near Campbell and Valencia at a duplex. Eric was down south looking for Shelley. He found her in an abandoned apartment. She shot at him, and he took cover. When he came up to return fire she'd disappeared into a bedroom. She slipped out a back window while he was taking cover up front."

"What? How would an eleven-year-old white girl get a gun in that neighborhood? Who was she staying with?"

"I don't know, but they're bringing in a K-9 to track her. Look, I have to go. I'll call you later, all right?"

We hung up. If Shelley was hanging out near Valencia, which was several miles further south than the Vistas, there wasn't much point in me continuing to look here, but I decided to talk to a few more people to make sure I'd covered all the bases. I hit five or six more houses where I knew I wouldn't get shot just for being a white cop walking by herself in the neighborhood. Not surprisingly, I learned zip. As I started the long hike back to my Jeep, someone behind me yelled, "Hey, Wolfe!"

I turned to see Trisha's ten-year-old granddaughter skating toward me on her skateboard. She rode down into a gulley, up the other side, and then jumped off right in front of me, kicking the board up into her hands at the same time she dismounted.

"Not bad! Where'd you learn to ride like that?"

She shrugged and looked around, obviously not wanting to be seen talking to me. "Here. Grandma got home... said to give you this." She shoved an envelope into my hand, jumped back onto the skateboard and kicked off before I could ask any more questions.

I watched her skate away as I opened the envelope and took out a hand-written note: *Alex, that girl's been in the neighborhood, sleeping in people's back yards with their dogs.* She hadn't written anything else, but she'd told me what I'd needed to know. Great. Now I just had to come back at night to get eaten by all the junkyard dogs people kept in their back yards. My head ached again and my shoulder throbbed. I continued my walk back to my Jeep and drove home, grateful for the stash of painkillers and the bed that awaited me.

That evening Ruthanne stopped by to see how I was doing. She took one look at my face and winced. "Yuck! Those bruises look gross, Alex. Maybe you should try some make-up or something."

"Your heartfelt description of my face is equaled only by your tender compassion and sorrow in the presence of my infirmities."

She snorted, "Yeah, what you said."

I motioned for her to sit on the couch and went into the kitchen to get some drinks. I yelled, "I have wine coolers and vegetable juice; take your pick."

"I love vegetable juice. I'll have one of those."

I stuck my head out to see if she was kidding. She wasn't, so I went back and grabbed a can for her and a bottle of Cherry Fizz for me.

She popped the top, drinking it as though it were carton of milk instead of a lethal concoction of vegetables.

I shuddered. "Talk about gross. Anyway, what about the kid? Did the K9 find her?"

"No, he couldn't even pick up the scent. They walked around for about an hour trying to get some type of odor, but no luck. The handler said maybe Brick was just having a bad day. He's a new handler too, so that might have had something to do with it."

"You said Shelley's been staying down on Valencia? How'd Eric figure that out?"

She pulled her notebook out of her back pocket and flipped through the pages. When she found the right page, she read for a minute. "I guess someone told him they'd seen her down around those apartments over there and he went to check it out. I didn't get the name of the person he talked to though."

I lay on one end of the couch and she sat on the other. I didn't feel like going back to the Vistas, but apparently nighttime was the only time I'd be able to find Shelley. "Just so you know, I've been looking for her in the Vistas. I'm gonna go out again tonight to look for her."

"You're going into the Vistas at night? By yourself? Does Kate know?"

I shook my head.

"Does *anybody* know?"

I could tell "you dumb shit" had tactfully been left off the end of the question. I shrugged. "You do." Now that she'd said it like that, the whole idea did sound pretty stupid. "Well, I can't take Megan, 'cause she'd freak out. I can't ask Casey, 'cause I'm not supposed to be working on any work-related investigation. I don't have much of a choice."

She was well aware of my on-going issues with Kate, and she narrowed her eyes suspiciously. "What do you mean you're not supposed to be working on any work-related investigation?"

I realized my mistake, and quickly backtracked. "Nothing. Forget I said anything."

"C'mon Alex. The whole department knows you've kept out of trouble for three months now. Kate's actually been bragging about you to the other sergeants."

That was news to me. "She has?" I suddenly felt guilty, but not guilty enough to stop searching. "Well, *you* can't go with me because that would definitely make it an official investigation. Look, I'll be careful, and I'll call you when I'm out of there so you know I'm still alive, all right?"

She didn't look happy about it, but there wasn't a heck of a lot she could do. "Can you at least take Megan so she can call 911 while you're getting the shit kicked out of you?"

"Megan doesn't do well in tense situations. She panics."

"Yeah, but at least she can hit speed dial. You can't go into the Vistas at night by yourself, Alex. That's just plain stupid."

I knew she was right, but I'd taken Megan on investigations before and she either got scared and freaked out or she got mad at me for some reason. I reluctantly took out my cell phone and called her. "Hey."

"Hi there." She sounded like she had something stuffed in her mouth.

"So is whipped cream boy there tonight?" I looked over at

Ruthanne, who'd perked up at the mention of whipped cream.

"Unfortunately, no. It's just Sugar and me and we're watching reruns." Sugar was her perfectly obedient chocolate lab, whom I absolutely adored.

I had half hoped her new boyfriend would be there so she couldn't come out with me. "I have to go look for Shelley tonight, and Ruthanne doesn't want me to go alone. She was wondering if maybe you'd come with me."

"Sure. I can be there in about forty minutes."

Ruthanne yelled loud enough for Megan to hear, "Tell her to bring the whipped cream!"

Megan yelled back, "It's all gone!"

"Ow, Megs. That hurt my ear." I covered the phone and relayed her message. "She says it's all gone."

"Dang."

I sighed. "I'll see you when you get here." When I hit the "end" button, I picked up my notebook and sat back into the couch. "Don't you ever think about anything besides sex?"

She looked puzzled. "Do you?"

"Okay then... moving on... do you have anything new with Shelley's case? What do they do with eleven-year-olds who commit murder?"

"Well, they'll have a hearing, and if she's adjudicated delinquent, they can keep her locked up until she's eighteen. Sometimes, when they turn eighteen, they transfer them to adult detention and they serve the rest of their sentence." For some silly reason, juveniles aren't found guilty or not guilty. Instead, they're "adjudicated delinquent" if the judge decides they've committed a delinquent act. "The department's trying to find other people who may have been molested by the man she killed. We have to walk a tight rope though so we don't 'impugn his good reputation.' Finding other victims would sure help corroborate Shelley's story that he'd come into her room to molest her, though."

I wrote down, *Check for other molest victims.* I could make a few unofficial inquiries easier than she or Eric could. "What'd the victim's wife say? Did she know he was molesting the kids?"

"No. According to her he should've been canonized. She said he always coached the kids' teams, even though they were only foster children and they might end up going back to their parents before the season ended. He didn't care. She's playing the grieving widow thing to the hilt."

I looked at her out of the corner of my eye, trying to decide what I was hearing in her voice. "But...."

"But... something just doesn't feel right. Eric believes her, but, call it women's intuition, I just don't trust the lady." The shoelace on one of her sneakers had come loose, and she reached down to retie it. "She seems to be able to cry at will, and she can really wrap men around her little finger. I don't know... I can't really put my finger on it."

I scratched notes while she spoke, and when she stopped, I underlined the word "wife," which I'd just written in all capital letters. "Have the interviews been transcribed yet?" It usually took a week or two for the transcriptionist to type out the interviews that the detectives recorded during an investigation.

"They're in the process. Who knows when they'll be done, but our ladies are really good so it shouldn't take too long. Why?"

I shrugged and tugged on the cuff of my jeans. "Can I have a copy when you get them?"

She sat quietly a minute before answering. "For you or for Gia?"

I smiled. "For me. I haven't sunk so low that I'd give official documents to a Mafia Queen."

She returned my grin. "Can you get me a date with Gia?"

"Ruthanne, Jesus! Have you no shame?" I felt my face color because Gia's incredible breasts suddenly came to mind. I'd never even thought of a woman in that way before and I had no intention of thinking of her that way now.

"You're blushing. Admit it, you think she's hot too." She reached over and lightly punched my shoulder.

"She's not hot, she's just Gia. And why can't you make up your mind whether you like men or women? It must get pretty confusing wondering what kind of equipment your next date's gonna have."

"What, and cut out half my possibilities? I don't think so." Her pager went off and she pulled it from her belt to look at it. "Damn, its Eric. I hope I don't have to go back out again tonight." She called and talked to him for a few minutes, then motioned for me to bring her a pen and paper. When I produced them, she wrote down an address and told him she'd be on her way.

She stood up to go and tossed the pen back to me. "Shit, another body turned up downtown. Sometimes I wish we'd have two consecutive weeks without a gang shooting or a homicide. I could really use a good night's sleep."

"I'll let you know how it goes tonight in the Vistas. And do me a favor... keep it to yourself, okay?"

She stepped over to the door just as Megan walked in. "Hi Meg. You two be careful out there. I'd hate to have to investigate your homicides right after I investigate this one. A woman needs her beauty sleep, you know."

I put my hand on the door handle to close the door after her. "Your concern is touching. Let me know if anything else comes up with Shelley." She waved as I pushed the door shut. I turned to see Megan standing behind me with her hands on her hips. I held my hands out to my side, palms up. "What?"

"What did she mean by that? When you said come with you, I assumed you meant on some easy interview thing. Why do we need to be careful? Because I'm not going anywhere I might end up dead, or worse."

I scratched my head. "What can be worse than dead?"

"Married."

I nodded. "Good point. Well, I can pretty much guarantee you won't get married while we're out tonight." I gathered up my equipment: gun, cell phone, flashlight, extra ammo, and a wallet containing my badge and ID.

Megan walked over to the box of ammo and dumped about twenty rounds into her hand. She filled both front jeans pockets while I laughed at her.

"You look like a chipmunk with her cheeks in the wrong place."

"Yeah? Well this chipmunk has no intention of coming back dead."

"What are you gonna do? Throw 'em at them?"

"I'm gonna throw them at you if you get me hurt."

"I'm not gonna get you hurt." I picked up my keys and mumbled on my way out the door, "I hope."

Megan followed me out the door. "What was that last thing you said?"

"Nothing. Let's go." We jumped into my Jeep and drove back to the Vistas. I parked in the same convenience store lot and gave a different clerk twenty dollars to watch my wheels. I definitely needed to hit Gia up for expenses the next time I saw her.

We had to cross a fairly busy road and I stopped to let some cars pass. Megan had been following so close she bumped into me and stayed there. I hid my smile and crossed when the road was clear. I had to stop twice when she accidentally gave my sneakers a flat tire by stepping on the back of my shoe and forcing it off my heel. When she almost did it a third time, I turned and put my hands on her shoulders. "You're following me so closely I was wondering if we're gonna have sex or whether you're just being really friendly?"

"It's dark out here, Alex. I want to go home."

Her shoulders were shaking and I gave her my best, reassuring smile. "When you work in the dark a lot, you get to realize that the darkness actually helps you because you're harder to spot. Give your eyes a minute to adjust, then look around. I'll bet you'll be surprised at how much you really can see."

We were standing in a small, unpopulated desert area on the outskirts of the neighborhood. When I thought her eyes had adjusted to the darkness, I began pointing out different objects. "You see that old barrel over there?" When she nodded, I continued, "How about that pile of broken cement?"

"Yeah! There's an old tricycle, and a shoe. All kinds of junk." She took in a shaky breath. "Okay, let's get this over with. I really do want to get out of here."

We made our way into the neighborhood, keeping to the shadows to avoid being seen. I poked my head over back fences to check the yards and nearly had my face bitten off several times for my troubles. One thing about south-side dogs is they don't like anybody coming onto their property. We ended up at Trisha's house where the door was standing open to let in the cool night air. I stepped to the side of the door and pushed Megan behind me. "Hey Trisha? It's Alex. You home?"

The volume on the television quieted several decibels. I heard the squeak of a recliner as someone lowered the footstool. From inside I heard Trisha sigh. "I'm here, Alex. What you want?" Trisha ambled to the door, all two hundred twenty five pounds of her. She crossed her arms and leaned up against the doorpost, checking me out. Her eyebrows came down and she peered a little closer. "Is that a white woman hidin' behind you?"

I turned my head to look back at Megan, then met Trisha's gaze again. "Yup."

"What she doin'?"

"Hiding."

Megan bravely stepped out from behind me and crossed her arms —I think to keep them from shaking. "I am not. I just didn't want to interrupt anything."

Trisha studied Megan, then glared at me. "What are you thinkin', bringin' a white woman into the 'hood after dark? Are you crazy?"

I shrugged. "I needed someone to call 911 if I needed help." I rolled my eyes at Megan's shaking body. "It seemed like a good idea at the time."

"Wolfe, you gonna get her killed!"

Megan turned steely eyes my way and grabbed my shirt. "If I get killed, I will haunt you for the rest of my life."

Trisha and I exchanged puzzled looks. I raised my eyebrows and gently pried Megan's hands off my collar. "You won't get killed. Trisha, we're just looking for that eleven-year-old you said was hiding in back yards. Can you give me any more than that?"

"Yeah. Monique called a while ago. She in her back yard right now." She pointed down the street.

"Which house?"

"Two houses down. The one with the red car up on jacks in the carport. You can't miss it."

"Thanks. I'll see you around."

"And don't bring no white woman around to get killed. Nothin' worse than moppin' up white woman blood."

I looked back and saw a twinkle in her eyes as she winked at me.

Megan turned around to see whether she was joking and Trisha put on her mean-mother face. Megan stepped closer to me and we walked down the path and out to the sidewalk.

When I slowed to get my bearings, Megan stepped on my shoe again and whispered, "Can we go home now? I really don't like it out here."

I reached down to slip my heel back into the shoe. "If Shelley's in that back yard, I'll just grab her and we'll go. Okay?" We walked to the back yard of the house Trisha had pointed out and I stepped up onto some old boards to slowly raise my head over the wood-slat fence.

A rickety doghouse leaned up against the chain link fence that bordered the alley. I couldn't see any dogs, but a big ass dog bowl took up most of the small cement slab next to the back door. Shelley was nowhere to be seen.

Megan pressed her shoulder up next to my legs and I could feel her body shaking as she leaned into me.

I whispered down at her, "Megan, stop shaking."

"I think I'm gonna pee my pants if we don't get out of here."

My giggling pissed her off enough that she stopped shaking and punched me really hard on my bruised thigh. I yelped as quietly as I could. "Ouch! Knock it off! That hurt!"

"I'm gonna hurt you even more if I get killed." She put her back up to the fence and squatted down. "I'm not going in that yard. I'll be right here when you get back."

I stepped off the boards and knelt down next to her. "Listen, if anything happens, you run back to Trisha's house, okay? She'll make sure you're all right."

She stared at me a few seconds, then nodded.

I ruffled her hair before stepping back onto the boards and hoisting myself over the fence. When I dropped down on the other side, I saw movement inside the doghouse. A miniature Gia flew out of the doghouse door, raced to the chain link fence, and began climbing.

My foot slipped in the soft dirt, giving her the extra second she needed to clear the fence seconds before I reached her. I vaulted the fence into the dirt alley and chased her about a half-block before she slammed into a wooden gate and rushed into someone's yard. I rushed in after her, but she clotheslined me across the eyes with her stiff right arm as I ran through the gate, then disappeared back though the opening into the alley. My already black eye began throbbing and I felt a trickle of blood seeping out of the stitches in my forehead. "You little—"

I picked myself up and ran after her again. She disappeared around a corner with me following at a much more careful pace. When I saw her climb another fence, I moved further down the fence line and vaulted over, hoping she wouldn't expect me to come over in a different spot than she had. When I landed, I saw her standing behind two very large, very mean looking dogs, holding onto their collars. Gia's mischievous grin was plastered across her face, and I pointed at her. "Don't even think about it!"

She did more than think about it. "Get her!" She let go of their collars and both dogs bared their teeth and started for me as she ran toward the other side of the yard and up onto the front fence.

My first thought was to go after her, but my second thought was how much it would hurt to get eaten by eighty-four very sharp teeth. I turned, raced to the back fence and threw myself over, landing hard on my shoulder and rolling into the soft-packed dirt that layered the alley. I painfully stood up, every bruised muscle and aching joint screaming for more of my blessed painkillers that were waiting for me back on my coffee table. I hobbled around to the front of the house hoping I could at least see which way she ran.

A black woman stood on the front stoop, chuckling at me as I limped up. "You lucky you didn't get eaten. Those boys don't like white folks in they yard."

I grinned at her while I brushed dirt off my pants. "That kid's just as white as me. Why didn't they eat her?"

"She been sleepin' with 'em some nights." She turned serious eyes on me. "You know that man that done took her, right? He was with you, wadn't he?"

I stopped brushing and straightened up so I could try to read her face. She didn't look like she was kidding. "What man?" Her silence worried me. I stepped closer and repeated, "*What man?*"

"Big guy in a business suit. Looked like a cop. He grabbed her, hauled her to his black car and drove off."

"Damn it!" I took out my cell phone and called Gia while I limped back to Trisha's house. I figured Megan had hightailed it back there when I'd taken off running.

Gia answered on the third ring. "Angelino's residence."

I didn't want to get specific since she was worried about people listening in on her conversations. "Gia it's me, and I'm really pissed off. I just need to know one thing. Tell me yes, or no, because if it's no, I've got a huge problem on my hands."

I heard her chuckle on the other end. "Yes."

"God damn you, Gia!" I slammed the phone shut and turned toward Trisha's house. Gia always kept one step ahead of me. She knew what I was doing when I was doing it, and it was starting to piss me off. She'd had Gabe follow me because she knew I wouldn't turn Shelley over to her when I caught her.

My anger inched toward the breaking point and I didn't even bother knocking before I stormed through Trisha's front door. Megan and Trisha were sitting on an old, ragged sofa eating ice cream and watching TV. I tramped into the kitchen where Trisha's grandson had just taken a bowl from the cupboard for himself. I jerked the bowl out of his hand. "Give me that goddamn thing."

He stepped back and raised his hands. "Well excuse the shit out of me!"

When I turned and growled at him, he slowly backed towards the freezer and pulled out a carton of ice cream, which he carefully held out to me. "You need some chocolate? Grandma says women need chocolate durin' their time."

I grabbed the container from him, scooped out a huge serving of chocolate chunk ice cream, and went to join Megan and Trisha in front of the television.

Trisha laughed, "Where's the girl?"

I turned hateful eyes on her and Megan put her hand on Trisha's knee. "I've known her a long time, Trish, and now is not the time to make jokes."

Trisha sat back in the couch and covered her grin by shoveling a huge spoonful of ice cream into her mouth. I pushed back in the recliner, put my feet up and ate every last drop of chocolate I could find.

CHAPTER 6

W hen the city physician finally released me to full duty, I
walked into the office ready to work. Casey sat at her desk
and grinned as I walked around to mine. "Welcome back. Are you
through playing possum?"

Kate came over to my desk and held out her hand. I wasn't sure
what she wanted. "What?"

"Do you have your medical release from the city physician?
Because if you don't, you're headed right back home."

I pulled the paperwork out of my back pocket, smoothed out as
many of the wrinkles as possible, and handed it to her. When I glanced
up at her face, I was surprised to see her studying my eyes. She reached
over and pushed my bangs to the side. "Why didn't he take the stitches
out?"

I put my hand to my forehead to feel the new stitches the doctor
had put in the night before. When Shelley clotheslined me, she'd
reopened the wound above my eye. "Uh, he just thought the cut
needed a little more time to heal." I swiveled around to open my file
drawer, hoping she wouldn't notice the new bruising around my
other eye.

She grabbed the arm of my chair and swiveled it back so I was facing her. She focused on the new bruise, then shifted so she could look me straight in the eyes. "Why is there a bruise on your other eye?"

"Oh... um... successive bruising." I pursed my lips authoritatively and nodded my head.

"Successive bruising?" She moved closer to get a clear look at the bruise.

"Yeah... you know, like when bruises appear after the fact? It happens sometimes." I continued to nod while I rubbed the bruise to conceal it from her scrutiny.

She reached up and pulled my hand down. "Alex."

I lowered my chin and raised my eyes to hers. "Hmm?"

"Why is that bruise newer than the one the bull gave you on your cheek?" At one point in her career, Kate had been the supervisor for the child abuse unit, and no one could tell the age of a bruise better than she could.

"Well, uh...." I lowered my eyes, swallowing hard. "I guess because with successive bruises, they show up later and they look newer because they show up later... or something." *Wow, that sounded stupid.*

Kate stared at me long enough to make me to squirm in my seat. When I realized I'd shifted into about the fifth position in five seconds, I pushed back in my chair and sat up straight and tall. Then I thought maybe that looked too nervous, so I slouched back down and played with the arm of my chair. I decided I should take the initiative. I turned to Casey. "So where are we on the kidnapping victims? Anything new?"

Neither woman spoke, and I watched Kate's finger tapping a staccato on her forearm. She flicked a finger toward Casey. "Why don't you fill her in on what's going on? Then the two of you go interview the clown again." She glanced at me one more time, then headed back to her desk.

Casey leaned forward and rested her arms on her desk. "What did you do to end up with new bruises when you were supposed to be at home in bed?"

I shrugged. "Nothing. And if Kate finds out about the nothing, I'm screwed. I think I'm screwed anyway." I needed to go talk to Gia, but I thought I needed to calm down and think things through before I completely burned all my bridges. Basically, she'd kidnapped an eleven-year-old kid, and I was pretty sure I was an accomplice. "I am so screwed." I lay my head down on my arms, trying to sort out exactly where my life had started to go haywire.

Casey knocked on the desk. "Hey, you want to go get some breakfast and talk about it?"

"No, I don't want to get you involved. It's serious this time, Case, and I don't know what to do about it." I sat back in my chair. "So what's up with the boyfriend? Have we heard anything else?"

She stood up and grabbed her keys. "Come on. I'm hungry, and I'll bet you haven't eaten yet." Without waiting for an answer, she headed out of the office.

I watched her go, and as my gaze traveled past Kate's cubicle, I caught her watching me. Nothing would have pleased me more than to pour my heart out to her so she could tell me exactly what I needed to do. Unfortunately, I didn't want to get her involved in my mess either.

Maybe if I just let time go by, everything would work itself out. Maybe I could join the mafia when I got fired. Maybe I could join a prison gang when I got convicted of aiding and abetting. All that went through my head while Kate and I looked at each other. I sighed and grabbed my keys to follow Casey out.

When I passed Kate's desk she stopped me. "Alex."

I stood by the door and waited for her to speak.

"Come here, please."

When I walked back to her cubicle, she motioned for me to sit in the chair next to her desk. I sat down, polishing one thumbnail with the other thumb, waiting for her to say whatever she had to say. She leaned back in her customary position, one foot up on the partially opened bottom drawer, one leg crossed over the other. "Alex, you and I have worked together for a while now, and I've gotten very good at reading you. That bruise is new. There is no such thing as successive bruising."

I chuckled and nodded but didn't say anything.

"You can tell me how you got it if you want, but I'm not going to push. If you've gotten yourself into trouble, we can work it out together. Unfortunately, I know you'll just keep digging until you're in the hole so deep maybe even I can't get you out." She sat quietly, waiting to see whether I had anything to say. When I didn't, she sighed. "If you change your mind, you can call me any time of the day or night, okay?"

I nodded and stood up to leave. "Thanks, Boss, but I'm all right." I turned to head out of her cubicle.

"And Alex?"

"Yeah?"

She watched me a minute, then reached over and picked up her pen. "Never mind. Go grab some breakfast with Casey."

A heaviness settled over me. A little black cloud was following me wherever I walked and I felt like everyone I passed could see it and was pointing it out to whoever would listen. Out in the hallway, I met Ruthanne as she stepped out of the elevator. She was carrying several evidence bags along with her briefcase and a drink cup. I took her briefcase from her so she could redistribute everything.

"Hey, thanks, Alex. I didn't want to make two trips from the car. That last homicide was strange." She paused and looked more closely at me. "What's the matter with you? You look like you lost your best friend."

I carried her briefcase back to the homicide offices and set it next to her desk. She put down the bags and grabbed my arm as I turned to head back to the elevators. "Alex, what's the matter?"

Just as I was about to answer, her partner, Eric, walked into the office carrying his own bags and briefcase. "Hey, Alex. Good to see you. What's new?"

I hadn't expected a friendly greeting from him after what Ruthanne had told me, but I acted as though I didn't know what he'd said. "Nothin'. Anything new on that eleven-year-old kid?"

"I heard you were interested in the case. What's with that?"

I shrugged. "Just curiosity I guess. It's not everyday an eleven-year-old kills somebody."

He studied me a minute, finally deciding to let loose of some of his information. "Well, after she shot at me, I started talking to neighbors up there on Valencia. Apparently she's been staying in the area the last few nights. They think she's been breaking into houses and stealing food. The undercover tactical units are going to set up a stakeout to see if we can catch her."

Alarm bells rang in my head and I stared at him, not sure exactly what to say. Ruthanne opened her briefcase to pull out several file folders while she listened to our conversation. Eric's desk phone rang and he walked over to answer it. I watched him go, wondering exactly who he'd been talking to up on Valencia.

Ruthanne set the folders on her desk. "What's the matter, Alex?" She stepped closer. "Is that a new black eye?"

Apparently the bruise was darker than I'd originally thought when I'd checked myself in the mirror this morning. That kid and I were definitely gonna have a "come to Jesus" talk when I got my hands around her scrawny little neck. "Yes, it's a new black eye." I leaned in close and whispered, "Can you meet Casey and me at the café? Something's not jiving. Can you get the names of the people Eric's talked to up on Valencia? It's important."

She glanced at Eric, then turned her back to him, pretending to show me something in one of her folders. "I can't come right now, but I'll get the names and call you, okay?"

"Thanks." Casey was probably wondering what was taking me so long, so I hurried out to the garage and climbed into my 2003 Chevy Malibu. A manila envelope had been slipped under the driver's side windshield wiper and I looked around to see whether anyone was hiding nearby waiting to jump out and yell "surprise" when I pulled it out and opened it. Our unit was famous for practical jokes, so I very carefully retrieved it and held it at arms length while I opened the clasp.

Inside, a picture of me impaled on one of Gumby's horns hung glued to a piece of white notebook paper. Someone had obviously used a computer program to merge and edit two separate photos. Underneath, he'd written, *Next time you'll come out with more holes than you had when you went in.*

I carefully lay the paper and envelope down on the hood of my car, then went to my trunk to retrieve a pair of disposable gloves. Once I'd placed the picture back in the envelope, I returned to Kate's cubicle.

"Hey Boss? This was left under the windshield wiper on my car." My cell phone buzzed with Casey's ring, and I answered it while Kate—who'd obviously noticed the gloves I was wearing—opened her desk drawer, retrieved a set of her own, and pulled them on. I handed the envelope to her at the same time I put my phone to my ear. "Hi, Case. Sorry to keep you waiting; something came up."

"Well, Maureen already brought your bagel, and she's a little grumpy today. Are you gonna be able to make it or do I have to tell her she brought it out for nothing?" Maureen was our very temperamental waitress who believed God had put everyone else on this earth just to bother her.

"Tell her I'll be there in about fifteen minutes, so she can just chill."

"Oh yeah, I'm gonna tell her that and then get some secret sauce in my hash browns the next time I come. I don't think so. I'll see you when you get here." Casey hung up and I watched Kate while she carefully slid the picture out of the envelope.

Her jaw clenched before she pushed the picture back inside. "Nate, come here please."

Nate walked over, glanced at me, then looked at Kate expectantly. Out of the corner of his mouth he whispered, "Nice shiner. Think I could get one of those?"

I whispered back, "I'll give you one if you don't shut your face."

Kate chuckled. "All right, children, knock it off." She pulled out another pair of disposable gloves and handed them to Nate. "Put these on and submit this for fingerprinting. I want you to write up a case report, classify it under threats and intimidation. Alex will tell you where it came from. Also, get with Jason in facilities management and have him pull the tape for the parking garage camera for the last..." She looked at me. "What? Two hours?" I nodded. "See if it's possible to tell who put this envelope on Alex's car."

Kate had gone into detective mode. She'd been a detective for ten years before being promoted to sergeant, and she'd been a detective sergeant for ten years after that. Detectives assigned to train rookies use her as an example because she'd had a reputation as being one of the most tenacious investigators the department had ever had. That usually meant I couldn't put anything past her, but it never stopped me from trying.

Nate and I went over to his desk and I filled him in on what details I had. My anger rose steadily the more I talked about someone threatening me, and by the time we'd finished, I'd decided to head back to the rodeo grounds after breakfast with Casey to do some more digging. I turned to leave and almost bumped into Kate, who'd come up behind me. She held up three fingers. "Three months, Alex. Don't blow it."

I grinned before stepping around her and walking over to grab my keys off her desk where I'd accidentally left them. "I'd hate for you to be bored much longer than that, Boss. Besides, I have my reputation to think about."

"I like being bored. My ulcers are finally starting to heal." She walked me to the door and held it shut a second. "I intend to work on this one personally. I don't like my detectives hurt, and I don't put up with them being threatened. If you come up with anything, tell me so I don't have to duplicate your work." She took her hand off the door and walked back to her cubicle. I trusted her completely, and having her in my corner helped take the edge off my irritation.

When I finally walked into the Sleepytime Café, Casey was just finishing her eggs and hash browns. She mopped up the last of the egg yolk with her toast and pointed the bread at me. "So what was so important you had to leave me here with only Maureen for company? I mean, she's a nice enough lady, but I can only take her for a short time before I want to strangle her."

Ruthanne surprised both of us when she came walking through the back door and sat in the booth next to me. "Hi guys." She grabbed the glass of iced tea out of my hand. "I decided I'd rather come spend some time with you instead of processing all the evidence from our latest homicide scene. You should have seen it—kinda like the whole thing was staged... weird." I tried to get my iced tea back, but she turned away from me and took a long pull on the straw. She called across the restaurant to Maureen who was picking up a food order from the kitchen. "Hey, Maureen, can you get Alex an iced tea? She's trying to steal mine."

Casey held her coffee cup in the air. "I could use some more coffee when you get a second." Maureen humphed before returning to the kitchen for the pitcher of tea and the pot of coffee. Casey watcher her go, then pointed at me. "Alex was just getting ready to fill me in on why she left me sitting here alone for the last half-hour."

I turned sideways so my back was up against the end of the booth and filled them in on the picture I'd found under my windshield wiper. "Kate's going to investigate the threat herself."

They both listened quietly. Then Casey asked, "What do you think's going on out at the rodeo? The girls are missing, but they don't seem to be in any real danger, and the mom's boyfriend is gone, but I can't find anybody who really gives a rat's ass about him. Apparently he hangs out on the fringe of the rodeo scene, kind of a cowboy wannabe." The toast disappeared into her mouth and she followed it up with the last little bit of coffee in her cup.

Maureen walked up with a glass of iced tea, the coffee pot, and the bagel I always order. "I took the bagel back to get it off the table, but if you want a fresh cut one, you'll have to pay. I ain't gonna throw this one out 'cause you can't get here on time." She clinked the plate down, set the iced tea and coffee pot on the table and then crossed her arms, daring me to complain.

"Maureen, Casey here was just wondering if you've ever spoken to your doctor about Prozac."

Casey sat bolt upright and choked on the coffee she'd just swallowed.

Maureen froze with the coffee pot suspended inches above the tabletop. She glared at Casey. "You *what?*" Her face went from mildly tan to pink to red in a matter of seconds.

I continued. "She mentioned some new types of drugs. What'd you call 'em Case? Extended release? She thinks they might work better for you since you're here for so long and..."

Casey kicked me under the table so hard it felt like she chipped my shinbone. "Maureen, I never said any such thing. Alex is—" She stopped mid-sentence when a commotion started at the front of the restaurant. I pushed halfway up in my seat to get a better view of what was happening.

A tall, emaciated transient was berating a customer as they both came through the front door. All three of us were familiar with him from our years working patrol. I had the best rapport with him so I shoved Ruthanne out of the booth and walked over to him, knowing that both she and Casey would be close on my heels.

"George, what are you doing in here?" I stopped a short distance away, knowing from past experience that if I crowded him he'd go berserk. As it was, he abruptly turned, screaming obscenities at me as he waved his arms and did a kind of puppet dance with his feet. He was wearing the same clothes he'd been wearing for the last five years: dirty jeans held up with an oversized belt and a faded brown suit jacket over a bright orange tank top.

I glanced at the customer he'd followed in. She'd backed up against the wall to get as far away from him as she could. I motioned for her to go behind me into the restaurant, and once she'd slipped past me, I said, "George, it's me... Officer Wolfe. Calm down a second and talk to me."

His arms and feet gradually slowed until they were still. I watched his eyes. They had an excited look that bothered me. He'd stopped yelling obscenities, but his lips curled back, exposing rotting teeth and giving him a ghoulish appearance that worried me more than the yelling had.

Casey slowly moved to my right, Ruthanne to my left.

George stepped toward me and drawled a singsong greeting that sent shivers down my spine. "Hello, Officer Wolfe. I've been waiting for you." A disgusting finger pointed at my chest. "Would you like to come with me to the dance?" He crooked his finger back at his chest in a circular motion, his nails black with dirt.

I calmly pointed to the glass doors directly behind him. "Sure, George. Let's go outside and talk about it. It's too stuffy in here anyway."

His head whipped around and he stared out the door. When he spun back toward me, his black eyes flashed with anger.

Ruthanne slowly stepped behind me and I heard her unhook the radio from her belt. She spoke quietly as she let the dispatcher know what was happening.

George pointed outside, spittle forming at the edges of his mouth as he yelled at me. "*Who's out there?* You want me out there so they can *kill me,* don't you?" His expression went from insane to friendly and back to insane so quickly that I wasn't sure I'd seen the transformation. In an instant, he screamed and charged, his hands curled and ready to choke the life out of me if I gave him half the chance.

I sidestepped him and grabbed his left wrist and elbow, using his momentum to drag him to the ground while Casey fell on top of him with her knee squarely on his spine. She grabbed his right arm and twisted it up onto his back. I held his left arm straight out from his body, pulling up on his wrist at the same time I pushed down on his elbow.

His legs flailed dangerously close to the glass doors.

Ruthanne grabbed both of them under her arm and held them in a wrestling hold.

He continued screaming and we all knew it was pointless trying to calm him down. I put my knee on his elbow and took my cuffs out of the leather case attached to my belt. I ratcheted the cuff onto his left wrist, then Casey moved off his back so I could shift around and straddle him while I twisted his arm back and cuffed it to the wrist she was holding.

Ruthanne chuckled. "Nice ass, Alex, but can you move it out of my face?" She shrugged, "Or not..."

Casey laughed and moved down to the legs to took over from Ruthanne. "Why don't you go out and coordinate the back-up before I have to hurt you?"

Ruthanne smiled and raised her eyebrows. "Could you be more specific on my choices?"

Casey laughed again and shoved her with a foot. "Get out of here."

We heard sirens in the distance, and Ruthanne went outside to get on the radio so she could tell everyone they could shut down lights and sirens. She also ordered an ambulance to transport George to the psychiatric hospital.

George lay on the floor, ranting about conspiracies and assassinations and whatever else happened to pop into his head. When the paramedics arrived they bundled him up and took him away in the ambulance.

The three of us went into the bathroom to wash up before returning to our table. When we sat back down, my sorry, stale bagel stared up at me from the plate. I picked it up and rapped it on the table. "Maybe I could hook this on my belt and use it the next time I have to hit someone." I set the bagel back on the plate, reached for six packets of sweetener, and emptied them into my tea.

Maureen surprised me by bringing a fresh bagel and setting it in front of me. "Here. It's on the house since you took care of George. I swear he's gettin' worse every year. I been here seven years, and so's he."

I picked up the fresh bagel and examined the underside, looking for secret sauce. Maureen crossed her arms. "What're you lookin' for?"

"Lookin' for? Nothing. I'm just always amazed at how perfectly brown you always get my bagels. They're always done just the way I like them."

Maureen walked back to the kitchen and Casey shook her head. "You are such a bullshitter, Wolfe. And after your Prozac B.S. I'm the one who has to worry about the sauce, not you." She took a sip of coffee. "Anyway, back to our missing boyfriend. I've been checking the missing boyfriend's apartment every day. His mail's piling up along with the morning paper. The neighbors basically say good riddance, and one woman was so worried she wanted to know if she'd get in trouble if she took his newspapers since he obviously isn't reding them."

I finished slathering on the cream cheese. "You said earlier that he was a cowboy wannabe. Have you talked to anyone at the rodeo about him?"

"I did, but since this is a special promotional rodeo and it's lasting longer than the normal week, cowboys are coming in, competing in their event and then moving on to the next town."

I'd just assumed Carl would be in town as long as the rodeo continued, but maybe he'd have to move on too. "Are they all the same clowns, or are they changing also?"

"The clowns are booked for the duration. That was one of the first things I checked."

Ruthanne piped in. "Maybe the missing boyfriend has moved on to another rodeo. Has anyone thought of that?"

I looked at Casey because I hadn't registered that possibility.

She nodded. "Yeah, Kate did. The next big rodeo is in Reno, and the Reno Police are keeping an eye out for him, although I doubt they'll be looking very hard. Besides, I think he'd have stopped his mail and said goodbye to his girlfriend if he had taken a planned trip."

Ruthanne finished off the tea she'd stolen from me. As she set down the glass, she elbowed my arm and nodded toward the door. "Look what the cat just coughed up."

Casey and I followed her gaze to the front of the café where Ruthanne's ex-husband had just walked through the door. He'd recently taken a special assignment as a bike officer, and actually looked pretty darn good in his Spandex. He knew it too, because he paused at his table long enough for us to appreciate his tight hind end before sliding into the booth next to a very buxom blonde who'd probably been on the cover of *Helpful Hooker Magazine*.

Ruthanne grabbed my old bagel that Maureen had left on the table and flung it across the room at her ex, hitting him square in the middle of the chest. Then she yelled across the restaurant, "Alimony's a wonderful thing, Asshole! You're three months behind!"

The blonde picked up the bagel and hurled it back. "Keep talking, Bimbo! Someday you might say something intelligent!"

Ruthanne pushed out of the booth with assault in her eyes.

I pulled her back down by her belt. "Down, Girl. You started it. What'd you expect?"

The blonde just wouldn't let it ride. "Oh don't get angry, Ruthie. I'll be nicer if you'll try being smarter." She pointed to me. "Is that your latest hump bunny?"

I growled as I leapt over the back of the booth. I almost got my hands wrapped around her throat before Casey grabbed me from behind and swung me around facing the other way.

Ruthanne raced past us with murderous intent in her eyes. Her ex grabbed her and wrestled her to the ground at the same time I wrenched out of Casey's arms and took off after the blonde, who'd decided she should probably make a hasty retreat.

Casey tackled me again, jerked my arm behind my back, and escorted me out to our vehicles where the ex had taken Ruthanne. They were involved in an earsplitting argument.

Kate chose that moment to drive by the café, and I heard tires squealing as she swung around into the parking lot just as Casey threw me up against the hood of the car. Kate jumped out and slammed her door. "All right! You three!" She pointed to Casey, Ruthanne, and me. "Back by the trunk!" She pointed to the ex just as the bimbo came striding out the back door toward us. I started for the bimbo again and Kate stepped in front of me. "Alex! Trunk! Now!"

I reluctantly turned back toward the trunk, mumbling profanities. Kate pointed to the ex one more time. "You. Get yourself and your —" She struggled for a politically correct term. "*Friend* out of here."

He glared one more time at Ruthanne, then nodded at Kate. "Yes Ma'am."

The bimbo threw one last shot over her shoulder as he led her back into the café. "At least I got the man. You only ended up with an ugly muff...." Her last words were muffled as the ex covered her mouth with his hand and dragged her through the door.

I'd jumped up on the trunk and scrambled over the roof of the car on all fours before Casey had time to grab me again.

Kate reached up, grabbed my shirt, hauled me off the car, opened the back door, and shoved me inside.

I reached for the other door handle and she growled, "Don't you dare." Swallowing my temper, I crossed my arms and slouched down in the seat, seething. She slammed the door and went after Ruthanne. "Damn it, Ruthanne! How many times do you have to be told to keep your mouth shut when you're around Andy?"

"Andy owes me money and—"

"Not on duty he doesn't! Now, I am giving you a direct order. When you are on duty, you will *not* say one word to him or to his new —bimbo. Got it?"

Kate wasn't Ruthanne's direct supervisor, but I didn't know any officer who didn't respect her more than almost any other sergeant on the department. Ruthanne glared at her, then shifted her gaze to the ground. "Yes Ma'am." She waited to see whether Kate had anything else to say. When Kate remained silent, Ruthanne nodded, got in her car, and drove away.

I watched the exchange out of the corner of my eye, and when Kate turned my way, I shifted in the seat so my back was to her. After a short time, the door opened and I expected her to ream me a new one. Instead, I heard Casey's voice. "She left, and I think we probably should head out too before Bimbo and Andy come back out."

I swiveled around in time to see Kate pulling out of the parking lot onto the main street. "She left?" Having been the brunt of Kate's anger on many occasions, I never trusted her when she didn't respond the way I expected her to. "Uh... so... what exactly does that mean?"

Casey shrugged. "I'm not sure, but she muttered something about Andy and his 'lousy street whore' before she got in her car."

I grinned. "She did?" I knew there was a reason I loved working for Kate. She has more common sense in the tip of her little finger than most people use during their entire lifetime. I stepped out of the car and tucked in the shirttail Kate had pulled out when she'd dragged me off the car. "You ready to go back to the rodeo?"

Casey pursed her lips as Ruthanne drove back into the parking lot. "Great." She walked over to the car and put her knee against the driver's door, preventing Ruthanne from opening it and stepping out.

The window rolled down and Ruthanne smiled. "Don't worry, I just came back to give Alex this list of witnesses she asked for." She handed Casey a manila envelope, then waved at me. "See ya later, Alex. I'll call you tonight."

Casey opened the envelope and examined the list. "What's this a list of? Witnesses for what case? Not ours."

I thought fast, but not fast enough.

Casey repeated, "Witnesses for what case, Alex?"

"Well, it's a case, um...." How could I tell her it was for a case I wasn't supposed to be working? It was obvious to me she suspected something, but my mind refused to come up with a quick not-quite-a-lie type answer. Then it came to me. "They're people who may have some information on the girl's disappearance." She didn't need to know which girl. I could have meant the two girls we'd had missing for a while. I reached over to try to grab the list, but she pulled it out of my fingers before I could get a good grip.

"What girls?"

I gave her my best shocked look. "What do you mean, what girls? How many girls are we looking for?"

She stared at me for a minute, then put the list back in the envelope before handing it to me.

"I'm sure it wouldn't be for anything you did while you were recuperating at home getting a second black eye. You wouldn't be that stupid." She raised one eyebrow and looked at me while she climbed into the driver's seat of her car. "I'll meet you at the rodeo."

Stupid? I thought about that a second. Yeah, I guess that described it all right. I got in my car and followed her out of the parking lot and down south to the rodeo grounds. The protestors were still walking in a circle waving their signs, but I didn't see Megan in the group this time.

We walked over to the police command post—a thirty-five foot recreational vehicle specifically equipped for police operations—and said hello to the various officers working the event that day. My buddy, Lt. Caruthers, was apparently inside the venue watching the bull riding, so we took a seat at the back table and chatted with a couple officers who were eating their lunch.

I filled them in on the picture of me impaled on Gumby's horns.

One young officer who was fairly new on the department pulled out his notebook. "Sgt. Dougherty briefed us about someone throwing you in with the bull. I've been talking to people. Some seem to think that Carl Boyd, the clown you interviewed, was the one who threw you in, but I talked to Carl, and I just don't think he's the one who did it. I spoke to one cowboy—" He flipped through the pages of the notebook. "Name was... Hondo Forbish." He grinned at me. "Can you believe a name like that? Anyway, he's a friend of Carl's, and he thinks Carl's ex-wife's boyfriend is the one who did it."

The other officer at the table, Henry Latas, scratched his protruding beer belly and laughed. "Kid thinks he's a master detective or something. He needs to learn real police work instead of trying to be a bird-brained pencil-pushing detective." He held up his hands. "No offense meant to you two lovely ladies."

The young officer blushed at the implied insult to Casey and me. I smiled to put him at ease. "Don't worry... uh, what's your name?"

"Weatherby, Ma'am. Jimmy Weatherby."

"Don't worry, Jimmy. The three of us go back a long ways. Henry's even gonna name his baby after me when he delivers." I patted Henry's gut. "Aren't you, Pork Chop?"

When Henry put his head back and laughed it sounded like a donkey had gotten loose in the R.V. We all laughed at the sounds coming out of his mouth until Lt. Caruthers opened the door and stepped up onto the steps. The room became silent, and Casey rested the heel of her boot on top of my foot, ready to dig in if she needed to shut my mouth.

Caruthers surveyed the four of us, then locked eyes with me. "I understand you wasting your own time, Detective Wolfe, since that's par for the course, but don't come in here and bother real policemen who have a job to do."

I couldn't help myself. "I guess that means it's okay to come in and bother you then, huh Lieutenant?" Casey stomped on my foot hard enough to make the blood drain from my face. I managed not to break eye contact with Caruthers, whose jaw line rippled as he ground his teeth.

Weatherby and Latas gathered up what was left of their meals and slid past the lieutenant on their way out the door.

Casey sighed and slid out of the booth.

I slid out after her and nodded to Caruthers. "Take care, Lieutenant."

We stepped out of the vehicle and headed underneath the stands. I looked back at Caruthers, who was standing on the R.V. steps watching us. I muttered quietly, "When that man dies, I'll be the first to pee on his grave."

Casey chuckled as she stepped up to a concession stand to buy us a couple of hot dogs and a soda. "I think you'll have to fight for the lead position during the stampede." She handed me a hotdog and soda before brushing off a table to sit down.

I sat on the other side to watch the various cowboys and spectators walking through the dusty underbelly of the rodeo stands. "So I hear you and Terri have been seeing each other. What's up with that?"

Terri had come on the department a year before we had. The other members of her squad respected her for her extensive knowledge of Arizona criminal laws, and whenever she was asked, she told people she'd found her niche in life and had no intention of ever doing anything other than patrol.

Casey took a bite of her hotdog, wiping away a smear of ketchup that had dripped onto her chin. "I don't know. We both like U of A basketball games, so we went to a few home games together. One thing led to another, and now we're dating. Nothing serious—we just like each other's company, that's all."

"I didn't know she'd gotten a divorce from her husband." I'd loaded too much mustard onto my bun, and I held it above the wrapper to let it drip out so it wouldn't get on my clothes.

A far-off buzzer sounded on the other side of the stands, indicating the end of a ride for one of the bull riders. Casey stayed quiet for a minute, then looked up at me through her bangs. "This isn't for general knowledge, but her husband put her in the hospital a few months ago with two broken ribs and bruised liver. They told everybody, including the department, that she'd been involved in a car wreck in another town. She moved in with me last week because he's been threatening her." She angrily wadded up the rest of her hotdog in the wrapper, stalked over to a garbage can and threw the whole thing in.

My appetite had disappeared as well, so I threw away what I hadn't eaten and followed her back into the recesses of the stands. I thought about Terri, trying to recall exactly what her husband looked like. "What's her husband's name again?"

"Robert Asshole Evens."

"Interesting middle name." I smiled to try to chase away the black cloud that had settled over her.

She looked around, then pointed. "See that can of beer standing next to that post?" She walked up to it and crushed it beneath her heel. "That's what I'll do to that slime-brained intestinal rash if he ever sets foot on my property or touches her again. I don't care if she and I are dating or not; he touches her, he's dead meat."

"Call me and we can make an evening of it." Her moods tended to cloud her judgment sometimes, and I always found it better to try to tease her out of them than to feed into the angry tirades.

She grunted and then chuckled. "I think you've got enough trouble on your hands without buying into mine. Let's try to find that one witness Weatherby talked to. What was his name? Hondo something?"

"Yeah, Hondo Forbish. How could you forget a name like that?" I picked up the beer can she'd crushed and threw it into the garbage. "I'll bet if we find Carl he can introduce us. They're supposed to be friends or something." We asked around about Carl and a cowgirl told us he was currently working the bull riding competition.

The stands were moderately full as we made our way to the top to watch him at work. Rodeo clowns are amazing athletes. We watched Carl and his partners climb into barrels, untangle bull ropes that had trapped dangling cowboys by their hands or fingers, and lead dazed men to the rail after they'd been knocked senseless.

The scene brought back memories of my time with Gumby, and I leaned my elbows on the bench seat behind us, trying to remember any little detail I might have forgotten or overlooked about the whole episode. I remembered talking to several cowboys and cowgirls about Carl and his kids. They'd all been friendly, definitely helpful, and to a person, they thought he was one of the best rodeo clowns in the business.

There hadn't been anyone in the enclosure where Gumby's corral was situated, or at least I hadn't seen anyone. Obviously, someone had enough time to take a picture of me. If I remembered the photo correctly, it actually looked like they might have gotten a picture while I was in with the bull. "Hey, Case, I think we need to get a copy of the picture of Gumby and me so we can try to figure out where I was when it was taken. Maybe that will give us a clue as to who might have taken it."

"Good idea. Hey, look. Carl's leaving the arena. Let's go catch him and see if he knows where Hondo is. I'd like to talk to him and get out of here. Sitting here makes me nervous with Caruthers out for blood. He'll say we were watching the rodeo while we're on duty."

"We are." My bruised ribs groaned as I levered myself up from my reclining position.

"You okay?" Casey reached down to help me to my feet.

"Yeah... I can hardly wait to get home to fill myself with pain killers and muscle relaxants. Everything's stiffening up again." I followed her down the steps and back into the underground world of backstage rodeo.

While we were scanning clown faces trying to identify Carl, she said, "I can do the interview if you want to go home early. Just call Kate and ask her to change the time on the roster. She won't care."

I recognized his orange wig and beefy shoulders before she did, so I edged in front of her and held out my hand. "Hi, Carl. How's it going? You looked great out there." He shook my hand and I turned to indicate Casey. "You remember my partner, Casey Bowman, don't you?"

He dipped his head. "Good to see you again, Ma'am. Have you found my girls?"

Normally, we keep the parents together at the command post when we're working a kidnapping, but Carl and Mona fought constantly and Kate decided it would be better if she sent Carl back to work with the promise that we'd notify him immediately if anything happened. He'd reluctantly returned to the rodeo, partly because he lived on a shoestring. Like most rodeo people, if he didn't work, he didn't get paid.

Casey shook her head. "No, nothing yet."

Carl crossed his arms across a barrel chest. "Did you have any luck finding my ex-wife's..." He paused to think of a word that wouldn't offend us.

Ever helpful with that kind of thing, I jumped right in. "Slime sucking piece of cow dung?"

He smiled, scratching his head before shrugging. "Yes Ma'am, I guess that just about covers it all, don't it?"

Casey rubbed the back of her neck. "Alex, you do have a way with words." She turned and indicated some empty seats. "Why don't we sit for a second?" Once we were all seated, she continued. "Mr. Boyd, we were hoping you could introduce us to a friend of yours, Hondo Forbish. Do you know where we can find him?"

"Yes Ma'am. He usually stays pretty close to the bull riders while they're waiting for their number to be called. I'd be happy to introduce you." After a pause, he added, "Do you think he knows something about my girls?"

Casey pulled her chair a little closer to the table so she could lean her elbow on it. "Well, our sergeant has made it a priority for Detective Wolfe and me. Right now, we're trying to dig up some kind of clue as to who might have thrown Detective Wolfe in with Gumby. It's possible the same person who threw her in is responsible for the disappearance of your ex-wife's boyfriend and quite possibly your girls."

He pulled off his wig so he could scratch the sweaty hair underneath. He was a rugged kind of handsome, and I watched him as he gathered his thoughts. His square jaw showed just a hint of a five o'clock shadow and the deep lines around his eyes testified to years spent working in the sun without the benefit of sunglasses. He must have sensed me watching him, because he raised his gorgeous bedroom eyes to meet mine. Alarm bells went off in my brain at the same time I experienced a very pleasant, if inappropriate, sensation between my legs.

Casey watched us a second, then cleared her throat. "Mr. Boyd, if you could take us to Mr. Forbish..."

Carl and I reluctantly broke eye contact. All of us pushed back the plastic picnic table chairs we were sitting in and stood up. "Yes Ma'am, I believe I saw him over by the loading chutes helping the contestants pull rope." He smiled at our confused expressions. "They help wrap the bull ropes around the rider's hand and jerk the flank strap when the chute opens."

The thought of climbing on the back of a two thousand pound bull had always mystified me, so I took a minute to satisfy my curiosity. "I've always wondered why a normally sane man would willingly climb on the back of a Brahma bull, then tie himself to it before pissing the bull off enough that he wants nothing more than to kill the little parasite clinging to his back."

Carl laughed. "Well, I s'pose if you got right down to it, it's probably 'cause there's a lot of incredibly beautiful women around who think if a guy can ride a 2000 pound bull, how much better can he ride them?"

I grinned. "Don't you guys ever think of anything else?"

He turned and caught my eyes again. "No Ma'am, not really." Then he shrugged. "I guess another reason is sometimes a fellah just needs to know he's got the cajones to get on and the know-how to stay on."

We followed him around to the working side of the rodeo stands. As we walked up, I saw several paramedics clustered around a young rider who'd apparently lost his battle with the bull. Blood drenched the side of his face, they'd enclosed one arm in an inflatable splint and a medic was inserting an I.V. into the poor guy's other arm. The kid was trying to sit up and the medics were pushing him back down. "I gotta ride later today! I ain't got time for no hospital! What don'cha understand about *let me up?*"

Carl knelt next to him so he could put a hand on the kid's shoulder. "You're done for a while, Tanner. Now just lay back and let 'em do their job. There'll always be another rodeo down the road."

"But Carl, I gotta ride! You know the deal!" The young man was close to tears, and Carl squeezed his shoulder.

"You can't ride the way that arm was broke and your head was cracked. That's just plain stupid."

Tanner grudgingly lay back while the medic finished inserting the I.V. Blood still seeped from the gash in his head and I watched as someone poured a solution onto it and lightly placed a square cotton bandage over it. I shook my head. "And I thought bein' a cop was a hard way to make a living. At least I get paid if I'm laid up."

The cowboy who'd helped me after I'd come tumbling out of Gumby's enclosure limped up and watched the paramedics load Tanner onto a back board, then onto a gurney and wheel him away.

Carl clapped the man on the back. "Well, speak of the devil! Hondo, these two are detectives who wanted to chat at ya a while." He turned to me. "This here's Detective Wolfe." He winked at me before indicating Casey with a wave of his hand. "And this here's Detective Bowman. I'm sorry I gotta leave you, but it's just about my time to get back to work."

Hondo grinned, and I noticed several of his teeth had gone the way of the Dodo bird. "That's all right, Carl. Those boys depend on you to keep 'em in one piece. I'm already all broke up; there ain't nothin' you can do to help me no more."

Carl nodded and left and we led Hondo to a relatively quiet spot away from the hubbub of the bull-riding event. Casey took the lead while I pulled my portable tape recorder out of my pocket and turned it on. She went through all the preliminary information: date, time, names, etc.

He listened politely, giving his full name and date of birth when prompted, then raising his eyebrows while he waited for the real questions to begin.

Casey started right in. "Mr. Forbish, I understand you and Mr. Boyd are friends."

"Yes Ma'am. I've known Carl for close to five years now. I used to ride bulls and he's pulled me away from more wrecks than I care to count. Cain't ride 'em no more." He slapped his stiff leg. The sound his hand made against the jeans didn't seem right to me and I tried to see if the leg was his or a prosthetic device.

Casey continued. "You must know his ex-wife pretty well then."

"Well, not too good. She never liked rodeo and we was on the road so much, I never seen much of her." He looked at the ground and shook his head, then looked at Casey again. "Don't know what he ever seen in her. She's a hard one. Couldn't keep her skirt on when he was away... least ways, that's what I heard." He grinned sheepishly and ducked his head. "Pardon me, Ma'am. I shouldn't a said that to a lady."

"One of the cases I'm investigating, Mr. Forbish, involves Detective Wolfe. I recognize you from when we pulled her out of the bull pen, correct?"

He nodded. "Yes Ma'am. She come flying over the wall and Petey and me caught her; then we reached in to pull you out. Damndest thing." He looked back at me and shook his head. "You're lucky to be alive, Ma'am. That Gumby's a killer." He knocked on his leg again. "He done this to me two years ago. Yes Ma'am, he's a killer all right."

"Someone threw her in the pen. Have you heard any rumblings around the rodeo people about who they think did it?"

He reached up and grabbed the front brim of his cowboy hat, adjusting it so it sat down further on his head. "Well, some folks think Carl done it. He weren't real happy with her comin' here and askin' all sorts a personal type questions 'bout his girls an all." He shrugged apologetically toward me. "Me, I think one'a Mona's boyfriends done it. I think he took the girls too, just to make Carl look suspect so's she can keep the girls all to herself."

"For the record, when you talk about Mona, who do you mean?"

"Carl's ex... Mona."

"Has Carl told you anything about what's happening with his case?" Casey leaned back against a post and rested the bottom of her foot on it.

"No Ma'am, not much. But I hear one of them boyfriends is missin'. That's what folks is sayin' anyways."

"That's the second time you've referred to 'one of her boyfriends.' How many do you think she has?"

"Well, two that I know of: some bum she picked up somewhere— he's the one gone missin'—and then Carl's ex-ropin' buddy, Smitty Cogburn. Ain't no love lost 'tween them two. It's a shame 'cause they used to be real close."

Casey and I exchanged glances.

She asked, "Do you think Smitty would have a reason to set Carl up?"

"Hell yes! Carl wiped the floor up with him when he found out he was doin' Mona. Broke his nose, knocked out two teeth... hell yeah!"

"Is Mr. Cogburn competing in this rodeo?"

"Yes Ma'am. He don't start 'till day after tomorrow though. That's when the ropin' starts."

Casey waited quietly for a second to see whether I had any other questions. I couldn't think of any, so I shook my head and shrugged. After she finished up the interview, I turned the tape recorder off and put it back in my pocket. We thanked Hondo and headed back to our cars. I called Kate to see whether she minded if I went home a little early.

"Actually Alex, I'm surprised you lasted this long. Did you two get any new information?"

I pulled out my notebook. "Yeah... a new officer, Jimmy Weatherby, dug up a guy named Hondo Forbish. We interviewed Hondo, and he told us about a second boyfriend of Mona's... guy named Smitty Cogburn. We should probably track him down tomorrow."

She was quiet, and I knew she was writing down everything I said, so I waited for her to finish. "All right, go on home. I've got a meeting to run to so I'll see you in the morning."

She hung up before I could tell her about my run-in with Lt. Caruthers. I put it in the back of my mind to tell her about it the next time I saw her. I stopped in a grocery store on the way home and bought two four-packs of wine coolers. When I got home, I downed some painkillers, two muscle relaxers, and two bottles of a lemon sparkle wine cooler. By the time Megan stopped by to check on me for the evening, I was three sheets to the wind. She led me into my bedroom, tucked me into bed and waited until I was out for the count.

CHAPTER 7

The next morning, my head felt like someone had come in during the night and filled it full of cotton candy. My thoughts weren't just fuzzy; they felt kind of sticky. A hot shower helped a little, and the four cups of coffee I downed before heading into work didn't hurt either. When I dragged myself through the office door, Sharon stopped typing. "You look like something my cat leaves on my front doorstep as a morning offering after her night of hunting."

I grabbed a handful of candy from her M&M man on the counter-top. "Thank you for those kind words. I'll cherish them always."

"The rest of your unit is still out at the call out. How did you escape the two a.m. wake up call?"

Panic surged through me as I grabbed for my cell phone. Kate always got majorly pissed when she couldn't reach me for a call out. "What? What call out? Nobody called me!" I flipped open the cover and groaned. I'd missed three calls from Kate and four from Casey. "Shit!" The M&M's were melting in my hand, so I threw them in my mouth and grabbed some more. Those disappeared as I bent down and lay my head on the counter. "Has Kate been in here yet this morning?"

She didn't answer so I raised my head to see why not. Her eyebrows rose a good inch and a half and she lifted her chin to indicate someone behind me. I didn't want to turn around and opted instead to put my head back down on the counter. I heard Sharon typing again and knew she was doing her best to blend into the background. It seemed to me it was always better to face my demons up front, so I swiveled around to see Kate standing behind me, arms crossed, jaw muscles rippling.

She didn't say anything, just turned and walked toward the lieutenant's office.

I figured maybe she had a meeting with the L.T. so I slipped out the door and headed for the elevators. When I was halfway there, someone grabbed my shirt from behind and dragged me back through the door and into the lieutenant's office.

Kate held onto my shirt, jerked a chair around and unceremoniously dumped me into it. She grabbed the arms of the chair, leaned over me, then changed her mind and reached back and slammed the door.

I was a little confused since I didn't think sleeping through a call out would bring on this kind of reaction, especially since she knew I was on painkillers and such.

The vein in her temple was pulsing faster than usual, and I stared at it for a few seconds before dropping my gaze to the carpet to study the patterns in the lieutenant's fake Persian rug.

Kate surprised me by re-opening the door, stalking out and slamming it behind her one more time.

I sat alone for about ten minutes until the silence in the room began to unnerve me. The rhythmic ticking of the desk clock didn't help either. I jumped when Kate stormed back in and slammed the door yet again.

"I tried to give myself time to calm down, but I just kept getting more pissed off the more I thought about you, so I knew if I didn't get in here and deal with you soon, I'd be so *furious* I'd come in and *throttle you to death!*"

I opened my mouth to say something and she held up a finger. "I still might, Alex! Don't say a *word* unless prompted, understand?"

I figured that wasn't exactly a prompt, so I opted for a nod instead of an outright answer.

"We had a call out in the Vistas this morning."

My heart stopped.

"Mrs. Trisha Bullard's grandson got himself shot again. She asked about you. Interesting, huh?" She stopped talking and leaned down on the chair arms again.

I was quick enough to realize that hadn't been a prompt either, so I kept my mouth shut and avoided making eye contact.

"She was laughing about the 'scared white woman' you brought with you on one of your cases the other day." She raised her eyebrows. "No, wait. It wasn't the other *day*, was it, Alex?" Her voice rose a couple decibels as she leaned in even closer. "It was the other *night!* By *yourself!* With a *civilian* as a back-up! *In the Vistas!*"

I squirmed. "Well, see I—"

"*Shut up!*"

I slid down in the chair and thought, *Yes Ma'am. Shutting up now.*

She turned around and punched the door with the palm of her hand. "Damn it, Alex!"

I looked at the door to see if she'd put a hole through it. Surprisingly enough, she hadn't.

She walked to the lieutenant's desk and leaned up against it with her arms crossed. "What case were you working—*while* you were on medical leave, I might add—and why would you take a civilian, whom I assume was Megan judging from the description, into the Vistas, alone, at *night?*"

Since she'd ordered me not to work on any cases while on medical leave, the prompt she'd just given me was actually a loaded question. I took some extra time to come up with an answer, only the extra time didn't help much so I decided to go with the truth.

"I'm waiting, Alex."

I nodded and took a deep breath. "Um, well...." I squinted up at her, terrified of her probable reaction. My heart pounded so hard in my chest I wondered whether my shirt was bumping up and down in rhythm with my pulse.

Kate raised her eyebrows, waiting.

"I thought maybe that girl Eric has been looking for might be in the Vistas since that's where'd I'd go to disappear if I ran away from juvenile court." The story formed in my head as I talked. "I was worried about her, and I knew I had a good rapport with Mrs. Bullard so I thought I'd go talk to her to see if she could help me find the little girl. She's only eleven you know." I thought I might play on her sympathies, so I threw in that part about the little heathen being "only eleven" as an extra measure. "I took Megan because you know she has a big heart, and she honestly wanted to—"

Kate stepped up to my chair, grabbed the arms, jerked it toward her and growled, "Try again, Wolfe."

Wolfe? I didn't remember her ever calling me by my last name before. "That's the truth. I was looking for that little girl."

"Why?"

"Because—" I couldn't come up with a plausible because. "Well, the thing is, I can't tell you why. But it's not because of anything to do with the department."

"She's wanted in a homicide, an aggravated assault on a police officer, and for escaping from custody! *Of course* it has to do with the department!"

I pursed my lips. "Well, the reason I went after her isn't related to department business, and I can't explain it any better than that right now. You're just gonna have to trust me, that's all."

"*Trust* you? Trust *you?*" She walked over and bashed the door again. "*Trust you?*"

I slid up in my chair, my face red. I shrugged and crossed my arms, not knowing what to say. I knew I made her mad a lot, but when everything was said and done, Kate's approval meant everything to me. As far as I was concerned, she was everything every cop should aspire to be. The thought that I might have lost her trust devastated me.

She glared at me with both hands on her hips, her tone harsh. "Do you know what other supervisors told me when I agreed to take you into the unit?"

I had a pretty good idea they'd told her she was crazy, but I shook my head. I continued staring at the floor, black thoughts filling my head. *Now even Kate hates me.* I felt like pushing my way out of the room and quitting. *I don't belong here anyway.* I'd never been able to hide my emotions from her, so I turned away and hoped she hadn't seen them.

She watched me for a second, then put one hand under her bangs and kept the other on her hip. "Shit."

The light from the oversized window cast shadows on the rug behind the desk. I stared at the maroon floral patterns that edged out from the shadows, wondering how I kept getting myself into these messes. The thing is, I didn't get myself into them. Other people always seemed to paint me into a corner, and the only way out of the corner was to do something that pissed Kate off. I couldn't look her in the eye, so I leaned my elbow on the arm of the chair and rested the side of my head on my fist.

She leaned back on the desk again, resting one foot up on my chair next to my leg. "Never mind what they said. Look, I'm going to need more than 'trust me,' Alex. I told you before, I know when you're digging yourself into a hole, and I'm not going to let you self-destruct. Talk to me."

I looked up at her. Most of the fury had gone from her eyes and she raised her eyebrows, waiting for me to begin. The black cloud around me thickened and I looked back at the rug. I couldn't get past the idea that she couldn't trust me.

She reached over and tapped my knee with her shoe. "Trust goes both ways, Kiddo. If you want me to trust you, you gotta give."

When I looked up again, her brown eyes had softened even more into what I might have misinterpreted as something close to affection. I put my head back onto my fingers and sighed. "Well, do you know much about the Shelley Greer case?"

"Yes."

"What do you know?"

When she didn't answer, I glanced up to see amusement in her eyes. "You're the one talking right now, Alex, not me."

I gave her a sheepish smile since I'd hoped she'd give me something I hadn't learned so far. "Do you know that she might be Gianina Angelino's great niece?"

She started, then reached for the chair next to me, turned it so we faced each other and sat. "No. Tell me about it."

"Gia got a call from Shelley's case worker. The lady was trying to locate relatives, and she came across some paperwork naming

Tancredo Angelino, Gia's twin brother, as the girl's grandfather." I paused to gather my thoughts. "Gia is having a DNA test done to see if it's true."

Kate sat back, thinking, so I waited. She finally nodded. "Go on."

If I didn't have to mention that I was keeping an eye on the homicide investigation, I thought I'd keep that to myself. "When Shelley escaped, Gia was concerned that law enforcement couldn't find her, so she asked me to try."

Kate looked up at the ceiling. "Alex, she is a Mafia Don. Can you see the headlines if anyone finds out you're doing favors for the mafia?"

I lowered my eyebrows. "I'm doing favors for a friend. Nobody's gonna tell me who my friends can and can't be." We locked eyes. "She's never been arrested, never convicted of a felony. No one has ever proven she's a criminal."

Kate tilted her head sideways and shrugged, apparently conceding the point. "Okay, so I'm assuming that's what you and Megan were doing in the Vistas. Then what happened?"

"Nothing. I found the kid, but she got away from me." I felt a blush coming on, and I rested my forehead on my hand to hide the red suffusing my face. I couldn't tell her about Gabe taking Shelley.

"Nothing? You found a girl the department was looking for in a homicide, and when she got away from you, you did *nothing?*"

Shit. I hated it when she went into interrogation mode. "Kate, this is the part where you need to trust me. There are some... issues... I've noticed in the investigation, and I want to work things out in my own head before—" I was about to say "before I turn Shelley into the authorities" but I caught myself in time.

She stood up and leaned back on the desk again, her arms and legs crossed. "What issues?"

"Can I get back to you on that?"

"No."

That was pretty straightforward. No grey areas there. "Well, they're not clear in my mind, and I can't really pinpoint what's bothering me. It's things like, how did an eleven-year-old girl get a handgun? How did she know how to use a semi-automatic pistol, and how was she able to escape from juvenile court so easily in the first place? How did she get from Valencia down to the Vistas so quickly? And now, Eric says she's been seen back on Valencia again. How is she moving those distances?" What I didn't tell her was that I knew she wasn't back on Valencia—that whomever Eric was talking to was giving him incorrect information. "And more importantly, why did Eric go to the apartment by himself? He could see there was a back window, so why didn't he call for someone to cover the obvious exit?"

"Okay, so why aren't you talking to Eric about your concerns?"

I thought about that one a second. "I guess because Gia's involved, and the fewer people who know about my friendship with her, the better it would be for both of us."

Kate nodded slowly. "Okay." She bent forward and put her hands on the arms of my chair. "You listen to me, Alex, and listen well." She paused until I looked her in the eyes. "I don't care how insignificant you think the information might be. You *will* discuss every aspect of your involvement in the Shelley Greer case with me everyday—*everything*, Alex."

Did that include the fact that I knew where Shelley was at this particular moment? I mentally shook my head. "Yes Ma'am." I needed to go talk to Gia, immediately.

"All right, then get out of here."

CHAPTER 8

I left the office intending to go straight to Gia's, but I picked up the phone and called Ruthanne instead. When she answered, I got right to the point. "Hey, would you do me a favor? Would you look up the name of Shelley's CPS case worker for me?"

"Sure, hold on a second." I tucked the phone between my ear and shoulder and rooted around in my briefcase for a pen and pad of paper. The light in front of me turned red, and I slowed to a stop. Ruthanne came back on the line. "Okay, the lady's name is Roxie Cole. You want her cell phone number?" I told her I did, and when she gave it to me, I thanked her and hung up, dialing Ms. Cole's number as the light in front of me turned green.

A singsong voice answered the phone and I wondered whether the lady always answered her phone as though she knew a joke she was dying to tell the rest of the world. "Hello? Roxie Cole here!"

"Mrs. Cole, this is Detective Wolfe with the Tucson Police Department. I was wondering if you'd have a few minutes for me to stop by to speak with you about Shelley Greer?"

"Well, I'm not in my office, but I'm just now pulling into the convenience store on the corner of Speedway and Sixth. If you're anywhere near where you could swing by, that would be great."

"Sure, it'll take me about five minutes to get there. How will I know you?"

"Just look for the ravishing beauty with Double D breasts and a waist to die for. I'll be the one standing next to her." She giggled into the phone and I took an instant liking to her.

"All right. And I'm the one with two black eyes and stitches in my head."

"Oh my! I'll have to hear all about how that happened. I'll see you when you get here, Detective."

When I pulled into the lot, I recognized Mrs. Cole immediately. She stood next to the doors of the convenience store holding two cups of coffee and a bag clutched in her hands. As I got out of my car and walked over to her, a huge grin swept across her face. "Detective Wolfe? I'm Roxie Cole." She held out one of the coffee cups and shook the bag. "Donuts! I couldn't resist." She giggled. "All cops eat donuts, right?"

I grinned back at her. "This one does. I hope you got chocolate." I stuck my nose in the bag and saw a chocolate donut covered with chocolate glaze and sprinkles.

"Of course there's chocolate! We're women aren't we?" She held the bag open and I reached in to grab the one I happened to know was called brownie fudge glaze deluxe. We walked over to the hood of my car so we could set our coffee down and dunk. "All right, Detective. What do you need to know about Shelley? I've been working with Eric Langstrom, the homicide detective who's investigating the stabbing. I've told him as much as I know."

My gut instinct told me I could trust this woman, and I decided to take a chance. "Ms. Cole—"

She held up her donut. "Roxie."

I grinned at her. "Okay. How'd you end up with a name like Roxie, anyway?"

She laughed. "Oh God. My name's really Olympia, but when I was a toddler, I used to put tiny stones up my nose and they'd get stuck, so my father started calling me Roxie, and the name stuck too!"

"Olympia huh? I'll have to remember that for future bribery material. Anyway, *Olympia*, I'm not exactly working with Eric on this. I'm a friend of Ms. Angelino." I stopped there to see what her reaction would be. Afterall, Roxie had been the one to put two-and-two together as far as Tancredo Angelino's connection to Shelley Greer.

She quietly dunked her donut again and I waited for her to process what I'd said. She'd apparently come to the same conclusion about me that I'd come to about her. "Ms. Angelino is quite a formidable woman. I think Shelley would be in very good hands if she were able to live with her."

I watched her take a bite. "Yeah, I think she would be too." We looked at each other and our eyes held for a moment. There was no doubt in my mind she knew Gia had Shelley, and a sense of relief and conspiratorial trust filled the air. I shoved the rest of the donut in my mouth and put my hand to my face to hide my chewing while I spoke. "What can you tell me about Shelley's past?"

She turned around, put her hands behind her on the hood of my car and pushed herself up until she was sitting comfortably with her feet dangling over the side.

I pointed to her with my coffee cup. "Make yourself comfortable, why don't you?" The mischief I saw in her blue eyes reminded me of Megan at her best. I guessed she was about my age, maybe not as fit or as strong as me, but not bad looking either.

She brought her legs up and crossed them, sitting Indian style, and leaned back on her hands. "Don't mind if I do. Well, let's see... Shelley's had a pretty hard life. Born out of wedlock, her mother was a prostitute and who knows who her father was. Pretty typical of a lot of my cases. Our files go back to when Shelley was three and a neighbor reported she was home alone a lot." She paused and grabbed the coffee out of my hand. "You drink way too slow." She finished it off, then handed the empty cup back to me, smiling.

I smiled back and shook my head. "Here, give me yours." I took both cups into the market, refilled them and brought them back outside.

She accepted hers while she continued the story. "Anyway, the apartment was fairly clean, and when the caseworker located the mother, she gave a hard luck story. The worker arranged for state-aid day care and said 'don't do that again,' which in reality is exactly what I would have done. We have too many extremely serious cases we're working, and unfortunately, a lot of times we have to let those kinds go."

I happen to be very familiar with how the system works, and I wasn't surprised by what she'd said. She paused, thinking. "I think the next time we came into contact with Shelley was when she was nine and her mother was in the hospital dying of HIV/Aids. The nurses called us, we took custody. She bounced around foster homes for a while." She shook her head. "All the records from the foster families say she was out of control, belligerent and a—" She held her fingers up in quotation marks. "Difficult placement."

My cell phone beeped, and I held up a finger. "Could you excuse me for just a minute?" When she nodded, I opened the cover.

"Alex, it's Ruthanne. How's your face?"

I chuckled. "It's fine; how's *your* face?"

"Very funny. Listen, can I stop by your place tonight? I have a few things I want to run by you."

"Sure, come about seven and bring dinner."

"Okay, see you at seven."

I shut my phone and turned back to Roxie. "Sorry about that. So she's bounced around foster homes and at some point she killed this last foster father?"

She raised her eyebrows. "Well, actually, she disappeared from our radar for about eleven months. She ran away and we didn't hear anything about her until about a month ago. She reported a dead body to a patrol officer who did some research and discovered she was a runaway. We put her back into the foster care system, and shortly after that she stabbed the foster father and I was assigned to the case." She put her hand to her chest and tried for a comic humble look. "I get all the difficult cases because I'm actually *the* star case worker for our unit."

"Which means you were in the office when the call came in and you got stuck with it."

"Bingo. Anyway, I took a liking to the foul-mouthed little brat and did some extra digging. I located Ms. Angelino, and the rest is history."

"Has there ever been any history, even a whisper, about that foster father molesting kids in his care?"

She shrugged. "Well, with these kinds of kids, there are always accusations, and frankly, I'm amazed people still volunteer to be foster parents. It's a thankless job. Anyway, don't get me off on that particular tangent. As far as Norm Kindler, the man Shelley killed, there were a few accusations that were later found to be false. In fact, you could probably talk to Detective Langstrom about them. I think he was a child-abuse detective at the time and may have investigated them. I'm not sure on that, but I think that's right."

I walked back to the door of my car and leaned in the window to grab my notebook off the seat. Sometimes I like to keep things in my head and write them down later, but I was getting too much information and was worried I wouldn't remember it all. I took a minute to record what I needed while Roxie sipped her coffee on the hood of my car. Mental math has never been my strong suit, but I subtracted eleven months from Shelley's current age of eleven, then subtracted one more for the month since she'd stabbed Kindler. "Let's see, Shelley would have been nine, almost ten when she ran away for those eleven months, right?"

Roxie nodded. "Yeah... in fact she stabbed Kindler on her birthday. How's that for a birthday party?"

"Do we have any idea where she was for those eleven months?"

"Nope. She wouldn't tell me. She's a street savvy kid, though—and tough."

I thought of Gia's tough personality and wondered when the DNA tests would come through. After chasing her through back yards and hearing about Shelley's personality traits, I believed more and more that the two of them were related. I took out a business card and wrote down my personal cell phone number.

She in turn gave me hers, then pushed off my hood and held out her hand. "Stay in touch, Alex. I'll let you know if I come up with anything interesting."

"I will. See you around."

As I sat in my car finishing my notes, I looked up to see Roxie headed back my way. I rolled down my window and she leaned her arms on the window frame and stuck her head in. "I forgot to mention, I was at a fund raiser the other night, and when I mentioned to one of the other guests what kind of work I do, he began talking about the Kindler case. That segued into a story he told me about a friend—actually an employee of his—who'd always blamed his problems on the fact that he'd been molested while in the foster care system here in Tucson. He was appalled that the man was too ashamed to report the abuse." She shrugged. "It's probably not anything to do with anything, but I thought it was strange when he laughed and said wouldn't it be a coincidence if the guy had been molested by Kindler. That just struck me as odd that he would say something like that." She pointed to her business card sticking out of my little notebook. "If you want, give me a call later. I'll call the other guy from the fundraiser and see if I can get a name for you. I know you guys like to follow up on weird little things sometimes."

"Thanks, I will."

She patted the window frame, then returned to her car.

I pulled her card out, entered her numbers into the address book of my cell phone then put everything away and backed out of the lot.

CHAPTER 9

The next stop I needed to make was Gia's house. As I drove into her driveway, I thought about how she'd manipulated me into finding Shelley for her, then had blatantly kidnapped her right in front of my nose. I walked up the path to her front door, unsure of exactly what I wanted to say. My anger toward her hadn't cooled, and I knew my mouth was what always got me in trouble. In fact, Casey had recently given me a plaque for my desk that read *Engage Brain Before Opening Mouth*.

I rang the bell, listening to the familiar gong echoing throughout the home. Gabe answered the door instead of Gia, and I raised my eyebrows, silently questioning him about why he was there instead of her.

He raised his eyebrows in return and leaned forward to say quietly, "That kid knows more foul words than I do. I shoulda' let you have her."

I whispered back, "No shit, Einstein."

He stepped back and motioned me into the house. "You know where to go. They're in the library."

I touched the frame on the Leonardo for good luck as I walked past, then stuck my head through the doorway into the library. "Knock, knock."

I stepped in and stopped dead in my tracks.

Gia had the kid backed into a corner. She held the girl pinned up against the wall with the side of her body while the girl struggled to free herself. Gia glanced at me, then turned back to Shelley and said calmly, "Either you sit on the couch like I instructed, or we will end up back here again. Your choice."

Shelley snarled at her. "Let go of me, Bitch!"

I chuckled. "Shouldn't that be Aunt Bitch?" I didn't know whether Gia had told Shelley about their possible connection, but seeing the two of them side by side left absolutely no doubt in my mind they were related.

Gia shot me a fiery look and I held my hands in front of me. "Whoa, okay then, I think I'll just go grab myself a glass of Scotch." I headed for the bar where I pulled out a bottle of Glenlivet and took two glasses down from the shelves above the counter. "I assume you'd like one, Gia. How 'bout you, Shelley?" I couldn't help but laugh again as Shelley tried to squirm free and Gia pushed her farther into the corner.

I held the bottle up to the light to admire the dark caramel brown color. Judging from past personal experience, this particular Scotch tasted better than anything I'd ever had before, so I poured some into my glass and took a rather large sip before refilling it to the top. I poured a glass for Gia, then took both glasses with me to the sofa. I set hers on the coffee table and held mine carefully while I made myself comfortable in the leather cushions.

Gia pushed off Shelley, pulled her by the shirt and escorted her to the sofa. "Sit down, Shelley. We aren't even close to being done with our discussion yet."

Shelley roughly slapped Gia's hands off her shirt before throwing herself into the sofa.

I raised my glass, trying to keep the contents from sloshing all over me. "Hey, watch it! This is good stuff."

Shelley glared at me. "You're the cop who chased me in the back yard. I hope those dogs chewed your ass off!"

I grinned at her. "You're a pretty tough little kid. Not even many bad guys can clothesline me like you did."

She looked pleased with herself. "Anya taught me that."

"Who the hell's Anya?"

The curtain fell back down on her emotions. "None of your business."

I looked sideways at her. "You don't mean Crazy Anya who lives in the tunnels, do you?"

Her face morphed into a rage as she fell back and kicked the glass of Scotch out of my hand, sending it flying across the room. I grabbed her arms just as she launched herself at me.

"She wasn't crazy! You take that back! She wasn't crazy!"

I caught a glimpse of Gia out of the corner of my eye as she took advantage of our role reversal, picked up her Scotch and sank into one of the armchairs next to the sofa. "Gia! This isn't tag-team wrestling! Get your brat off me!"

Shelley kicked at me with her knees, and I rolled onto my back and brought my legs up trying to fend off the blows. When I caught sight of Gia again, she'd fired up her cigar and was watching the two of us with quiet amusement. I'd had just about enough of her little heathen beating up on me. I launched both of us out of the sofa, faced her away from me and wrapped my arms completely around her in a bear hug. Then I sat back down and wrapped my legs around hers, holding her like that until she began to calm down.

Unfortunately, it didn't take her long to get her second wind, and I could feel her ramping up for another assault. I decided to take the bull by the horns. "Anya is *too* crazy, and if you'd really spent any amount of time with her, you'd know it! But I like her anyways. I like her a lot because she's got a good heart and she can't help it if her brain's a little screwed up."

Shelley screamed at me. "I *did* spend time with her! I—" She choked on the rest of the sentence as she buried her head in the crook of my arm and cried something I couldn't hear.

I pulled my elbow away from her face. "What'd you say?"

She turned in my arms and I was surprised to see how red her face had gotten and how many tears were running down her cheeks. She ground her elbow into my chest and screamed again. "She's *dead*! She's dead, and she was all I had and now she's dead!"

We locked eyes a second until I sighed and relaxed my bear hug enough to turn her so she was facing my chest. I put my hand on the back of her head, pulling it down onto my shoulder so she could cry out her grief. She was a tough street kid, but her heart had broken when her friend had died. The way she fell apart in my arms made me wonder whether she'd ever given herself the luxury of grieving for Anya before now.

Gia and I exchanged glances over Shelley's head. When she finally began to relax, I rubbed her back and said quietly, "She really was a good person, Shelley, and we were both very lucky to have known her."

After a few minutes, Shelley wiped her tears on the sleeve of my shirt, and I sent Gia a disgusted look. I'd never been good with kids, and one of the reasons just happened to be all the various disgusting fluids that flow out of their bodies.

She pushed off me and returned to her side of the sofa while I thought about what she'd said. "Did you stay with Anya when you ran away from one of the foster homes? Did you live with her down in the tunnels?" The thought that a ten or eleven-year-old kid could survive for—what had Roxie said—eleven months undetected under the streets of Tucson amazed me. The tunnels run beneath Fourth Avenue. They're used by drug addicts and other vermin to hide from the cops, shoot up their drugs, have sex or sleep.

She turned away from me, pulled her legs up and wrapped her arms around them. I thought she looked smaller than most kids her age, and I suspected that lack of proper nutrition probably had contributed to her slight stature. Her hair color and Gia's were an identical raven black, but the most striking and telling characteristic were the unusual, dove-grey eyes that flashed cold steel whenever she became angry.

A thought occurred to me. "What happened to Muddy?" Whenever I'd seen Anya, a scruffy brown mutt named Muddy was walking sedately at her heals.

Shelley covered her eyes again, burying her head on the arm of the sofa.

I looked pointedly at Gia and motioned for her to move to the sofa to comfort the kid.

She in turn made little shooshing motions at me, as though I should move over and hold her again.

I gave her my best "do it" glare and made a sharp, quick stabbing motion with my finger to get her to do something.

She glared back at me before leaning over and awkwardly patting Shelley on the back.

My mouth dropped open and I raised both my arms, palms up to silently ask Gia what exactly *that* was supposed to accomplish.

Gia's eyes opened wide, and her lips pursed into an exasperated scowl.

I mimed gathering Shelley into my arms and holding her, then jabbed my finger first at Gia, then down at Shelley's back.

Gia, mouth still tightly closed, moved stiffly to the cushions next to Shelley and at least began massaging her back with the palm of her hand instead of patting her like she was an obedient dog. The contact seemed to relax both of them. Gia leaned over Shelley and spoke quietly. "I don't know what a 'Muddy' is, but I'm sorry thinking about it makes you so upset."

Shelley sniffed and said angrily, "He's a him, not an *it*." "Dummy" was implied but left unsaid.

I crossed my arms and whispered, "Way to go, Mrs. Freud."

Gia shot me one of her liquid lava looks and I grinned at her. "Muddy was Anya's four legged, curly haired friend with floppy ears." Gia had set her glass of Scotch on the coffee table. Since mine had gone flying a few moments earlier, I picked up hers, enjoying it all the more since I'd taken it from her. "Did the people from the Animal Care Center come take him when the police came to get Anya's body?"

Shelley nodded.

"Do you want me to go see if I can find him at the shelter and bring him to you?"

Gia and Shelley spoke at the same time: "No!" "Yes!"

Gia repeated, "No! Absolutely not!"

Shelley pursed her lips and buried her head back into the arm of the sofa.

My backwoods Pennsylvania grandmother used to tell me, "You have the gift, Alex. Always listen to what it tells you. Your soul's instinct will always be right." I often wondered whether my "soul's instinct" was what kept getting me into trouble. Anyway, she meant I had the ability to sense what people were feeling. I always thought about that when I interviewed people and had a sixth sense about whether they were lying or telling me the truth. Right at that moment, an overwhelming sense of loss came at me from Shelley, and I remembered what my grandmother had taught me.

There was no question in my mind that Shelley needed Muddy, if for no other reason than she'd lost both Anya and Muddy in the same day. I raised my eyebrows at Gia and vigorously nodded.

Gia lowered hers and shook her head exactly two times.

I mouthed, "Yes!"

She silently barked, "No!"

It suddenly occurred to me that God had just presented me with a wonderful way to get back at Gia for having Gabe follow me. I relaxed and pretended to acquiesce, nodding my head while sipping some more Scotch.

Shelley sat up and moved to the corner of the room where she slumped down on the floor and stared out of the floor-to-ceiling window.

There were some questions I wanted to ask her, so I went over and sat next to her. "You mind if I ask you some questions?"

She continued to stare out the window.

I decided on an extremely indirect approach to getting the information I wanted. "Did you know that Anya was really Dr. Anya Anderson?"

Shelley scratched her cheek but still refused to say anything.

"She had a PhD in literature from the University of Berkley. Sometimes, when her mind cleared, she and I would sit and talk. I didn't believe her at first when she told me about her PhD, but she bet me fifty dollars and dared me to look her up." I smiled at Shelley's reflection in the window. "I lost fifty bucks on that bet." I reached out to tap her arm. "Do you know what schizophrenia is?"

Shelley shook her head slightly.

"It's a mental illness that can be hidden when someone is young, but then people start to develop... well, certain symptoms. That's what happened to Anya. She was a professor at a university, and she gradually she began to lose her grasp on reality. Sometimes she'd see things or hear people talking to her who weren't really there."

Shelley lowered her eyes and spoke so quietly I had a hard time hearing her. "She used to talk to invisible people all the time. Sometimes, she'd get mad at me 'cause I didn't answer their questions."

I chuckled. "Yeah, me too. Once she took a stick to me because I sat on an invisible friend of hers."

She looked up at me, startled. "Me too!" Her arm stuck out of her sleeve and she discretely covered a two-inch long scar on her forearm.

I pretended I didn't notice her movement, then reached down and pulled up my pants leg. I pointed to a scar I'd gotten on my shin when a burglar had thrown me into a pile of scrap metal as he was trying to get away. "She really whacked me hard a few times." Okay, so she hadn't given me that particular scar, but she had laid into me with a pretty hefty stick.

Shelley moved closer and studied the scar before slowly moving her hand off her forearm. I reached over, rubbed her scar with my finger and smiled at her. "She made me apologize to her invisible friend. Boy, did I feel stupid talking to thin air."

She giggled. "Me too." Her eyes turned serious again. "But she wasn't always crazy."

"No, she wasn't. I'll bet she taught you more things than just how to clothesline a cop." I reached over and messed her hair and she moved away from me again. I let her settle, then said, "She was actually a pretty tough lady. I remember one day we were talking, and just that quick," I snapped my fingers. "She pulled a knife out of her sock and threw it at my head. It stuck into a piece of wood right next to my ear." I reached out to tap her again. "You know what she told me?"

Shelley shrugged and recited something she'd obviously memorized. "Drawing a knife's quicker than drawing a gun, a gun's quicker than a fist, and a fist's quicker than a word, but a word is stronger than all three put together."

Actually, Anya had thrown the knife at me during one of her delusional episodes and she'd told me that if I was planning to shoot her, I'd better think again, but I said to Shelley, "Exactly. She was really good with a knife."

Shelley reached down, pulled a knife from a sheath hidden beneath her sock and buried it into some wood ten feet away. She got up, pulled it out of the wood and returned to her space.

I swiveled around and exchanged "Oh shit" looks with Gia whose face had gone completely white. I turned back to Shelley. "Um... I guess Anya taught you pretty well."

The knife disappeared back into her sock. "She told me don't never let nobody touch you if you don't want to be touched, and if they get you down and you can't get away, stick 'em."

I found it interesting how her dialect moved from fairly well educated to inner-city thug depending on the situation. Her prowess with the knife made me worry about Gia's safety, so I decided to get some clarification on the point. "So how come when I came in here and Ms. Angelino had you up against the wall, you didn't stick her?"

Her face crinkled in concentration while she tried to come up with a way to explain her actions. "It's 'cause... Anya said I'm a kid, and—" She shook her head. "Well, she said I would know if someone was tryin' to help me or if they were tryin' to hurt me, and if they were tryin' to help me, even if I got super mad, I shouldn't stick 'em. And Anya was right." She pointed to Gia. "Even if she'd've turned me over her knee like she told me she was gonna...." A blush crept up her face. "I wouldn't've stuck her 'cause she was just doin' what she thought was right. She wasn't doin' it to hurt me." She studied me to see whether I understood what she was trying to explain.

I thought about what she'd just said. "Wow, even a lot of adults don't understand that concept as well as you do. I think you're a pretty bright kid."

She nodded as she looked from me to Gia, then back to me again. She said quietly, "Anya said I was." A far-off look came over her.

It seemed like she was trying to decide something, so I let her sit quietly for a minute. I watched her face carefully, wondering what was going through her mind.

Finally, she reached behind her back and pulled something from her waistband. She held out a filthy paperback that I really didn't want to touch without gloves on, but I swallowed my disgust and took the book from her. I wiped some dirt from the cover with my thumb so I could read the title—Mansfield Park by Jane Austen. I stared into Shelley's eyes a moment, then reached back and handed the book to Gia.

Shelley began to recite from memory. "About thirty years ago Miss Maria Ward, of Huntingdon, with only seven thousand pounds, had the good luck to captivate Sir Thomas Bertram of Mansfield Park, in the county of Northampton, and to be thereby raised to the rank of a baronet's lady, with all the comforts and consequences of an handsome house and large income." She paused, turning toward Gia, who'd gotten up from the sofa and was walking to the bookshelf, still holding Shelley's book.

We watched her run her finger across several books before resting it on the edge of one and pulling it off the shelf. To my surprise, she kicked off her heels and folded herself onto the floor next to Shelley. "Where did you learn to read books like this?"

Shelley took her paperback from Gia's hands and held it to her chest. "Anya made me read it to her every day. She made me memorize stuff, to keep my mind good, she said."

Gia held out the leather bound copy of Mansfield Park she'd pulled from the shelf. "I'd like to give this to you, as a gift. It's yours to keep, as are any of these other books here in my library. The only stipulation is, you have to read the book to me before it becomes yours."

Raised flowers decorated the outer edges of the light brown leather. Shelley reached out to run her finger over the flowers. She carefully traced the letters in the title. "You have Anya's book?"

Gia smiled as she touched the shabby, worn out book in Shelley's hand. "*You* have Anya's book, well worn and truly read, as all books should be. Mine is only a drab imitation that has languished on these shelves and possibly never been opened. We'll find a place of honor for your book, Shelley, so we'll always have it to remember your very wise friend, Anya."

Shelley carefully reached behind her and tucked her book back into the waistband of her pants. She obviously wasn't ready to entrust her prize possession to anyone but herself.

I leaned against the window, enjoying the warm sunshine as it streamed through. "So Anya taught you how to clothesline a cop, throw a knife, and read classics. What else did you learn from her?"

"A lot of stuff."

"Did she teach you how to shoot a gun?"

"No. She said if I was good enough with a knife, I didn't need a gun." She reached down to pull the top of her sock over the hilt of her knife, then sat cross-legged with her chin in her hands. "You gonna take me back to jail?" Her nonchalant posture didn't fool me. She refused to meet my eyes but she'd focused her entire attention on me, waiting to see what my answer would be.

Gia brought one knee up and draped her arm around it. "No, Shelley, you're going to stay with me for a while. Alex isn't here to take you back to the detention center."

The hackles on the back of my neck went up. "Gia." I locked eyes with her and said quietly, "You don't dictate how I do my job —ever."

Shelley watched both of us, listening.

Gia broke eye contact first, which was a minor victory for me. "You're right, Alex. I apologize. If you remember, I told you we both need to modify our behaviors toward each other. I'm used to being the decision maker in all aspects of my life."

The muscles in my shoulders felt tight. I reached up to massage my neck while I thought about Shelley's question. "I know this is a silly question, but why did you run away? You stabbed Mr. Kindler in self-defense. Detective Langstrom is working to prove there were other kids he molested. You would have been out fairly soon, but now, you have escape and aggravated assault charges against you."

Shelley lifted her chin off her knee. "He said he was gonna prove Kindler didn't do nothin'. He said he'd make sure I went to prison for the rest of my life."

I shifted toward her. "Who said that?"

"That asshole detective." The scowl on her face intensified. "He said nobody believed me."

"Was anyone else with you when he told you that?"

She shook her head. "Only me and—"

Gia interrupted her. "Wait a minute, Alex. What do you mean, aggravated assault? From when she hit you in that back yard?"

I watched Shelley as I answered Gia. "No, from when she shot at Detective Langstrom in the apartment."

Shelley bolted to her feet. "That's a lie! You're lying!" She hauled back and kicked me in the shin, which was momentarily unprotected since my reactions were somewhat slower than hers and when she jumped up it took me a half-second longer than her to push to my feet.

Pain raced up my leg and came partially out my mouth before I could stop it. "You little...!" I grabbed for her, but Gia stepped between us before I could get my hands around Shelley's scrawny little throat. Gia's eyes sparkled with amusement as I hopped around on one foot holding my shin and glaring at the little shit glaring out from behind Gia's shoulder.

I growled like a feral dog and limped over to the liquor cabinet. My glass lay across the room where Shelley had kicked it, so I grabbed a cognac snifter, stalked to the coffee table and filled it to the brim. I downed half the glass before I got my temper back under control.

Gia reached around and put her arm across Shelley's shoulders. She brought her to the sofa and the two of them sat, waiting for me to calm down.

Once I could open my mouth without spewing hateful invectives, I pointed at Shelley. "I... you...." My mind flew in circles, wanting to yell at her but needing to find out what had happened on Valencia. I took a deep breath and another swig of Scotch, then lowered myself into an easy chair. I tried for a smile, but I'm pretty sure what showed up didn't come anywhere near close to friendly. "Okay, tell me what happened in the apartment then."

Shelley crossed her arms, squeezing her lips shut to show me she didn't have anything else to say to me.

Gia picked up her cigar and sat back into the couch chuckling. "Good one, Mrs. Freud."

Her mischievous grin brought a real smile to my lips this time. "If your kid keeps attacking me, I'm gonna end up with an early medical retirement."

"I'm not her kid."

"Oh, you can talk? So, tell me what happened at the apartment."
She didn't move.

I finished my Scotch and got to my feet. "You're gonna have to tell me sometime, and the sooner you decide I'm on your side, the sooner we can all get back to a normal life."

The kid continued to glare at me.

I winked at Gia, "She's all yours, Aunty. I'll let myself out." I walked to the end of the hall where Gabe met me and held open the door.

He usually came across as completely competent and slightly bored, but today he had circles under his eyes and his hair fell slightly out of place. I pointed to the dark circles. "I think she'd do that to the best of us."

His eyes met mine as he said quietly, "My grandfather used to work for Ms. Angelino's father when the twins were young. He used to come home totally exhausted. Now I think I understand why."

I smiled sympathetically as I stepped out and he shut the door behind me.

CHAPTER 10

Megan called and we decided that since her protest buddies were headed to a vegetarian restaurant for lunch, she and I would meet at one of our favorite Mexican hangouts. We both pulled into the restaurant at the same time, and I raced her for the parking spot closest to the front door. I slid into the space first, and she lay on her horn until several waiters stuck their heads out the front door to see what was wrong. I strolled inside while she backed up three spaces and parked her car.

I waited for her to come in before finding a table toward the back of the restaurant. She knew I always sat facing the front door, so as we neared our seats, she pulled me back by my shirt and made a dash for the far side of the table. Her hind end claimed the chair inches before mine and she sat grinning while I pulled out the chair on the other side. "All right, but if someone comes in to rob the place, I hope you can pull your gun before they shoot me in the back."

The waiter came to the table and eyed Megan's ample cleavage before asking for our drink order. Megan bent forward and adjusted her shoe, which accomplished exactly what she intended; her breasts rested on the tabletop and pushed up out of her bra even more than usual. She smiled up at the appreciative young man. "We'll both have some iced tea, and I'd like some chips and salsa, please."

When the waiter left to get our drinks I said, "Your shoe okay?"

She grinned back at me. "It is until he gets back with our drinks."

Two angry voices carried through the restaurant and I swiveled around to see who was arguing. The booth the people were sitting in hid them from view, and I fervently hoped I wouldn't have to get involved in breaking up a family fight. They lowered their voices again just as our waiter brought our drinks and the chips.

Megan indicated the booth with her chin. "What's that all about?"

He shrugged. "They come in all the time. Lately it seems like all they do is argue." His eyes traveled to Megan's chest again, then back to the booth. "She's got a couple men she comes in with, but I haven't seen the other one in here lately. Just this guy."

We gave him our order and when he left I told Megan what had happened with Shelley and Gia. It helped to talk about my cases with her because she always had a unique point of view when it came to suspects, victims, and me. I dipped a chip in the salsa while I spoke. "It bothers me that Eric would tell a little kid that nobody believed her and she's going to prison for the rest of her life. That doesn't sound like something he'd say."

"Maybe the kid's lying to you."

I thought about that a second. "I don't think so. She's tough, smart, independent and...." There was a particular word I wanted, and it took me a little while to come up with it. "Genuine. She wears her heart on her sleeve, and there's no question about what she's thinking or feeling."

Megan knew me well enough to know when I was thinking out loud, so she ate the chips and let me work out what was on my mind.

"You know, usually kids like her know how to manipulate people to get what they want. She's not like that. If she wants something, she'll tell you. If you make her angry...." I put my foot up on my chair and rolled up my pant leg to show her my newest bruise. "She lets you know."

Megan pushed partway out of her chair so she could look over the table at my shin. "Ouch! She really got you. What did you say to piss her off?"

I thought back to that point in our conversation. "I think I asked her what happened in the apartment. She got pissed off, kicked me, then clamed up. She wouldn't say anything else."

"She kicked you because you asked her what happened in the apartment? There has to be more than that. What else did you say?"

"Nothing. I said, tell me what—No, wait. Gia asked me why she would be charged with aggravated assault, and I said because she shot at Eric in the apartment. That's what set her off. She screamed that I was a liar."

"Well, I guess the question is, do you believe a respected homicide investigator or an eleven-year-old murder suspect?"

"I believe Eric."

"What about what you just told me about Shelley?"

I scowled at her. "Now you're going in circles."

"No, *you're* going in circles. I'm just trying to keep up." She dipped a chip in the salsa, poured some extra salt on and stuck it in her mouth. "Were her prints on the gun?"

"I don't think they found the gun."

"So what evidence did they come up with at the apartment?"

Our food arrived and we were quiet a minute while we settled into our meal. The waiter filled our water with a big grin on his face.

Megan took a sip and looked up at him over her glass. "Why the big grin? You love your job so much you walk around with a smile on your face?"

The waiter glanced over at the booth where the man and woman had been arguing earlier. "Naw, I just filled their water, and she's got her toes up his crotch. His face is practically purple he's enjoyin' it so much."

We still couldn't see anything on the other side of the booth, but we swiveled around anyway to stare at the vinyl backing.

"Funny thing is, she does the same thing with the other guy she comes in with. We always take bets to see how long it'll take before her shoe comes off."

Megan laughed at the conspiratorial whisper the young man used as he described the torrid rendezvous. "Let us know if the table starts to rise on his side. If it does, I definitely want to make his acquaintance"

I set down my glass of water and sighed. "Megan, this guy's only a kid." I looked at him. "How old are you, anyway? Nineteen? Twenty?"

"Twenty."

I turned back to Megan. "You're corrupting our youth. Will you knock it off already?"

Megan gave him her best come-hither look. "I'd be glad to corrupt him anytime he'd like."

The waiter laughed and left to deliver some food to another table. "Megs, what's the matter with you? I thought you were hot and heavy with that cowboy. What's his name again?"

"Petey. And what's the matter with *you*? You used to flirt all the time. I'll bet you haven't had any since your last birthday, and that was what, nine months ago?"

Truth was, I didn't get any then either. I just let her think I did. I shrugged. "I don't know. I've been wondering the same thing lately." I thought about Carl and immediately dismissed that from my mind. Kate would definitely frown on my dating the suspect in a kidnapping.

Megan's gaze shifted from me to something going on behind me. I turned in time to see the arguing couple get up from the booth. When I took in a startled breath, I choked on inhaled lettuce and ground beef instead of air. My coughing and wheezing could have raised the dead and I was afraid the noise would attract the couple's attention. I definitely didn't want them to recognize me. I picked up a napkin to cover my face and made my way to the woman's restroom where I could die in private.

Megan followed me in and began pounding my back, trying to dislodge whatever food had caught in my throat.

Since I could still pull in a wheezing breath, I brushed her arm off because the only thing the pounding accomplished was to give me several more bruises on my already battered body.

Our waiter stuck his head in the door. "My boss wants to know if she's gonna be okay or should we call the fire department?"

When my airway finally cleared I wiped tears from my cheeks with a paper towel. "Tell him I'm fine. And what if I'd been naked in here or something? Why would he send a guy in to check on someone in the woman's restroom?"

"No waitresses here right now, and to be honest, naked would have been fantastic!" He leered at my body while I stood there with my hands on my throat watching him.

Megan bumped me from behind and whispered, "Nine months, Alex."

He looked shocked. "Nine months! Heck, I don't wanna get her pregnant, I just want to put a smile on her face."

Megan shook her head sadly. "No, I mean it's been nine months since she's gotten any."

"Megan!" I pushed past the young man, who shot me a startled look.

"Nine months? You gotta be kidding me!" He followed me out into the restaurant as he blared out his newest discovery.

The manager walked over to see what he was shouting about. "Nine months what?" He turned to me. "I hope you're going to be okay. You really looked like you weren't going to make it."

The waiter pointed at me as he exclaimed at the top of his voice. "She hasn't had sex with anybody for nine months!"

The restaurant went silent. I held my arms out to my side and slowly moved in a circle so the whole restaurant could see me. "Okay, okay! I haven't had sex in nine months! Go ahead, make your jokes!" I walked up to a middle-aged couple, my arms still held straight out. "My sex life sucks! How's yours?"

The man smiled up at me. "Once a day... twice if I can manage it." The room broke out into spontaneous applause as the woman took the man's face in her hands and delivered a long, deep french kiss.

I dropped my arms to my side. "I give up." I turned to the waiter and pointed at Megan. "Give her the bill. She gets it pretty regularly."

The manager walked up and put his arm around my shoulders. "No, no, this is on the house." He grinned at the rest of the people in the restaurant and said loudly, "At least she'll get *something* nice today!"

Hoots and hollers followed his announcement as I chuckled and took a bow. "Thank you, thank you. I'm glad I could entertain you today. Thank you." I grabbed Megan around the shoulders and escorted her out to the parking lot. Her smile reached to both ears and I grabbed her hair gently on either side of her head. "I hate you, but I couldn't live without you, Megan Gertrude."

"Well Alexandra Frieda, same goes for you." She grabbed my head and planted a wet one right smack square on my lips.

I pulled back, sputtering. "Eww! Yuck! What is the *matter* with you?" I vigorously rubbed my lips with the back of my hand. "That's like getting kissed by a sister!"

People across the street stopped and looked as she threw back her head and laughed. "I know! I felt sorry for you!" She danced away to her car as I swiped at her and tried to grab her hair again.

"You'll be sorry, Gertrude!"

She waved at me on the way out of the parking lot. I waved back and wondered how I'd gotten so lucky to have such a nut as my best friend. My cell phone rang just as I fastened my seat belt. I flipped it open and saw a number I didn't recognize pop up on the display. "This is Detective Wolfe."

The silence on the other end stretched out, making me wonder whether my photographer friend had gotten hold of my phone number somehow. I heard someone clear his throat. After a few seconds, he spoke. "Detective Wolfe, this is Carl Boyd."

My heart jumped—just a little bit. I decided it hadn't jumped enough to feel guilty about, just enough to wake me up. "Carl, what can I do for you?" When he didn't answer, I wondered whether he'd hung up. "Carl? You there?"

He cleared his throat again. "Yeah, I'm here. Listen, this was probably a bad idea. Never mind, okay?"

I wanted to catch him before he hung up. "Wait. What did you want? I'm gonna be wondering what you called about the rest of the day if you don't tell me. I kinda' obsess that way. You don't want me to obsess, do you?"

He chuckled. "No Ma'am. I wouldn't want to be the cause of that. What I was wonderin'... well, I guess what I wanted to ask...." He stopped again and then blurted out, "Would you like to meet me somewhere for coffee? It's okay if you don't. In fact it's probably a bad idea anyway."

I completely forgot about the plaque Casey had given me and surprised myself by accepting his offer. "Sure! That'd be great. When and where?" Alarm bells echoed throughout my head and I completely ignored them. Nine months is an extremely long time to dance with your toys.

"How about right now at the coffee shop at 12th and Irvington?"

I checked my watch. "I'm on my way. It'll take me five minutes." My internal juices went into hyper drive as I thought of Carl's incredible body lying under mine. Okay, so I was getting ahead of myself. I knew I couldn't do anything with him until the case was solved. Could I? *No, I couldn't.* His body came to mind again and I raised my eyebrows. *Maybe just once.*

Every nerve in my body tingled as I pulled into the parking lot and saw him sitting in front of the shop. He stood up, removed his hat, and pulled out a chair as I walked up. I sat in the offered chair. "How did you beat me here?"

He blushed. "I've been sitting here trying to get up the nerve to call you. Can I get you some coffee?"

I felt like I was going to have an orgasm right there on the patio. It had definitely been too long. "Iced tea would be great thanks—six packets of sweetener."

"I'll be right back." I studied his tight hind end as he walked into the shop. I really liked cowboys stuffed into form-fitting jeans. When he returned, I embarrassed myself by studying the front of his pants.

He sat in a chair next to mine. "You're blushing."

I sipped the iced tea. "I think it's just a little warm, that's all."

He raised his hand as though testing the air. "Yeah, it must be at least seventy degrees out here."

I laughed self-consciously, wondering what I was doing here having tea with the suspect in my kidnapping case. *Am I completely out of my gourd?* I focused on the funny place between my legs. *Yes.* He'd brought out several napkins and I began playing with the edges of one, rolling up the side before flattening it out again.

He covered my hand with his and electric currents shot through my body. *Did I just have an orgasm?*

He held my eyes and said, "You feel it too, don't you?"

My cell phone saved me from answering. I pulled my hand out from under his and flipped open the phone. My voice sounded shaky as I answered. "Detective Wolfe."

"Alex." Kate didn't sound pleased.

Every sexual fantasy I'd ever entertained went flying out of my brain. My body returned to normal and I wondered what the hell I'd been thinking. "Yes?"

"Don't you dare look around. Now tell me, what are you doing sitting in front of a coffee shop holding hands with the suspect in our kidnapping investigation?"

It sounded like they'd been following Carl and I didn't want to give them away by saying the wrong thing. "I'm just having some tea with a friend right now, but I'm available if you need me for a call out." I covered the phone as though I didn't want Kate to hear and mouthed, "My sergeant."

He nodded and leaned back in his chair, stretching his long legs out in front of him.

Kate growled. "I'm going to call you out all right. Get your ass back to the office, *now!*"

"Yes Ma'am." I shut the phone. The look of disappointment on Carl's face told me he knew what was coming. "That was my sergeant. I have a call out I need to go to. Listen, this probably isn't such a good idea right now, anyway. I'm sorry."

He stood up at the same time I did. "You feel it too. I know you do." He paused, fumbling with the brim of his cowboy hat, which he still held in his hands. "I can wait." He put his hat on and started to walk me to my car.

I stopped, not wanting to give the cops watching us anymore fodder for jokes than they already had. "Carl, don't. I can walk myself to my own car." He stayed where he was and I drove out of the parking lot wondering exactly what I'd been thinking and just how pissed Kate was going to be this time.

When I got to the office, I went to my desk and waited for her. Other detectives were quietly working at their desks, writing reports, and taking interviews on the phone. But me? I had to be caught with my pants down, salivating over a kidnapping suspect. Well, okay, they hadn't been down yet, but it'd been close.

The office door slammed opened and Kate came striding in. She didn't stop, didn't pass go, just headed straight to the lieutenant's office and stalked in.

I sighed, walked in behind her and gently shut the door.

She stood in the middle of the room with her arms crossed, waiting.

"You want the truth?" I figured I was toast anyway, and I couldn't come up with anything plausible that would work.

"That would be nice."

"I haven't had sex in nine months, I'm horny, and he's cute."

She lowered her head and stared at me.

It looked to me like she was trying to hide the amusement that flitted across her face, but I couldn't be sure. She turned toward the window, scratched her head, then shook it. Without looking at me, she said, "Get it somewhere else, Alex."

I was sure she was hiding a smile this time. "Yes Ma'am."

"Get out of here."

"Yes Ma'am." I opened the door and walked out. After a few steps I remembered there were a few things I needed to tell her so I turned back. "I almost forgot—Megan and I had lunch at Carne Loco, and Hondo Forbish and Mona Boyd were sitting together in a booth. They argued about something, then she put her toes in his crotch and—"

Kate turned from the window and held up her hand. "Whoa. I don't need the details about the toes. What did they argue about?"

"I don't know. I couldn't see them in the booth, and I didn't realize it was them until they got up to leave. The waiter said she comes in all the time with Hondo, and sometimes she's there with another guy. He hasn't seen the other guy in a while though."

"Interesting. Do you still have the picture of Mona's boyfriend, Kenny Finch?"

"Yes Ma'am." I figured it wouldn't hurt to try to earn back some brownie points by being polite and respectful.

"It won't work, Alex."

I grinned and shrugged. "I figured it wouldn't hurt."

A small smile played on her lips as she watched me a minute.

I gave her my best innocent look and waited.

She finally shook her head before continuing. "Anyway, take the picture back to the restaurant to see if that's the other man Mona comes with. It won't tell us much since we know he's her boyfriend, but it'll still be another small piece of the puzzle."

"Yes Ma'am." I heard her chuckle as I turned to head to my car. I drove back to the restaurant and asked the cashier if I could speak with the young man who'd served us. While I waited, my mind wandered to my conversation with Shelley. I pulled out the list of witnesses Ruthanne had given me and decided that since I was already on the south side of town, I might as well see whether I could make contact with any of them.

The young man walked out of the kitchen carrying a tray full of plates loaded with tacos, enchiladas, burritos, and a few other miscellaneous bowls and bottles. He raised his chin toward me and yelled across the room. "I'll be right there as soon as I get these people their food."

I waved to him as I went back to studying the list. Two of the witnesses lived in the apartment complex where Shelley had shot at Eric. I decided to start with them.

The waiter came over with a smile plastered on his face. "I don't get off until seven tonight, but after that, I'm all yours."

My confused look must have given me away because he pumped his hips back and forth in a comic imitation of a turtle humping a cake pan. I blinked and burst out laughing. "Are you kidding me? I could be your mother! Granted, I would have been a really young mother, but hey, it happens."

He gave me a wounded puppy dog look. "I like older women. It wouldn't be a problem."

"Older women? *Excuse me?* I am *not* an older woman!"

"But you just said—"

I held up my hand. "Never mind what I just said." I pulled Kenny's picture out of my notebook. "Do you recognize this guy, or not?"

He took the offered picture. "Yeah, he's the other guy that lady plays toe-ball tag with."

"Toeball tag? How long did it take you guys to think that up?"

"My brother came up with it, but it fits. What do you want this guy for? He a criminal or something?"

I took the picture back from him. "No, he's not. How long has it been since you've seen him in here?"

His eyes traveled to the booth where Mona and Hondo had been playing tag. "It's been a while... about two weeks I guess. I remember when he comes in 'cause he's a lousy tipper and I always make sure to give him lousy service."

I pulled out my business card. "Would you call me if he comes in again? And I'd appreciate it if you could give him my number and ask him to call me if you do see him."

He took the card and stuffed it into his front shirt pocket where I was sure it'd be washed with the next load of dirty laundry. I pointed to his shirt pocket. "You think maybe you could set that in a drawer by the cash register so you know where to find it if he does come in?"

He shrugged as he pulled the card back out of the pocket. "Yeah, I guess so." I watched him walk over to the cashier. He handed him the card, then said something I couldn't hear. The cashier waved the card at me and then placed it into the drawer with exaggerated care.

I waved back and muttered "Smartass" before heading out to my car.

CHAPTER 11

I pulled into the parking lot of the apartments on Valencia. The three-story complex surrounded a central courtyard where an empty pool lay abandoned and cracking. A weathered sign hung on the wrought iron fence encircling the pool. Out of curiosity, I walked over to read it: *NO WATER IN POOL. DIVE AT YOUR OWN RISK.* That gave me a pretty good idea of the intelligence level of the people living in the complex. The peculiar, dirty-diaper smell particular to older, filthy apartments hung in the air. I pulled out my witness list again. The first lady lived on the third floor in apartment 308. I studied the numbers on the doors on the first floor trying to decide which set of cement stairs would get me the closest to 308.

Of course, the building the farthest away from where I stood had the numbers 101-111 stenciled on the doors. I climbed the three flights and went looking for 308. At 307, I realized these were all odd numbers, and 308 was located in the next apartment building over. "Goddamnit." I'd started back for the stairs when a disembodied voice spoke quietly from the open window of 307.

"You probably shouldn't use His name like that in case you need Him later on."

I glanced in the widow but the reflections on the glass kept me from seeing inside. "Um, right." I looked up at the sky. " Uh... sorry, God."

When I turned to head to the stairs again, the man said, "You don't need to look up, you know. He can hear you just fine down here. Open the door and come in. Its not locked."

As I stopped next to the door, I mumbled, "Damn it."

The voice called out the window. "I heard that."

Any time I wore my gun and badge visible on my belt, I felt obligated to act completely professional when dealing with members of the public. It might have had something to do with my long-standing relationship with Internal Affairs, but I preferred to think it was because I was a public servant whose job entailed helping people in need. I thought back to Internal Affairs and decided that was the more likely scenario.

I sighed as I mentally prepared myself for the stench I knew would hit me the moment I opened the door. All these old apartments reeked, even if the place had just been cleaned or if the current occupant kept the rooms immaculate. I turned the knob, pushed the door in and stepped back a step to allow the first wave of foul air to rush out before I had to breathe. When I thought the air had cleared enough to enter without gagging, I stepped inside.

The man lay in a bed that had been pushed up against the window so he could face outside to watch the world go by. Arthritis had twisted his body into impossible, painful looking contortions, but his smile welcomed me into his home. He waved a gnarled claw at me, beckoning me inside. "Come in, come in. Shut the door so Stacy can't get out, would you?"

I grimaced at the thought of staying in the little twelve by twelve room without fresh air from the open door, but I reached over and pushed it shut anyway. "Who's Stacy?"

"Hello." A high-pitched crackly voice greeted me from the foot of the bed. I don't know how I'd missed her when I walked in, but I smiled at a beautiful Scarlett McCaw perched next to the window.

I stepped closer, smiling from ear to ear. "Hello! Are you Stacy?"

"Yes. Do you want to take a shower?" She waddled closer to where I stood mesmerized by her.

The man laughed. "No, Stace, she's not here to give either of us a shower." He shifted around in the bed and gave me a pain-filled smile. "Her absolute favorite activity in the world is standing in the shower with the water cascading down her back."

I stared at her while she bowed up and down and said, "Stacy wants her shower."

I knelt down so I was on her level and asked the man, "Do you want me to turn on the shower for her, just for a few minutes?"

Stacy yelled. "Yes!" She jumped off the side of the bed and started waddling toward the back of the apartment.

"How does she know what I said?"

I looked up at the grinning man, who waved his claw at me again. "I don't know. Her intelligence never ceases to amaze me. Go ahead; it'll make her day."

Stacy disappeared through a door, which I assumed went into the bathroom. I followed her into a tiny space that held a rusty porcelain pedestal sink, a fairly clean toilet and a tub and shower combo. She jumped into the tub, quietly mumbling, "Shower, shower, shower, shower...."

I reached in to turn on the water. When it rained down on her she began screaming and flapping, "Cold! Cold! Cold!"

I heard the man laughing in the living room. "Oh man! Sorry, Stacy! I forgot to tell you to warm the water first. She hates cold water!"

I grinned at Stacy as she jumped up onto the side of the tub and berated me while she fluffed her bedraggled feathers. "Cold!" She jumped down and waddled over to some pliers on the floor.

The hot water nozzle had broken off so I called into the other room. "How do I turn on the hot water?"

Stacy piped up. "Pliers! Pliers!"

The old man called back, "There should be some pliers on the floor next to the door."

I picked up the pliers, squeezed them around the hot water nub and turned. Stacy and I waited until the sound of the water made a distinct change, indicating the hot water had kicked in.

She squawked "Shower!" before plunging under the stream.

I thought it would be polite to give her some privacy, so I walked back out to the bed.

From inside the bathroom, a stirring rendition of "I've Been Working on the Railroad" rang throughout the little apartment.

The man held out his hand. "I'm Seth by the way—Seth Rivers."

I studied his hand, afraid I'd hurt it if I gripped it too hard. The problem was, I didn't know how hard too hard was. I reached out and carefully enfolded his fist into my hand since he couldn't open his fingers. "Nice to meet you Mr. Rivers. I'm Detective Wolfe. Actually, you can just call me Alex if you like."

"Seth."

Stacy decided to change songs, bursting forth with "The Hallelujah Chorus."

"Whoa, she's got quite a pair of lungs on her."

"Wait until she gets to something from the Rolling Stones. You can't hear yourself think. So what brings you to this little slice of paradise, Alex?"

"I'm just doing some follow-up on that shooting the other day. I wanted to talk to some of the people who saw the little girl over in apartment..." I pulled the paper out of my pocket. "Apartment 122."

He pointed back with his fist. "You probably should shut the water off now. I can't afford to run my bill up too high."

"Oh yeah, sorry."

As I headed back to the bathroom, he called after me. "122 is right across the way from me. I can see it clearly out of my window. I saw that detective go in, heard the shots and ducked." He looked a little sheepish. "I knew it wouldn't help to duck since I was still here in the bed, but it was just a gut reaction to close my eyes like I was hiding. When I opened them, he came running out and looked around, then got on his radio."

Stacy screamed at me when I reached in with the pliers to turn off the water. "No! Traitor! No!"

I called out to Seth. "Traitor? Where'd she come up with that?"

"The guy who comes twice a week to bathe me taught it to her. He thought it would be funny if she yelled that whenever he turned off her water."

"Sorry Stacy." I followed her back out to the living room. "Do you live here all by yourself?"

"No, I have Stacy to keep me company. My neighbor stops in twice a day and I get Meals on Wheels so I eat regularly. It could be worse." He smiled at me. "Things could always be worse."

I thought of how lonely I'd be if I were confined to a bed twenty-four hours a day. I knew Seth probably wanted me to stay and visit, but unfortunately, I needed to get back to work. I pulled my little notebook and pen out of my pants pocket. "You said you saw Detective Langstrom go into the apartment, you heard a gunshot, and then saw him come back out again. Did you see anyone else go in or come out?"

He lifted a fist, indicating the window in the wall behind him. "No, but as you can see, all the units have windows at the back of the rooms. Whoever shot at him probably went out the back window."

"Has that unit been empty long?"

"About a month I think. Some kid overdosed in there about a month ago. The police thought it might have been foul play, so detectives came out. I guess they decided the kid just took too much Meth."

Stacy climbed back up on the blankets. Her favorite place to stand seemed to be at the foot of the bed near the window.

I watched her waddle back to the spot she'd occupied when I walked in. I reached for the door. "Thanks for the information, Seth, and sorry you heard me cuss. You seem kinda' religious or something."

"I was a missionary for thirty years. I've toned down the hellfire and brimstone, but when I heard you, I couldn't resist."

I grinned at him. "Thanks for toning it down. My sergeant gives me all the hellfire I need." I surveyed the sorry little room and came to a decision. "If it's all right with you, I'd like to stop in every once in a while to see how you're doing." I looked at Stacy. "And to give you a shower."

"Shower!" She waddled to the edge of the bed, ready to head back to the bathroom.

Seth chuckled. "No, Stace. No more shower. She's leaving."

Stacy turned around and headed for the end of the bed, muttering the whole way back. "Traitor, traitor, traitor."

I let myself out and waved to Seth and Stacy as they watched me from their window. People amazed me sometimes. His whole world consisted of the courtyard of this filthy apartment complex, but he seemed happy and content. A little lonely maybe, but he definitely didn't feel sorry for himself.

I walked back down the stairs, found the even-numbered building and walked back up the three flights to the third floor. I knocked on apartment 308 and waited. A woman in a frayed bathrobe and slippers answered the door holding a cigarette in one hand and a half a sandwich in the other. "Yeah?" She took in the badge and gun on my belt, then shoved part of the sandwich into her mouth.

"Mrs. Richey?"

"Yeah." Some food fell out of her mouth as she spoke and I almost gagged.

"I'm Detective Wolfe. I'm investigating the shooting that happened in apartment 122 the other day."

"Well, ya don't need me then." She stepped back and pushed the door shut.

I stuck my foot out to stop it from closing completely. "I understand you saw the girl who was trespassing there?"

"Didn't see shit."

I pushed the door open so I could see what was going on inside. Mrs. Richey opened the refrigerator and pulled out a bottle of beer. A cockroach picked up the piece of food that had fallen from her mouth and I had to look away to keep from gagging. I just wanted to get my questions answered and get the hell out of Dodge. "You told Detective Langstrom you'd seen the girl going in and out of that apartment. Were you lying to him?"

She twisted off the cap before taking a swig. She glared at me from above the neck of the bottle through beady eyes. "Fuck you."

I smiled my most gracious "stay out of IAD" smile. "No thanks. Sorry to have bothered you." I walked back down the stairs while I read the other name and apartment number on the witness list. "Jared Scone. Apartment 124." Jared's apartment was right next to 122. I fervently hoped he wasn't as disgusting a slice of humanity as Mrs. Richey. The door stood open, so I moved to the side and knocked.

A middle-aged man wearing shorts and knee socks answered the door. His bare belly hung over the top of his pants, stretching out the spider web tattoo decorating the majority of his sunken chest and globular stomach. The spider on his D-cup breasts had been stretched by age and extra weight until its three bottom legs were four times the length of the three on top. He reached up to scratch the spider and belched. When I curled my lip in disgust, he growled, "What?"

"What do you mean, 'what?'"

He stared at me a second, then waved me away as he turned to go back inside.

"Mr. Scone, I'm Detective Wolfe and I have a few questions about the shooting the other day."

"Fuck you."

Definitely not in this lifetime. "No thank you, Sir. I wanted to ask about the girl you said you saw next door. Can you describe her for me?"

"No."

"Were you here when she shot at Detective Langstrom?"

"Yeah."

"Did you hear her say anything?"

He picked up a remote and fell back into the sofa. "Look, I didn't see shit. He went in; a few minutes later I heard a shot. She came out, he came out. End of story."

"*She* came out? The front door?" That didn't fit with what Eric had said, but then again, this wasn't the world's most reliable witness. "You sure *she* came out the front door?"

His left boob twitched. "S'what I said ain't it?"

I studied him a minute. I couldn't tell whether the information moving through his coagulated brain pathways had any basis in reality. "How long had the girl been staying in that apartment?"

When he answered, he pulled back his lips as though he was a dog about to snap at me. "Ask the fuckin' detective."

"I'm asking you."

"Fuck you."

I sighed. "No thank you." This was getting me absolutely nowhere. I turned to wave at Seth and Stacy up on the third floor, then made my way back to my car.

I got in and pulled out my cell phone to call Roxie. When she answered, I could barely hear over the background noise on her end. I said loudly, "Roxie?"

"Yuppers! Who's this?"

I smiled. "It's Alex Wolfe. Where the hell are you? It sounds like you're in the middle of a riot."

I heard her laugh. After a second, the background noise quieted. "There, is that better? I stepped outside. I've been looking for a kid and I found out she's been stripping at one of the clubs on Miracle Mile. A really hot babe came out and started her dance right when you called, and the guys in the joint went crazy."

"A hot babe? How many scabs and sores did she have on her body?" The only women who stripped on Miracle Mile were the ones who couldn't work anymore for the higher-class joints in other areas of town.

"I didn't look that closely, but I did recognize the stripper as one of the girls I worked with about five years ago. Goes to show you how well the system works, huh?"

"Yeah. Hey listen, do you have the name of that man who said he'd been molested while he was in foster care?"

"Yeah, it's in my car. Hang on."

I doodled on my notepad while I waited for her to get the number. I looked back at the apartment complex, and it dawned on me that Eric had said Mrs. Richey and Mr. Scone were the ones who'd told him Shelley had been in the apartment. How had they contacted him? Or did he contact them?

Roxie came back on the line as I slipped out of the car to talk to Scone again. "Okay, the guy I talked to was Randall Bollinger. His friend is Chad Caldwell." She gave me a phone number just as I walked up to Scone's door.

Scone saw me coming, shoved out of his chair and charged the front door like a bull elephant.

I switched the phone to my left hand and rested my forearm on my Glock. "Hang on, Roxie."

"What the fuck are you doin' back here? You fuckin' cops! You goddamn fuckin' cops!" He stepped out of the door, both fists clenched at his side, his boobs wobbling with pent up tension.

"Whoa, there Mr. Scone! Take it easy! I just had one more question."

"Fuck you!"

"Yeah, I got that. Listen, Detective Langstrom said you told him—"

"Fuck him!"

"Yeah...um, you told him Shelley was staying here, right?"

He moved toward me and I took another step back and moved my hand to the grip of my gun. He surprised the hell out me when he put his head back and howled like a coyote at the top of his lungs.

One of his neighbors yelled out his window, "Shut up, Asshole!"

I heard Roxie's far away voice on my cell phone. "Alex, are you okay?"

I held up my finger to the maniac howling in front of me. "Just... um just a second Mr.—" His name escaped me for a second so I put the phone to my ear and said quickly, "Hold on, Roxie, okay?" She'd worked in the system long enough to realize I needed her on the line in case anything happened, and I trusted her to be patient.

The howling stopped abruptly. Unfortunately, I was just stupid enough to ask one more time. "You told him Shelley was staying here, right?"

The howling started again, and the neighbor yelled out the window. "What the fuck, lady! Leave the asshole alone or he'll howl for the next two hours!"

I nodded and slowly backed away. "Okay, okay, I'm goin'." I pulled out one of my business cards, knelt down and set it on the ground. "If you think of anything—"

He pounced on the card and stuffed it in his mouth, chewing viciously.

I continued to back up. "Or not." There wasn't much point hanging around, so I backed the rest of the way out of the complex and into the parking lot. I put the phone back to my ear as I approached my car. "So, Roxie."

The line was quiet a second. "So, Alex."

"How 'bout them Dodgers?"

"You scared the crap out of me, Wolfe. Don't do that!"

"Wolfe? Since when did I become Wolfe?"

"Since I'm gonna have to change my underwear! Shit!" The way she chuckled at the other end of the line made me grin.

"Hey, thanks for the names. Can I have the phone numbers again? I didn't get a chance to write them down. I'm gonna see if I can't locate Mr. Caldwell to find out if he'll talk to me."

"I only have Bollinger's number on the business card he gave me." She gave me the number. "Don't forget, I was really only grasping at straws. When Randy mentioned the guy, I got the feeling he was hinting at something, and I just thought it was weird that he mentioned it right after we'd talked about Shelley's case. There's no basis in fact, Alex. I was hypothesizing, that's all."

I pulled out into traffic, thinking I should call Ruthanne to see what time she planned to come over that evening. Roxie said something I didn't quite catch, and I turned my attention back to her. "Sorry Roxie, my mind wandered a second. What'd you say?"

"I said, your department filed aggravated assault charges against Shelley this morning. I was at the hearing. Your Detective Langstrom is really painting a picture of a seriously mentally ill child who's a danger to herself and society. Unfortunately, the records from previous foster placements add to his argument. She's never been an easy kid to handle."

I thought about the mischievous look Shelley had given me as she stood holding the collars of those two huge dogs. She wasn't crazy; she was a miniature Gia, surviving some appalling life circumstances in the only way she knew how. "I don't think you 'handle' a kid like her. Anyway, would you let me know when things happen with her case? I'm a little worried about it, but I'm not really sure why."

"You and me both. Yeah, I'll call you if anything comes up. Take care, Alex."

I pushed auto dial for Ruthanne while I merged into traffic on Interstate 10. After a few miles, I passed a highway patrol officer who had a semi-truck pulled over. When I glanced in my rear view mirror, I saw the truck driver yelling something at the officer. On a whim, I pulled off at the next exit and circled back around to see what was going on. Ruthanne answered her phone, and I told her I'd call her right back. I disconnected and threw my phone onto the seat beside me as I pulled up behind the patrol car.

I heard the two men arguing up near the front of the rig, so I walked around and stepped up next to the officer. The trucker continued his harangue on the injustice of being stopped for nothing more than going five miles over the speed limit and having a hick highway patrol officer pull him over because he had nothing better to do.

The officer turned to me and immediately noticed my badge. "Would you mind waiting with him while I look around the rig? He has some wires hanging in back and I need to see what else is wrong with his set up."

The driver put his hand on his hips, leaning toward the officer as he sputtered his objections. "You don't have shit! I keep this rig in perfect condition, and you're costing me money holding me here, you little—"

I stepped between him and the departing officer; keeping my left side toward him with my hands resting on my belt buckle, ready to react if necessary. "Look, you'll probably get out of here a whole lot quicker if you just keep your mouth shut. He's just doing his job."

The man turned a full circle, throwing his arms in the air before turning again and heading for the wall that bordered the freeway. He squatted down and leaned against the wall and I followed him over to make a stab at polite conversation in an effort to calm him down. "Where you from?"

He picked up some stones, shooting them like marbles at some trash along the highway. "Originally? From Pennsylvania. Now I live in northern California." He followed the patrolman with a suspicious eye, then glanced back at me, waiting to see what other inane question I'd come up with.

I shrugged. "My Dad's from Pennsylvania. A place called Beaver."

He nodded. "Outside of Pittsburg. I've been there. I'm from Roxbury, a little bump in the road in southern P.A. What's that fuckin' cop doin' now?" He stood up and started over to his truck. I walked along beside him.

The cop slid under the back of the rig, pulling on various objects hidden from my sight. It was obvious he suspected the guy of something more than loose wiring, and I wanted to distract the driver long enough for the cop to finish his inspection in peace. "You still have family back there?"

The driver knelt down to watch the patrolman poke around under the trailer. "My granddad."

The patrolman pulled himself out from under the trailer, dusted himself off and pointed to the wall. "Would you mind waiting over there, Sir?" Another highway patrol car pulled up. I could hear a K9 barking in the back, and I glanced at the semi driver, who'd suddenly gone from pissed off to pale in a matter of seconds. Another car pulled up behind the K9 vehicle, and Eric Langstrom stepped out.

He walked up, holding his hand out to me in greeting. "Alex, I thought that was you. I was going the other way and I saw you standing here. Thought I'd stop by to say hello. I've been meaning to have a chat with you anyway."

I took his hand. "Hey, Eric. You guys have been busy lately. Hold on a second." I directed the semi driver to the wall and waited until he squatted down again.

Eric followed us over. "What are you doin' on a highway patrol stop, anyway?"

I shrugged. "I don't know. Ever since Ed got shot, I like to make sure they're okay until their back-up arrives." Ed Tuckerman, a Highway Patrol officer just months away from retirement, had been shot and killed a few months earlier while making a solo traffic stop along Interstate Ten.

He smiled at me. "Yeah, you seem to get involved in all kinds of things that you're not officially assigned to."

He reached up and pushed some wisps of hair across the top of his balding head. A light breeze caught them and pushed them out of place again. I'd always liked Eric. He had a ready smile that belied the dogged professionalism he applied to every aspect of his job. He'd risen through the detective ranks quicker than most, mostly because he chose to follow the rules instead of skirting around them. I wondered whether I should maybe try that sometime. His 6'2" frame supported a muscular physique that he kept in shape by working out four days a week in the department gym. That was something else I thought I should maybe try.

He pushed the hair over again, then stuffed his hands in his pockets. "I hear you're interested in the Shelley Greer case."

My radar went on full alert. "Where'd you hear that?"

"Nate said Kate chewed you out for looking for Shelley down in the Vistas when you were supposed to be on medical leave. What's up with that?"

I wasn't ready to give him any information I'd collected on Shelley, so I gave him an explanation that was just a little ways down on my absolute truth meter. "Yeah, it pissed me off that the brat would actually take a pot shot at you up on Valencia, and I started thinking, if I wanted to hide from the cops, where would I go?" I shrugged innocently. "The Vistas popped into my head, so I thought I'd go look for her there. Found her too, but she set two dogs on me and got away."

"Why didn't you call for back-up? We probably could have caught her right then and there and saved ourselves a lot of time and expense." He sounded like he wanted to cross-examine me, which didn't sit very well.

The semi-driver watched the K9 as it circled around the front of the truck, first sniffing around the tires before standing on its hind legs to smell around the engine compartment. The officers must have had some type of probable cause that I didn't know about, because they opened the passenger door so the handler could lift the dog up onto the seat. The driver rested his chin on his fist while he watched the search.

I turned back to Eric. "Well, I know I should have called for back-up, but I wasn't supposed to be there, ya know? I've been trying to stay out of trouble lately, and I didn't want Kate to know I'd gone down there looking for the kid when I wasn't supposed to be working."

The K9 hoped down out of the cab to continue its search toward the rear of the truck. About midway back, the shepherd put its head down and under the trailer. He scratched tentatively at one spot, then moved down a few feet before frantically trying to roll upside down to scratch the underbelly of the trailer.

When the driver stood up from his squatting position, I pointed to the ground. "Sit."

He sighed as he lowered himself back down. "I'm screwed, huh?"

I didn't answer because he really was screwed. The K9 had just alerted to some type of drug hidden underneath the belly of the trailer.

The highway patrol officer walked over and held out his hand to me. "Thanks for standing by for me. I think we can take it from here."

"No problem." I took him aside to let him know what the driver had said. He assured me he'd include it in his report. After Eric and I had shaken his hand, we walked back to my car to continue our conversation.

Eric pushed the flyaway hairs back across his head. "I wish you'd have called, Alex. That kid really is a danger to society. I think she killed Norm Kindler in cold blood, and I intend to prove it. From everything I can gather, he was a good man who was loved by a lot of kids who needed a safe place to stay."

I thought this seemed like a good time to get some of my earlier questions answered, but I wanted to ease into the subject instead of appearing too interested. "How are the boys? They must be, what— nine, ten years old now? They still playing ball?" Eric proudly coached his twin sons' baseball team. He'd been a star second baseman in college and had played in the minor leagues until a torn rotator cuff in his shoulder had ended his career. Now his boys were following in their father's footsteps and Eric couldn't have been more pleased.

"They're ten. One plays left field. You should see the arm on that kid. The other followed his old man and plays second base. He's quick. Nothing gets by him. I think they both have a great chance to play college ball, maybe even go on to the pros. You never know."

"Ten huh? Man, one year younger than Shelley Greer. It's amazing how some kids turn out great, while others get all psychotic and kill people." I knew Shelley wasn't psychotic, but I wanted to keep Eric talking. I knew if I started defending her, he'd get suspicious and clam up.

"I thank God neither of my boys is like her. I'm a very lucky man when it comes to my family."

"Yeah. I wonder how she got from Valencia down to the Vistas. How'd you know she was in that apartment complex anyway?"

"I have a confidential informant," He shrugged, embarrassed that he'd used the full term when I knew perfectly well what a C.I. was. "Sorry... I had a C.I. call me. I'd put out word I was looking for her and she called and said she'd seen a young girl at that apartment complex. When I went down there, I talked to two of the 'residents'—more like mental patients if you ask me—and they said they thought she was in that empty apartment."

"How do you think she got from the detention center down to Valencia? And where did she get the gun? You think someone's helping her?"

He leaned against the hood of my car, crossing his arms as he stared at the cars rushing past us on I-10. "I don't know. She disappeared from her last foster home for a year. She was only nine at that point. Someone had to be helping her then. My guess is she hooked back up with whoever that was. I wish I knew."

"What kind of gun did she have?"

"A little .22 semi-auto. She took it with her. You're lucky she didn't shoot at you down in the Vistas."

I made a mental note to go back and look in the doghouse Shelley had originally run from when Megan and I first came across her. If she didn't have the gun when Gabe grabbed her, she had to have left it somewhere. "So she shot at you, then went out the back window?"

He smiled sheepishly. "Yeah, my officer safety sucked because I was just thinking she was this little eleven-year-old girl. I walked in, and she pointed the gun at me and fired. It surprised me so much I turned and ran for cover outside at the same time I pulled my Glock. By the time I got back-up units there and we'd cleared the apartment, she was gone."

I grinned at him. "Thank God she's a lousy shot, huh?" I remembered I'd been curious about how she could have escaped from the detention center in the first place. "Hey, what's up with that deputy she got away from? He need to go on a diet, or what?"

"Yeah. He and I went through the academy together. He was overweight when we first started, but he slimmed down by the time we graduated. I guess his wife's a fantastic cook and he can't resist her lasagna." He smiled before becoming serious again. "It wasn't all his fault though. Judge Masters is the presiding judge over Juvy right now, and he always insists the kids be unhandcuffed when they come into his court. The handcuffs came off and she took off running." He held up his hands. "The rest is history."

My cell phone rang and I reached into my car to retrieve it from the passenger seat where I'd thrown it after I'd hung up with Ruthanne. I looked at the caller I.D. and saw she was calling me back. I flipped open the phone. "Hi."

"Hi yourself. You forget you were gonna call me back?"

"No, I stopped to back-up a DPS officer. Then Eric stopped to talk and I just haven't had time to call."

"Well, I'm sitting on your front porch stoop watching your neighbor peep out the window at me. He's pretty strange... gives me the willies."

"He's harmless. He's definitely more scared of you than you are of him. You see a cup under the window that looks like I don't pick up my trash?"

"Yeah."

"Dig in the dirt right under the cup and you'll find a spare key. Just make sure you wipe it off before you jam it in the door or I'll have to get a new lock again."

The line was quiet a minute before she said, "Got it. How long before you get here?"

"About fifteen minutes, depending on traffic. We're pretty much done gabbing anyway. I'll see you when I get there."

Eric had wandered back to the truck and stood talking to the K9 officer. I yelled over to him. "Hey, Eric, I gotta run. Good luck on finding that kid." *Not.* He waved back at me as I climbed into my car and eased my way back into traffic to start for home.

CHAPTER 12

I pulled up to my house and was surprised to see Casey's car parked alongside Ruthanne's. When I opened the front door, Tessa, and the as-yet-unnamed two-pound terror came tumbling out the door, bouncing in absolute ecstasy because I'd decided to grace them with my presence.

Dogs are great that way. I'd sent them away for an extended period of time after Gumby danced on my face, and I was still the most wonderful, important person in their lives. I knelt down to hug Tessa, who licked every exposed patch of skin on my face and body. "Hi girl. You missed me, huh?"

The little guy jumped straight up and down, trying his hardest to get noticed even though he stood no higher than the top of my ankle. I caught him at the top of his leap and pulled him into my chest. "Hi there! Yes, I see you, Mighty Mite. I see you."

Casey called out from somewhere inside the house. "I thought I'd better bring 'em back to you or I'd end up keeping them. Come on in and make yourself at home." She chuckled. "We have."

I walked in and saw Casey and her new roommate, Terri, sitting together on my couch with Ruthanne lounging on the floor in front of it. She was holding a bowl of Chinese take-out while she shoveled noodles into her mouth with a pair of wooden chopsticks. Two empty bowls sat on the floor next to her, and Casey went into the kitchen to bring out a clean bowl for me. "Here, we already stuffed ourselves, but we left plenty for you. I think Ruthanne thought there were gonna be ten people here judging by the amount of Chinese she brought."

Terri reached down to pick up the two bowls at her feet. I accepted the clean bowl from Casey and filled it with noodles, chicken teriyaki and a liberal sprinkling of soy sauce.

"Terri, I haven't seen you in ages. You still working in Team Two?" Our police department divides the city up into six teams. Team Two encompasses the Northwest part of town.

Terri set the dirty bowls on the coffee table to make room for me on the floor next to Ruthanne. She nodded. "Yup. I want to stay right where I am until they scrape my old decaying body out of my patrol car."

I studied the pieces of chicken in my bowl. "Now that's a lovely thought just before I eat. Thanks."

Casey stepped over me and flounced back into the cushions on the sofa. "Kate said you saw Hondo and Mona together at Carne Loco. What's up with that?"

"Megan and I had lunch there today. The waiter said Mona is there a lot, either with Hondo or Kenny. He said he hasn't seen Kenny in a couple of weeks though. He also said Mona seems to be romantically involved with both men." I looked over at Ruthanne, who'd just slurped up a two foot-long noodle. The noodle swung up and hit her on the cheek, depositing a streak of soy sauce before disappearing into her mouth. I reached over with a napkin and wiped it off.

She raised her eyebrows, pulling them tightly together, giving her a devilish expression that always meant her mind had turned—or returned, in her case—to sex. "I'd much rather you'd use your tongue."

I swiveled around to see what reaction that would get from Terri and Casey. Terri's eyebrows shot up into her hairline but Casey just laughed. "You'd better watch out, Ruthanne. Alex told me Kate has a better sex life than she does, so she just might take you up on your offer one of these days."

Terri and Ruthanne chorused in unison, "Kate?"

I shifted back around and said with a nonchalant air that I knew would catch their attention, "I'll have you know I almost had an orgasm this afternoon, and if Kate hadn't butted in, I probably would have gotten some."

The room became silent, the only sound coming from my chopsticks clicking against the side of my bowl as I pinched a piece of chicken and brought it to my mouth.

Ruthanne put her hand on my sticks and pushed them away from my face. "Kate, as in Sgt. Brannigan, kept you from having an orgasm?"

"Yup."

"I don't believe you."

Casey shook her head. "Me neither."

Terri had to add her two cents. "No way. You're lying through your teeth."

"I'll bet each of you fifty bucks. You lose, you each pay me fifty bucks. I lose, I'll pay each of you fifty bucks."

Everyone exchanged glances with everyone else, the bet silently tossed from person to person like a hot potato. Finally, each woman nodded at the other, and Ruthanne spoke for all three of them. "Okay, but you have to prove it. You have to call Kate and get her to admit she kept you from having an orgasm this afternoon."

"Deal." I put my bowl on the coffee table, pushed up onto my knees and solemnly shook hands with each woman. The battery on my cell phone had almost died, so I went into my bedroom, brought out my charger and plugged it in. I hit the speaker button, then the number for Kate's auto-dial for her cell phone.

"Sgt. Brannigan."

"Kate, its Alex."

"What do you need, Alex? I'm a little busy."

"I need you to help me win a bet. Did you or did you not stop me from having an orgasm this afternoon?" The silence on the line stretched out. I checked to make sure we were still connected, and when I saw I still had service, I said expectantly, "Kate? You there?"

"Alex." Her tone left absolutely no doubt that she was not a happy camper.

Casey reached up and pushed her fingers into her eyes while

Ruthanne pinched her nose to keep from making any noise. Terri unconsciously slid down in the couch so that her head almost rested on the seat cushions and her knees bumped up against the coffee table.

I answered politely, "Yes Ma'am?"

"I'm in the middle of a Senior Staff meeting with the Chief, the legal advisor, and all of the assistant Chiefs. I'm briefing them on the kidnapping case we're working. Do you have some new information I need to give them, or can I call you back?" *And ream your ass* was left unsaid.

I grinned, thinking of Kate trying to sound politically correct on her end of the line while she wanted to get her hands around my skinny little throat. "Just say yes or no, Boss. I'll split my winnings with you."

She didn't say anything for a second and Ruthanne crossed her fingers, hoping Kate wouldn't respond. The silence stretched out into the room before Kate finally asked, "How much?"

Casey and Terri both gasped as I quickly answered. "One hundred and fifty dollars split right down the middle. Seventy five for me, seventy five for you."

"Ninety for me, sixty for you. Yes, I did." The line went dead right after she gave her answer.

I raised my fist in the air, jumped to my feet and did a little Irish jig in the middle of my living room. My feet tapped a happy staccato as I chanted, "*Oh* yeah! *Oh* yeah! Who's the woman? *Oh* yeah!" Tessa and the puppy bounced up and down with me while Casey reached for her wallet and pulled out two twenties and a ten.

As she handed them to me with her left hand, she solemnly stood and raised her right hand to her forehead in a formal presentation of arms. "Alex, I would have paid twice this much to hear Kate say that. I salute you." Terri and Ruthanne both came to attention and gravely saluted me as well.

Terri walked over to her purse to get her checkbook. When she returned with a check written out for fifty dollars, paid to the order of Alex Wolfe, she handed it to me and said, "And in a Senior Staff meeting no less. Alex, you are the Master of Moxie. You're my hero."

She reached up, pulled my head down to hers and kissed me on both cheeks.

I pushed her away, frantically wiping the kisses off my cheeks. "Yuck, Terri! Kiss Casey if you gotta kiss somebody... or Ruthanne."

Terri just shook her head, obviously overcome with admiration. She grabbed my face between her two hands, pulled me close and landed a wet one right smack on the center of my lips. I pushed back from her and fell into the couch, sputtering and spitting. The three of them cracked up, slapping Terri on the back and congratulating her on breaking my "lesbian cherry," as Ruthanne put it. I ran into the kitchen and ran my mouth under the water, wiping it over and over until I thought all the cooties had disappeared. I yelled back out to the living room, "That wasn't funny! I don't do women!"

Ruthanne yelled right back. "You'd do Gia in a heartbeat and you know it."

I heard Casey stage whisper. "She has a crush on Gia?"

When I stormed back into the living room, the three of them looked innocently at my dripping face. Gia's round, firm breasts came to mind and I felt my face flush while I pushed the thought all the way down to my feet and out onto the floor where it belonged. "I do not have a crush on Gia! She's my *friend*! We're *friends*!"

They all stood there trying not to laugh. Casey had her lips sucked back into her teeth, Ruthanne gritted *her* teeth so hard the muscles in her jaws danced, and Terri's chin was lowered onto her chest while she looked up at me from upraised eyes.

I ran my hands over my face and started giggling, unable to stay angry with the three people in the entire world who would understand if I did happen to have romantic feelings for Gia, which of course I didn't.

They all gave in, laughing at me while Terri led me back to the couch, pushed me down and handed me my unfinished dinner. Casey picked up my chopsticks and stuck them upright in my noodles while Ruthanne went to her fanny pack and retrieved fifty dollars to pay off her bet.

Casey sat down on the couch next to Terri and put her arm around her shoulders.

I watched them out of the corner of my eye, thinking how cool it would be if Carl were here and I could snuggle up to him the way Terri cuddled up to Casey.

Ruthanne plopped herself back down onto the floor and finished off the noodles still left in her bowl.

The little puppy jumped up into my lap, and I realized this would be a perfect time to figure out a name for him. "Hey guys, help me come up with a name for this little guy. I'm horrible at coming up with something that fits. Give me some ideas."

Casey reached over to scratch him behind his oversized ears. "We were calling him Stinker since he's always getting into trouble." She cooed to him in baby talk. "Aren't you, you little stinker?" She put her nose down to his and he took a playful nip at it.

Ruthanne put her bowl down on the ground for Tessa to lick clean. "How about Horny, since you got him 'cause Nate was trying to impress that woman?"

"Oh, I can hear me asking Newton to let Horny out while I'm at work. I don't think so."

Terri, who loved birds of all kinds and studied them as her hobby, said, "What about Jinx? That's a kind of tiny woodpecker, and the name seems to fit him. Little Jynx." The puppy chose that moment to bark, which seemed to me to say he liked the name.

"Yeah, I like it. Jynx it is then. What do you think, little Jynx?" He ignored me as he carefully stepped from my lap onto Ruthanne's head, balancing his two front feet on her hair while keeping his back feet on my knees. He leaned forward, intent on watching Tessa as she lay at Ruthanne's feet licking her bowl. His front feet slipped off her hair and he landed with his belly sprawled across her head, his front feet hanging over her forehead and his back feet scrambling for purchase on her shoulders.

She dipped her head forward and he happily tumbled into her lap. His pleased pounce startled Tessa into scrambling for cover, releasing her claim on his intended target, the now empty and totally clean bowl. When Jinx discovered that Tessa had left him absolutely nothing, not even the slightest bit of soy sauce or chicken flavoring, he put all four feet into the bottom of the bowl, took several turns around the inside and curled up for a nap.

Casey squeezed Terri's shoulders. "What do you say? We still need to get home to feed all the critters."

Terri sighed before sitting up, gathering all the empty bowls and taking them into the kitchen. "I guess... if we have to. I was about ready to go to sleep right here on the couch." She pushed through the kitchen door and I heard the water running in the sink.

I called after her. "Leave the dishes, Terri. I've got 'em."

"Just take me a second... I'm almost done anyway." When she came back to the living room, Casey held the door open for Terri to precede her and said over her shoulder, "See you tomorrow, Alex. I'll meet you for breakfast at Sleepy Time, okay?"

"Sure. I'll be there about eight thirty." When the door shut behind them, I turned to Ruthanne, who'd deliberately stayed behind. "So I know you didn't come over just to bring Chinese food and lose a bet. What's up?"

She seemed uncomfortable, walking across to my entertainment center and running a finger along the top of the console. Ruthanne had an excellent reputation on the department as being a thorough, hard-working detective. The lazier detectives begrudged her the elite assignment in homicide and often complained that she'd slept her way into the unit.

While she nurtured that reputation just to keep them guessing, I knew she'd actually earned her place by crossing her I's and dotting her T's in all her other detective assignments. I trusted her, and I knew that whatever she had on her mind was something I needed to pay attention to.

She kept her back to me, tapping her toe on the carpet behind her in a nervous rhythm. "I don't know exactly... it's about the Kindler case. Things are just... off, that's all. Did you know Eric filed aggravated assault charges against Shelley?"

"Yeah, I figured he would. She shot at him. Why do you think that's weird?"

Her toe tapping stopped. She looked at the floor, then with a big sigh put her head back to stare at the ceiling. "Alex, Eric and I have been friends for a long time. I'm worried about him. He's becoming obsessed with finding Shelley and making sure he has an airtight case against her."

She still hadn't turned to face me, so I walked over and leaned against the entertainment center next to her. "That's his job. That's your job." I reached up to put my hand on her shoulder. "Hey. I don't see what the problem is here. If she's innocent...." I thought about that a second. "Well, she's not *innocent*. We know she stabbed him, but if she did it in self defense, that'll come out in the investigation."

Ruthanne finally turned to face me, her expression closed, as she seemed to be weighing her options about something. She crossed her arms and turned her back to me again. I stayed quiet a minute, going over what she'd just said to try to understand what she wanted to tell me. So far, nothing she'd said sounded off to me. The toe tapping started again, a strange affectation I'd never seen her do before. "Alex, what if Kindler did try to rape her? Eric's not even looking into that possibility. He's absolutely convinced she stabbed him when he went in to tuck her in for the night."

I put my back to the entertainment center and leaned on one of the lower shelves. Tessa lay curled around the bowl containing little Jynx and they both slept peacefully. Sometimes, my mind works more efficiently if I just let it wander to other thoughts, keeping the main problem somewhere in the back recesses of my mind. Tessa's feet twitched as she chased some make-believe dream rabbit through fields and under trees. Ruthanne's tapping caught my eye again. "What's the matter, Ruthanne? This seems to be about more than just Eric and Shelley. Something's got you uptight. Can you tell me what it is?"

She reached up to quickly wipe a tear out of her eyes before laughing it away. "It's stupid. I was a child sex crimes investigator, for Christ's sake. Why this is hitting me now—" The sentence cut off abruptly.

I watched as she grabbed her purse and headed for the door. Normally, I'd have let her go. If people need space, I'm the last person to force myself onto my friends, but this also included Shelley and Gia, and I quickly made up my mind to try to get her to talk out whatever had so uncharacteristically upset her. The surprised look on her face when I moved in front of her to stand between her and the door made me smile.

"You're my prisoner until I know what's bothering you. We're talking about a little kid's life here, her freedom for many, many years. I need to know that everything's being done to make sure she's treated fairly, and so do you."

She growled as she threw her purse back at the couch, startling Tessa and the puppy, who raised sleepy heads, decided the world was still rotating the way it should, and lay back to enjoy their dreams once again. "Fuck!" She sat on the coffee table with her elbows on her knees, her hands clasped in front of her. "Alex, I've never, *ever* told anyone this. You've got to promise me—" She stopped mid-sentence again.

I walked over and sat down next to her. "I promise."

"I think the reason this case is bothering me so much is because Eric isn't even entertaining the question that Shelley might be telling the truth. In all my other cases when I worked child sex crimes, we listened to the kids, and we usually believed them until something proved they were lying for some reason."

There was more. I felt it just like my grandmother told me I would, so I waited to hear what it was. When she didn't continue, I said quietly, "What is it, Ruthanne?"

She shook her head and chuckled sadly. "You'd think you were a detective or something the way you hear things that go unsaid."

I waited patiently.

When she spoke again, her words barely rose above a whisper. "When I was nine, my father raped me. I told my mother, my teacher, and the cop at school, and no one believed me. Since he got away with it, he continued to rape me for the next three years." Bitterness crept into her voice and sparks flew from her eyes as she turned her head toward me. "It wasn't abuse or molestation. It was rape, every time, and I wish I'd had the guts to do to him what Shelley did to Kindler." She wiped away some tears that had escaped down her cheek. "I believe her, Alex, and it's so frustrating that I'm the only one who does and no one's listening to me. Eric even asked Jon to take me off the case."

Jon supervised the homicide detail. I wondered whether he'd done as Eric requested.

"Did he?"

"No, but he took me into his office and told me I needed to be a team player, as though believing Shelley's side of things suddenly makes me the bad guy. They all want her locked up forever because she had the nerve to shoot at Eric." She lowered her head onto her hands. "I don't know... fuck, maybe I *shouldn't* be on this case because of what my asshole father did."

I put my hand on her back. "Actually, I think you're the exact person for this case, and don't you dare let Shelley down by backing out. I believe her too, and I'm gonna help you prove to everybody exactly what happened, okay?"

She sat so quietly that I wasn't sure what to do. In the ten years I'd known her, she had never, ever, been a quiet person. As usual, I stupidly said the first thing that came into my mind. "I'm amazed you like sex as much as you do after what your dad did to you."

She lifted her head. "First of all, don't call him my dad. Dads throw the softball around with you, they don't rape you. And second, rape and sex have absolutely nothing in common with each other. One's about control and the other's about fun." Relief washed over me when her devilish grin returned. "And I do have fun." Her mood improved immensely when we moved on to her favorite subject. "So, my dear, I am making it my personal mission to get you laid. I assume you want a man?"

"I can find someone on my own, thanks. I don't need any help."

"Nine months a virgin and you don't need help? Shit, Alex, I'm close to havin' you committed. Nine months?" She grabbed her purse again. "You gotta be kidding me! I never go nine *days*, let alone nine *months*. I'll find you somebody." She opened the door and looked back at me over her shoulder. "And when I do, I'll make sure everybody knows about it. A woman's got her reputation to look after, you know."

"Don't you—" The door shut in my face as I muttered, "dare."

CHAPTER 13

The next morning I met Casey for breakfast at our usual café. I'd never seen the place so packed. Every table had at least three kids shoveling food into their faces, talking with their mouths full and waving their forks around like they had an American flag in their hand on the Fourth of July. Casey had somehow commandeered a table and I made my way over to it, dodging a new waiter who was carrying a water pitcher in one hand and a coffee pot in the other.

He executed a perfect pirouette around me, obviously having years of experience in keeping the water from sloshing all over customers who were clumsy enough to get in his way. He kept up a constant monologue on his way around me. "Excuse me, excuse me, sorry, excuse me."

Apparently a regional soccer tournament had come to town. All the kids in the restaurant were wearing green and black uniforms with *Warriors* stenciled across their backs. As I walked past one table, a particularly strange looking boy with oversized front teeth held the handle of his fork in one fist and carefully pulled back the tines with his other hand, creating a wicked catapult. He fired a syrup-loaded piece of waffle that hit me square in the chest. As I stopped and stared down at the gooey projectile sticking to my right breast, I heard Casey say quietly, "Uh oh."

The kid's mother whined, "Jeremy, that wasn't polite. Say you're sorry to the nice police lady."

The nice police lady trembled with the effort it took to keep from throttling the little brat. I'd just opened my mouth to chew the kid's ass when I felt Casey's hand on my arm. "I've got your iced tea all ready, Alex. Here." She picked a napkin up off the kid's table, scraped the waffle off my shirt and deposited the whole mess onto the kid's plate, accompanying her actions with an angry rebuke. "I think this is yours, and it had better not leave your plate again except to go in your mouth."

Another boy at the table high fived the first, and Casey quickly steered me by my elbow to our table, where she deposited me before returning to the offending kid's mother to speak quietly in her ear. I couldn't hear what she said, but the woman turned beet red, gathered up her four charges, paid her bill and left the restaurant.

Casey came back to our table and we watched them until they were across the parking lot piling into their mini-van. I dipped a napkin in my water, wondering why these kinds of things always happened to me instead of her. I spoke without taking my eyes off the widening stain on my shirt. "What'd you say to her?"

"I mentioned you were suffering from post traumatic stress disorder and any type of assault might trigger an episode and she should probably get her son out of here before you came unglued."

I stopped in mid-rub and raised my eyes to meet hers. My temper still hadn't subsided, so I chose to keep my mouth shut and go back to rubbing.

She loaded her coffee with the customary four packets of sugar and six tubs of creamer, then sat back and waited for me to calm down. We'd worked with each other long enough to know when to shut up, and I guess she figured this was one of those times.

The trembling gradually subsided, taking with it my ill humor. I took a deep breath, relaxed my shoulders, and set the wet napkin on the bench beside me. "Why don't people cull their young like the animals do? If she had asked, I would have gladly done it for her."

Casey's naturally even temper always seemed to bring me to some sort of equilibrium, and the twinkle I saw in her eyes as she looked at me over her coffee cup put to rest any vestige of anger I might have secretly harbored toward the little heathen. She sipped her coffee as she surveyed the other twenty or so soccer players finishing their morning meals. "I honestly thought you were gonna cull him when I saw the slow burn building in your eyes. I hear there are several hundred players in town from all around the country. This team's from Alabama, the twelve and under division."

"Why doesn't stuff like that ever happen to you? Why is it always me they pick on?"

"Oh you poor baby, getting picked on by a twelve year old kid." She grinned. "They don't pick on me because I look like a mean S.O.B. who's gonna eat them for lunch."

"You do not."

"Oh yes I do. You're just used to this crabby lookin' face, that's all."

"You don't have a crabby lookin' face. You're always puttin' yourself down. Build yourself up, why don't you?" We'd been through this argument countless times and I decided to change the subject. "What are we gonna do about the two girls and Kenny Finch? My caseload's backing up and they're still missing."

"Your caseload's backing up because you're spending all your time duplicating Eric's work on Shelley's case. You need to just trust that he knows what he's doing."

There were too many unanswered questions about Shelley's case. I wanted to let the fragmented pieces of data floating around in my mind digest in the hope that I could begin to sort out exactly what I needed to do to help Shelley get a fair shake. I held no illusions that the criminal justice system provided equal justice in any way, shape or form, and I often found myself championing people I thought might get screwed if the system was left to its own devices. Since I'd decided to let the brain juices stew for a while on Shelley's case, I steered the conversation back to our kidnapping case. "Do you think Kenny's dead?"

Her left eyebrow rose a fraction of an inch. She contemplated the swirls forming in her coffee as she gently rotated her spoon first in a clockwise direction, then counterclockwise, creating a temporary pocket of turbulence. "It's possible. We haven't come across any evidence to suggest otherwise, and the piled-up newspapers and mail and the abandoned apartment indicate he intended to return on the day he went missing."

"All right, so let's go over what we have. As far as we know, the gardener at his apartment complex was the last person to see him alive as he left in his blue Nissan. But he wasn't going to work because he didn't have a job. So where did he get money for his apartment and gas for his car?"

"While the rodeo's in town, he does odd jobs... you know, sweeping, shoveling manure, whatever they needed done."

That made sense since we knew he hung around the cowboy scene. "Kate found out he sometimes followed the rodeo around the country, right? Have we heard anything from the Reno police?"

She shook her head and sipped her coffee. "No. I talked to them yesterday afternoon. They haven't heard anything."

I continued with the recap. "He and Mona are in some type of relationship, but she's also seeing some guy named Smitty Cogburn, and apparently she and Hondo have something going too."

The volume in the restaurant increased by several decibels as several of the kids began leaving. A soccer ball came flying through the air, missing my head by inches. I caught it and set it on the bench between the wall and me while I continued talking. "We know Hondo lied to us at least once because he told us he didn't know Mona very well."

A blonde tomboy walked up to the table and interrupted me. "That's my ball."

I didn't even look at her. "Not anymore."

"Give it to me." She crossed her arms, standing with her legs slightly apart, challenging me.

Her rudeness set me back. When I slid out of the bench and stood in front of her, she noticed my badge. Her arms fell to her sides as a slight pink color rose in her cheeks. She'd been staring me straight in the eyes while I was seated, but now her eyes rested somewhere around my chin. "Sorry... I didn't know you were a cop."

"It doesn't matter if I'm a cop. Where do you get off talking to anyone like that, let alone a woman you don't even know?" I rested my hands on my hips; staring down at her while I wondered what type of manners they taught kids in Alabama. She wore her hair cropped short above the ears, and when she looked around to see where her friends were, I noticed a large bruise on her neck. "Where'd you get the bruise?"

She grinned as she brought her eyes up to meet mine. "I'm the goalie. I stopped the tying goal with that one." She pointed to the bruise on her neck. "Then I stopped the winning goal with this one." She pulled up the cuff on her shorts and showed me a second bruise on her thigh.

Other than the initial rudeness, she reminded me a lot of myself at her age. "Did you win?"

Her chin pointed in the direction of the ball on my seat. "They gave me the game ball and voted me player of the game." She reached up and rubbed her forehead with her fingers. "I really am sorry I talked to you like that. I was just being tough 'cause all the other kids were around. Can I please have my ball back?"

I picked up the ball, rolled it up onto the back of my hand, down my arm, behind my neck and across into my other hand. It rested on my fingertips, and I pulled it away as she reached for it. "You gotta promise me somethin' first."

"What?"

"Doin' things you know are wrong just because your friends are around—"

"Is stupid, I know." She looked back at the door where her teammates were waiting for her. "But you try being the only girl on a team with a bunch of boys. You gotta be tougher than they are or they sh—" She quickly caught herself. "They spit on ya."

I lowered my chin and held her gaze. "Tough isn't rude, and it isn't mean. Tough is the ability to stand up for yourself, to be who you are. Don't let them dictate who you become, okay?" I handed her the ball and watched as she bounced it on the floor and dribbled it out the door with her feet.

As the door swung shut behind her, she turned quickly, pulled the door open again and stuck her head back in. "Hey, our game's at Rodeo Park at two o'clock!" A huge grin spread across her face as she let the door swing closed.

I sat back down, ready to continue with our discussion of the two kidnapping cases. A woman at the next table leaned over and waved her napkin to get my attention. I saw the fluttering out of the corner of my eye and looked at Casey, trying to pretend I hadn't noticed the white flag.

"Woo hooo!"

I've always found it hard to ignore owl sounds in the middle of a restaurant. Casey raised her eyebrows, waiting for me to acknowledge the woman.

An involuntary sigh escaped my lips as I turned to the woman and smiled. She sat up straighter, inordinately pleased at my attention. "That was so nice of you. She really is a wonderful little girl. She's the best twelve and under goalie in Alabama, you know."

I'd learned very early in my career not to encourage inane conversation with strangers. I nodded and then picked up my tea, hoping she'd get the hint that I had other things to attend to. Apparently, she took that as an invitation to gather up her purse and coffee, bring them to our table and slide in next to me.

I moved as far away from her as I could and tilted my head sideways, glaring at her while she blissfully carried on about their team's goalie. "She's played with these boys for four years now. Her parents couldn't make the trip, so I'm keeping an eye on her. My son plays defense, and I'm always telling him it's his job to protect her." She giggled at her little joke while Casey and I remained mute, wondering how we were going to get this woman away from our table without garnering a rudeness complaint from IAD.

"She sleeps in our hotel room with us." She lowered her voice in a confidential tone. "Most people wonder about having a boy and girl sleeping in the same hotel room together, but I think she'll go the other way, if you know what I mean."

That got me going. "Why? Because she likes sports? Why do people always assume that any girl who likes sports or any woman who wants to be a cop or a fireman is a lesbian? Do I look like a lesbian to you?"

Casey swiveled her head from the lady to me and back to the lady again, suddenly enjoying the turn of the conversation.

The woman backtracked. "Oh no! Of course not! Heavens no! That's not what I meant at all! Heaven forbid! Oh my goodness!" She slapped me on the shoulder with the back of her hand, a gesture of familiarity that almost sent me into orbit.

Casey sat back, grinning as she rested her arm on the back of her bench, bringing her coffee cup to her lips and watching to see what my reaction would be.

I turned to face the woman full on. "Heaven forbid? What's *that* supposed to mean? How do you know God's not a lesbian?"

The coffee apparently went down Casey's windpipe instead of her throat because she spluttered it back into her cup and began coughing uncontrollably. The woman's horrified expression brought me back to my IAD senses and I forced out a laugh. "I'm just kidding. God's not a lesbian." I shook my head and muttered, "I don't know where the hell that came from." Casey really must have swallowed wrong, because her coughing began to sound very much like an enraged goose, and the woman and I watched with worried expressions as she struggled to clear her airway.

Maureen brought a fresh glass of water to the table and set it down in front of Casey. "Here, drink something; that always helps me."

The coughing gradually subsided and her breathing returned to normal. She picked up a napkin and wiped her eyes, then chuckled quietly. "Don't do that right when I take a drink, Alex. You're gonna kill me one of these days."

Maureen put her hands on her hips. "What'd she do this time? She never comes in here without causin' some kinda' trouble."

"I do not!"

Maureen began ticking off incidents on her fingers. "A lady attacked you; you and your friend attacked another lady; you wrestled with George...."

I held up my hand. "Okay, *occasionally* things happen when I'm around, but—"

The woman piped in. "She said God is a lesbian."

Maureen's expression didn't change.

"I did not! I said *what if* she was a lesbian!"

"God is not a she."

"How do you know?" How do I get into these inane arguments? Even *I* don't believe God is a she. What do I care what other people think? "Look, never mind." I turned to the woman. "Thank you for telling us about your goalie and good luck at the game this afternoon." I thought no one had ever given a more polite or succinct dismissal in the history of interrupted law enforcement lunches.

She apparently didn't agree. "I'd like to talk to your superior officer."

I sat back in my seat, rubbing my temples, and wondering why my head had suddenly started hurting. I couldn't help sighing, "No you wouldn't."

"Yes, I would."

I slowly reached into my pocket, pulled out one of my business cards, scratched off my number and wrote Kate's name and office number at the bottom. "Fine. Here." I shoved the card at her.

She grasped it delicately between her thumb and forefinger, placed her reading glasses on the end of her nose, and read the card carefully. When she'd finished, she glanced over her glasses at me. "You're a fine one to be correcting a little girl about manners, Detective. Your sergeant will be hearing from me immediately."

An angry retort died in my throat when I felt the familiar pressure of Casey's heel digging into my toes. Sometimes I just wished I lived on a deserted island, by myself, with absolutely no trace of humanity anywhere around. The muscles in my jaw tensed as I bit back my words and sat silently waiting for the woman to leave. When she realized I had nothing else to say, she gathered her purse, paid her bill and walked angrily from the restaurant.

Maureen returned to the table after taking the woman's money at the cash register. She picked up the woman's coffee cup and glanced my way. "God ain't a lesbian."

I rested my head against the back of the booth and said tiredly, "How do you know?"

She cackled, "'Cause George told me God was a dill pickle and we shouldn't eat 'em anymore!" Her laughter rang throughout the restaurant and I couldn't help but grin. How the hell do I get myself into these things?

Casey laughed with Maureen, and I eventually joined in. I picked up our bill and took out my money. "I can hardly wait to hear what Kate has to say about this one."

CHAPTER 14

W e headed into the office to get our marching orders for the day. Kate sat with her elbows on the desk and the phone up to her ear with her cheek resting on her fist. She took one look at me and silently banged her head with the receiver several times.

I shrugged as I walked past, then pointed to my chest and raised my eyebrows in a question mark.

Casey put her arm around my shoulders and guided me back to our desks. "Don't push it, you knucklehead. Hopefully she's talking to her stock broker instead of the soccer mom."

My e-mail had probably filled to overflowing since I hadn't checked it in over a week. With all the departmental bulletins and internal communications flowing into our accounts we could easily have three hundred unopened e-mails when we returned from a two-week vacation. I sorted them into categories, quickly deleting everything with the generic heading *All-TPD*. I figured if it was something I needed to know about, I'd hear it soon enough.

Kate walked over and pulled up a chair. Casey's chair squeaked as she rocked back, waiting to hear what Kate had to say. I glanced up from my e-mail and then returned to my deleting. Unlike Casey, I wasn't anxious to hear what she had to say. Kate addressed us in a conversational tone. "You two have been busy the last few days. So far this morning, I've had a complaint from Lt. Caruthers and from a Mrs...." She checked the piece of paper she held in her hands. "Mrs. Latkes, who just happens to be a deaconess in her church back in Alabama. She is quite certain, by the way, based on her detailed study of the scriptures, that God is *not* a lesbian."

I blushed and felt an inexplicable urge to hide my face. As I ducked my head, I braced my elbow on the arm of my chair and held my forehead in my hand.

She continued in the same conversational tone. "Now, I can check the Rules and Procedures Manual, but I'm pretty sure discussing God's apparent lesbianism with a member of the public isn't covered, so I'm going to *assume* you've never had training in that area and give you some remedial training instead of writing you up for rudeness to the public." She didn't say anything for a minute, and I peeked out to see whether she'd said her piece and left. I jumped slightly when she grabbed the back of my collar and pulled me up in my chair. She let go when my eyes met hers. "So Alex, if there's only one thing I teach you while you work for me...." She paused, thinking about what she'd just said. "And God knows there's a hell of a lot more I need to teach you than just one thing, but if there *is* only one thing, I'm going to teach you to think before you open your mouth."

I didn't like the sound of that.

"Lt. Caruthers and I have been assigned to do a Narcotics Destruction Board tomorrow, and you're going to help us."

I shot forward, ready to leap to my feet. She stopped me by stepping forward until her knees almost touched my chair. Her aggressive posture helped me hold my tongue and I glanced at Casey out of the corner of my eye. She had her hand over her eyes and was slowly shaking her head. Kate towered over me, waiting to hear what I had to say. When I remained silent, she nodded. "Very good. Lesson begun. Here's your warning. *Do not say anything* disrespectful to Lt. Caruthers tomorrow. We'll be with him from eight o'clock in the morning until three o'clock in the afternoon. Any questions?"

I looked at her belt buckle. "He's an asshole."

"Yes, he is. I asked if you have any questions. I intend to be absolutely sure you understand me."

"He always pisses me off. Why should he be able to say things about me, but I can't say things back to him?"

"Because he's a lieutenant and you're a detective. Anymore questions?"

I glared at her. "What if he's an asshole tomorrow? You expect me to just—"

"I expect you to be respectful, no matter what he does. One slip, Alex, and I guarantee you'll regret it."

Her look told me she meant it, but I didn't lower my eyes this time. Letting Caruthers get away with his bullying remarks didn't sit well with me, and I wasn't sure I could do it. I ground my teeth, angry that she'd set me up for his special brand of harassment.

She repeated herself. "Do you have any questions?"

I didn't answer and she turned to Casey. "Good. Now on to the kidnappings. Casey, you wrote in your report that one of Mona's boyfriends, Smitty Cogburn, is in town and set to compete today."

Casey nodded as her glance darted between Kate and me. She knew I was seething, and I could tell she wanted to communicate something to me. I turned my back to her and stared out the window. I knew what she was thinking: I should be thankful Kate didn't just give up on me and kick me out of her unit. After all, she'd threatened to do that before. My mind churned with angry thoughts. *I'm an adult. Why can't they just treat me like one? Kick me out if you want to! Maybe I don't belong here anyway!*

Kate continued. "I want you and Alex to go interview him. Find out if he has any ideas about where the kids might be."

If it was Casey, she'd just laugh about the God thing, but no, it's Alex, and Alex has to be taught a lesson. I tuned back in and realized neither Casey nor Kate was saying anything. I glanced over my shoulder at Kate, who looked like she was waiting for an answer from me. Casey motioned with her head for me to say something. I said to Kate, "Did you ask me something?"

Kate blew out a lungful of air and stepped up to my chair again. She bent down close. "Are you listening now?"

I nodded once, too angry to give her anymore.

"I said, if Caruthers is at the Rodeo grounds when you go interview Cogburn, stay away from him."

"He better stay away from me too, then."

Kate surprised me by the vehemence of her reaction. "God damn it, Alex! What is it with you? What don't you understand? You are walking on thin ice with just about every commander on this department! I believe in you! I think you are an excellent detective, but I can't save you from yourself! I'm trying, but I'm running out of options. If Caruthers confronts you today or tomorrow, *keep your goddamned mouth shut!*"

I pushed out of my chair, brushing her back as I stalked past. My keys lay on the edge of my desk, and I shoved her aside and grabbed them before heading out to the elevators. I aimed my key at the lock to call the elevators and just about jammed it into a hand that shoved past me and covered the keyhole. I recognized Kate's watch and flung my arm out to punch the elevator doors with the side of my fist. "I'm not a little kid, Kate! You want to write me up, then do it! You want to kick me out of your unit, then do it! But don't treat me like a ten-year-old child!"

She quietly backed me up against the wall with a finger poking into my chest as she punctuated each word. "Then... stop... acting... like one."

The elevator doors opened and two detectives started out. They must have recognized Kate's angry posture because they gingerly stepped around her and pretended they hadn't seen anything.

Kate stared at me while I stared at her shoulder.

Another detective walked up and called the elevator. He rocked back and forth on his heels, uncomfortable with the two of us standing there in some type of confrontation. The elevator doors opened and he stepped inside. I moved to do the same, but Kate stepped sideways, blocking my exit. I knew her well enough to know she was waiting for me to talk. When two more people walked up, she grabbed my arm, unlocked the temporary evidence storage room next to the elevators, and ushered me inside. When the door shut behind us, she stood in front of it with her arms crossed. "Now *talk*! I don't allow my detectives to stalk off in an angry fit when I'm in the middle of a conversation with them. We'll hammer this out and get it out in the open."

"Fine, if you want me to talk, I'll talk! Caruthers is an asshole! You're giving him seven hours to berate me and bait me and sneer at me! You're fuckin' setting me up to get fired because I can't take that shit for seven hours without kicking his fuckin' ass!"

"Yes, I am setting you up, and I plan to be there to make sure you keep your mouth shut. I want him to piss you off. If you want to survive on this department, Alex, you have to learn to play the games. This is lesson number one. And just so we're clear, I intend to *keep* setting you up until you learn to control your temper and act like an adult who works in a paramilitary organization where subordinates show respect to their superior officers and where you hold your sarcastic tongue around obnoxious civilians!"

She was right and I hated it. "Maybe I don't belong here anyway! I love being a cop. It's all I've ever wanted to do, but I'm not good at... at...." I couldn't find the right words so I paced to the wall and back to where she stood. "I'm not good at letting shitheads do stupid things and say stupid things just because they have one or two bars attached to their collars!"

She waited to see whether I had anything else to say. When I turned and leaned angrily against the wall, arms crossed and heart pounding, she nodded and stepped in front of me again. "No, you're not. But you will be by the time I'm done with you. Do you know why I even bother with you?"

I glared at her, wanting to tell her she needn't bother, but decided against it. I shook my head instead.

"This is why. You have a talent for seeing the truth in an investigation, Alex, even when it's hidden. Very few people have that ability, and very few people are willing to go to the lengths you go to in order to bring out the truth. You understand the concept of working within the gray areas, and at times you slip too far to the other side. It's my job to pull you back. I have never put this much effort into any employee before in my twenty-five year career. Do you realize that?"

I shook my head again. The muscles in my neck began to relax and I twisted my neck to help work out the kinks.

"You're unique. This might sound strange, but bear with me. Your heart is good. There is no evil in you. You're a pain in the ass, but I believe this department cannot afford to let the Caruthers and the Beulows drive people like you out. Work with me, Alex. You *do* belong here more than any of those assholes. Don't let them win."

I turned and put my back up against the wall. What she'd said made sense. There were people on the department who wanted nothing more than to get rid of me once and for all, and here I had the best sergeant on the department in my corner, pulling for me. I looked up at her and managed a weak smile. "I'm a great detective, huh?"

She smiled back. "Don't push it." We stared at each other for about half a minute. My anger and frustration levels had dropped and as I held her gaze, I realized how very important police work in general, and the Tucson Police Department in particular, were to her. She honestly believed in justice and fair play, despite the Caruthers and the Beulows and dishonest judges and uninformed juries. She'd never become jaded like so many of the other tenured officers on the department, and she believed in *me*.

She smiled again. "You ready to head to the rodeo grounds with Casey?"

"I guess going to the kids' soccer game this afternoon is out?"

She opened the door and put her hand behind my neck to usher me out into the hallway, not bothering to answer.

Casey was waiting in the corridor by the elevator. When we walked out of the evidence room, she jingled her keys at me. "You ready? I'm driving."

"No your not. It's my turn."

Kate reached into her pocket and pulled out a coin. She flipped it into the air and said, "Call it."

I said, "Heads."

She caught it, quickly glanced at it and shoved it into her pocket. "Tails, Casey drives."

"Hey! I need to see it. That's not fair. You—" The door to our offices closed on Kate's back in the middle of my sentence. I turned to Casey. "That's not fair!"

She held the elevator door opened for me and jingled her keys again. "I hear Gumby calling your name, Alex. Let's go."

CHAPTER 15

We pulled into the rodeo grounds parking lot forty minutes later. Parking spaces stood empty in the dirt lot, mute testimony to the excitement level of the day's events. Bull riding, steer wrestling and saddle bronc riding tended to draw the biggest crowds, while barrel racing and team roping, which required just as much skill and a lot more practice, were less exciting. Most of the trucks parked in the lot had stickers plastered on the rear windows and bumpers. I read them out loud as we drove past. "Don't interfere with somethin' that ain't botherin' you none." I nodded. "Well, there's some logic to that one. Hey, I like this one too: 'Sometimes you get, and sometimes you get got.'" We pulled into a space next to a red pick-up truck with oversized tires and a beautiful new paint job.

Casey pointed to the saying printed in an arc on the back window of the cab. The bold red words arched over a picture of a hapless cowboy standing in a ditch throwing a shovel full of dirt over his shoulder. "Now that, Alex, is one I'm going to have printed on a t-shirt, a bumper sticker for your car, and a poster for the wall back at the office. 'If you find yourself in a hole, the first thing to do is stop diggin'.' That's even better than 'Engage brain before engaging mouth.'" She put her foot up on the bumper of her car to brush some dirt off of the bottom of her pants. "Actually, now that I think about it, maybe I'll put one saying on the front of your shirt and one on the back since you seem to have major problems in both areas."

I playfully shoved her sideways and since she had one foot up, she just about ended up sitting in the dirt. As it was, she barely caught herself on her hands before her hind end hit the ground. Laughing, I held out my hand to her. "You look like a crab ready to run for its lunch. Here." I pulled her up and we jostled each other up to the entrance where a few stalwart protestors still remained.

Megan sat sunning in a lawn chair, chin tilted to the sky, holding a panel from a cardboard box under her chin. She had her eyes closed and I motioned for her friends to keep quiet while I picked up her water bottle and let the water slowly drip onto her hair. She reached up and swatted her head, apparently thinking a fly had buzzed her. I squeezed harder until a stream of water splattered into her hair. She bolted out of the chair and swatted me with the cardboard before I could jump out of her way. "Alex! You moron!"

I rubbed her wet head with my knuckles, messing her already messed-up red mop. "I love you, too, Gertrude."

The media apparently had more newsworthy subjects to cover since they were conspicuous by their absence.

Casey tapped my shoulder. "Here comes Caruthers."

I refused to turn around and acknowledge him as he strode across the compound apparently with some definite purpose in mind.

Megan whispered quietly, "He's such a hypocritical brownnoser."

I nodded as I heard him speaking to Casey, who'd stepped away from us to greet him. "Casey, good to see you back here. You babysitting again?" I imagined him indicating me with a lift of his chin and decided to ignore his jabs as best I could.

Casey, always respectful, answered carefully. "No sir. Alex and I are here to interview one of the cowboys about our kidnapping case. We should be out of here pretty soon."

His tone took on a quizzical quality that told me he was setting himself up for another jab. "You must have a day off tomorrow, huh?" I remembered Kate's lecture and remained silent.

Casey sighed, hating the games people like Caruthers always needed to play. "No sir. I work a regular shift tomorrow."

Caruthers appeared to think about that a little longer than necessary and I turned to see why. He looked me directly in the eyes as he thrust his make believe sword. "Oh really? Your sergeant called me a few minutes ago to say she'd assigned Detective Wolfe to help with the destruction board tomorrow. I just naturally assumed that if *she* had to baby sit her, *you* must be unavailable for the job."

I opened my mouth to respond, then thought about my conversation with Kate. Everyone watched me, waiting to see what my reaction would be. Casey stood up straighter than usual and kind of leaned back, apparently dreading what she knew she was about to hear. I heard Megan growl quietly behind me, but it was the gloating look of anticipation I saw on Lt. Caruthers' face that made me pull out my cell phone and hit autodial. I put the phone to my ear and waited until Kate picked up the phone. "Sgt. Brannigan."

"Sarge?"

"What's up, Alex?"

"Lt. Caruthers was wondering if you had to babysit me tomorrow because you were under the impression Casey wouldn't be here in the morning to cover the task."

Caruthers spoke loud enough for Kate to hear. "No, no! That's not what I meant! I was just pulling your leg, Alex. Here, let me talk to her." He held out his hand for my phone. The thought of him putting his puffy red lips anywhere near my cell phone made me queasy.

"He wants to talk to you."

"Alex, listen to me." She waited for me to say something.

"I'm listening."

I nearly jumped out of my shoes when the growling behind me exploded into a torrent of curses that would have done a sailor proud. Megan shoved me aside as she got into Caruthers' face. "Listen, Shithead! If Alex isn't gonna answer you, then *I* will, you sorry, worthless mother f...."

I had to tune her out so I could hear Kate. "Alex! Who is that?"

"It's Megan."

"Tell her to shut up!"

"Why?"

Megan continued her blistering tirade, making sure she included everything from the size of his manhood to his prowess in bed.

Kate yelled into the phone. "Alex!"

I sighed and stepped in front of Megan, who'd taken a few more steps toward a red-faced Caruthers. I had to raise my voice to be heard. "Megan! Kate says you need to shut up!"

Megan grabbed the phone from me and began lecturing Kate, telling her it was about time someone started defending me against all the pinheaded buffoons on the department. I had to swing my arm around her neck and clamp my hand over her mouth before I could yank the phone out of her hands and snap it shut. When she couldn't pull my hand off her face, her teeth found a purchase, and she bit down —hard. I jerked away and quickly stuck my injured hand under my arm to stop the pain. "You *bit* me!"

Megan yelled in my face, "*Yes*, I bit you! Maybe that'll wake you up! How can you just let that ass insult you like that without saying anything?" Her righteous indignation ignited a familiar fire in me and I spun around, intending to lay into Caruthers with both barrels. Casey saw the change, grabbed Megan and me by the back of our shirts and dragged us both into the rodeo grounds.

Caruthers yelled after us, "Do you get paid extra for babysitting two of them? You're a good cop, Casey, but that loser's going to pull you down if you don't watch out."

The snarl coming from Casey shocked me and I looked over my shoulder to see her expression harden into stone. "Case, don't—"

Just as she let go of us and swung around to snap at Caruthers, her cell phone rang. She jerked it off her belt and answered it without looking to see who was calling. "What do you want, goddamnit!"

I grabbed the phone from her. "Whoa, give that to me." I was used to Megan and me losing it, but I wasn't sure I could handle Casey going over the edge. I put the phone up to my ear at the same time I led the two of them further away from Caruthers. This was definitely a switch, me playing the mature one of the bunch. "Hello?"

Kate's voice shook with her attempt to control her anger. "Alex, I'm on my way down there. *What is going on?*"

"Well, Casey's gonna shoot Caruthers, Megan is going to—How did you put it, Megs?—cut off his balls with a dull-edged frog sticker, and I'm actually the one who's in charge right now."

The line remained silent and I checked to make sure I hadn't lost the signal. I heard Kate chuckle, and I put the phone in front of my nose so I could make sure the readout said *Kate Brannigan.* The chuckling turned to laughter, and I put the phone on speaker and grinned at the other two. Kate's uncontrolled belly laugh shocked the two of them out of their momentary insanity. Casey took a long, drawn-out breath while she pinched the bridge of her nose between her thumb and forefinger, a familiar gesture I recognized as her way of regaining her composure. Pretty soon, all three of us were giggling at Kate's reaction while Kate struggled to get herself back under control.

We heard her blow her nose before she came back on the line. I pictured her wiping her eyes, trying to clear the tears as she drove like a bat out of hell to get to us before World War III broke out. "I'm sorry, Alex, but the thought of you being the responsible one in that fiasco I just listened to made me wonder whether I'd just gone totally off the deep end. Look, are you three away from Lt. Caruthers?"

I glanced back toward the command post and saw his dark blue uniform disappearing inside the door of the R.V. "Yes."

"Then wait for me under the stands by the picnic tables. I'll be there in about five minutes."

I closed the phone and bought all three of us a soda. We sat at a picnic table as instructed and waited until Kate walked up. When she sat down, I went back to the concession stand and bought her an ice-cold lemonade, which I knew she preferred to soda. I set it on the table in front of her before taking my seat again. I was rather enjoying my unfamiliar role as the mature one in the group.

The three of us remained silent. For once, I hadn't done anything wrong, and I looked Kate in the eye with something close to camaraderie. The pleasure I took in for once being the only righteous one in the group fairly burst forth from every pore of my body. I felt as though everyone sitting with us underneath the stands could hear my triumphant thoughts. *How could these two have allowed that idiot to provoke them like that?*

Kate must have caught my subliminal message because I saw amusement in her eyes before she lowered her gaze and bit her lower lip. Casey studied the white plastic arm of her chair, worrying a small scratch in the finish with the tips of her fingers, careful not to look Kate in the eye. The way she hid her eyes behind her bangs reminded me of a puppy that had piddled in the house instead of going outside. Megan, who didn't even work for the police department, let alone for Kate, looked like a five-year-old child who knows she's about to be spanked.

Kate sat back and crossed her arms. "Casey?"

Casey still didn't meet her eyes, but she turned her head obediently in Kate's direction. Kate leaned forward and tapped her lightly on the knee. "Don't *ever* answer your department phone like that again."

Casey blushed crimson as though Kate had just given her the most horrendous reprimand possible. "Yes Ma'am."

I stared at Kate with my mouth hanging open.

Kate turned to Megan. "Megan?"

Megan brought her eyes up to meet Kate's, her eyebrows pulled up higher than I'd ever seen them before. I actually thought she might start crying.

Kate lowered her chin, but held Megan's gaze. "It's not a good idea to do battle with a TPD lieutenant. They wield more power than you realize."

Megan looked down at her shoes and nodded. "Yes Ma'am."

My chin dropped down onto my chest and I held my hands out to my sides. "That's it? That's all they get? *That's it?*" I thought of all the times Kate had raked me over the coals, disciplined my ass with a month of call outs, made me work eight hours as a hooker, which I hated, and yelled at me for five minutes straight. And here she wasn't even slapping these two on the wrists! "Kate! That's not fair!"

Casey jerked up from the table, humiliation evident in her stiff posture as she grabbed her cup to unceremoniously dump it and most of its contents into a nearby trash receptacle. I didn't understand how one measly sentence, one barely perceptible negative comment could have totally devastated her. She never got in trouble. Sure she'd lost her temper before—I'd seen that plenty of times when she was dealing with bad guys—and granted, this incident involved a member of the command staff, but so what? He deserved it.

I swung my attention back to Kate, who got up from the table and walked over to where Casey stood by herself, arms crossed, leaning up against a pole near the sidewall. Kate spoke quietly to her, her face not the angry mask that always scared the pee out of me, but with more of a gentle, instructing demeanor that irked the heck out of me. Casey met her eyes, nodding occasionally at whatever Kate had to say.

I'd forgotten about Megan. She sat dejectedly, her elbow on the table, her cheek resting on her fist. I knocked her fist out from under her face. "What's the matter with you? You look like Kate just jumped down your throat. All she did was tell you not to yell at a stupid lieutenant!"

She sat back in her chair, staring at me. "It's *Kate*, Alex! I don't want her mad at me! I mean... well, its *Kate*!" She repeated herself as though that one sentence explained everything. This was Megan, the person who'd paraded naked with me through an old folks home when we were fourteen-years-old just because we wanted to give the old guys one last thrill. Megan, who, on a dare, had slept with every starting member of our men's college basketball team in a hotel room with the coach in the room next door. Megan, who'd spent three nights in a Mexican jail because she'd kicked a Mexican cop in the balls for hurting a puppy in Rocky Point. It'd taken me three days and three hundred dollars to get her out of there.

Kate walked back to our table and pulled out her chair, obviously wanting to talk to me alone. "Megan, why don't you head back to your protest? Your friends are probably wondering if they're going to have to spring you from jail or something."

Megan picked up her cup, sighing as she nodded at Kate and walked sadly out of the venue. My whole belief system had just turned upside down. What was wrong with my two best friends? I sat shaking my head as I stared after her. My focus turned to Kate when she laughed at my perplexed face. "Alex, what's the matter? You look about as confused as a second grader who's just had calculus explained to her."

My obstinate little kid emerged, pouty face and all. "You didn't even yell at them. If it'd been me, you'd'a kicked my ass."

She nodded. "Yes I would have."

Her agreement confounded me even more. I'd expected her to lecture me on how she always treats her employees the same, how fairness was the keystone to her supervising philosophy. Instead, she as well as admitted that she treated me differently than everyone else. I raised angry eyes to her, the pout intensifying as I pursed my lips to keep from saying something I'd regret.

Amusement flickered in her eyes. "You don't kill a mosquito with a two by four, and you don't tame a raging gorilla with a fly swatter."

A giggle escaped my pouty face. "A raging gorilla?"

"A belligerent baboon?"

She'd done it again, and I loved her for it. How she manipulated me out of my moods, I'd never fully understand, but I shook my head as she stood and gathered up the trash on the table. "Go find Casey. She's off trying to find Smitty Cogburn. I'm going to talk to Lt. Caruthers. Don't forget. Eight o'clock at the evidence section tomorrow morning."

That thought soured my mood again, but I set off to do as I'd been told. The rodeo grounds weren't that big. Finding Casey took me all of about five minutes. A small crowd had gathered in a corner of the stands, listening to Carl the clown berate a cowboy for being stupid enough to believe Mona loved him. Casey stood between the two men, one hand on Carl's padded, oversized clown shirt and one on the other man's snap button cowboy shirt. The shirt fit him like a glove and I admired its double western yoke and two snap pockets on front. The blue denim material highlighted his fiery blue eyes as he braced himself, ready for a fight. He held his fists balled at his sides, one foot back, chest puffed out in the ever popular banty-rooster imitation common among men who feel the necessity to stand up for their lady's honor.

I stepped next to Casey and smiled at Carl, whose white clown make-up and painted on red lips didn't hold a candle to the menacing hatred pouring off him in black waves of aggression. "Hey Carl, this isn't the place. I'd hate to have to take you to the ground and handcuff you in front of all these kids. Who wants their kids to see a clown humiliated by a nice cop like me?"

Carl pointed over my shoulder at the cowboy. "He knows where my girls are!"

I stepped back to give myself room to maneuver in case he made any aggressive moves, either toward me or toward the other man, whom Casey had ushered down the steps and away from the crowd.

Carl could barely contain his rage. "He knows and he's laughin' at me, thinkin' I'm too stupid to figure things out! Well, I *figured* it out! Him and Mona's got the kids hid somewhere so I can't see 'em, and I'm gonna kill him if he don't tell me what he's done with 'em!"

"Why don't you let Casey and me deal with him? That's our job. We'll find your kids, Carl, but you need to calm down and let us work, okay?"

The angry reddish hue suffusing his face combined with the white clown paint gave him a comic pink complexion I'd bet money he'd cover up if he could see it in a mirror. I blinked several times, trying to reconcile the pastel color of his skin with the usual primary colors associated with a swarthy, normally sun tanned cowboy. When that didn't work, my brain made the necessary adjustments and accepted the fact that a pink-faced cowboy stood before me in oversized jeans held up with checkered suspenders. "Listen, Carl, if my guess is correct, that's Smitty Cogburn, right?"

He nodded.

"He's the reason Casey and I came today. We're here to interview him, and we can't do that unless you calm down and get back to work."

The crowd decided we weren't very interesting anymore. They began filtering back onto the uncomfortable metal benches in the stands, reclaiming their seats with exact precision, claiming seat 31B as theirs even though seats 31 C-L were empty. And heaven help the poor soul who dared rest his backside in 31 B when he'd originally claimed 30 C as his own. 31 B knew the only reason 30 C had usurped his position was because the view from 31 B far eclipsed the view from 30 C. All of this went through my mind as I watched them wandering away from where Carl and I stood facing each other, me waiting impatiently for him to make a decision, him radiating pink with pent-up emotion.

He finally gave me one quick nod, then headed to the other end of the stands. I hoped he had work to do, and guessed he probably did since the team roping had concluded for the day and the rodeo workers appeared to be preparing for the bull riding, which always took place toward the end of the day's events. I followed the path Casey and Smitty had taken down the stairs, but I didn't see them waiting for me underneath the stands. I knew where the first aid rooms were since there were large Red Cross signs posted at regular intervals throughout the venue. Each sign had a red arrow pointing the way to the nearest station, and I figured Casey had taken Smitty to one of them in order to have a little privacy while she interviewed him.

I followed the arrows to the first station, where two very handsome firemen stood, legs apart and arms crossed, enjoying the adoring glances from the passing women. I sighed at their muscular physiques, wishing circumstances were different for Carl and me. One of them, a man I'd known for years from our mutual calls on the streets, noticed my sigh. He held out his hand to shake. "Hi, Alex. That was a big sigh, and I saw you drooling over my backside." He smiled as he turned and patted his butt.

I reached out and grabbed it, giving it a playful squeeze. "If only you knew."

The two of them exchanged glances. "If only we knew what? That you haven't gotten any in the last *nine months?*"

"Michael! Who told you that?" I shouldn't have been surprised since rumors tend to spread like wildfire throughout the police and fire departments.

"Who *hasn't* told me that?" He looked sideways at me. "I'd be glad to help out." His eyebrows pumped up and down, emphasizing the comic leer spreading across his features. The crowd bustled around us, kids yelling, mothers pleading.

The door behind Michael opened and Casey stuck her head out. "You coming?"

"Definitely."

The two men guffawed as I pushed past them to join Casey and Smitty in the little medic room. She'd set up the interview in typical fashion. Two chairs faced each other, and a third sat off to the side where I could sit and observe without interfering with the pace of the questioning. Casey and I usually worked like this. One of us took the lead role and asked all the questions while the other one took notes, quietly assessing the honesty of the person being interviewed. I sat in the lone chair, which creaked ominously under my weight. The wooden legs wobbled as I reached into my back pocket to pull out my notebook. The rodeo had been around for about eighty years, and my guess was this chair had been an integral part of the original furnishings.

Smitty was already seated in one chair; Casey took the second. A small folding table was set off to the side and she pulled it closer so she could set her tape recorder on it after she pushed the record button. She went through all the formalities, including the names of people present, date, time and location of the interview.

My mind wandered while she spoke because I'd heard the introduction hundreds of times. The same thing happened whenever I read someone their Miranda rights or heard another officer reciting them. I'd said them so often that my thoughts raced on to other problems or issues, not even aware of the words coming out of my mouth or even really aware of asking the all-important questions toward the end: "Now, having been advised of these rights and understanding these rights, will you answer my questions?" Often the suspect surprised me by answering the question, and I had to think back to what it was I'd just said.

I watched Casey as she spoke. Her professionalism and knowledge had always impressed me, and as she asked questions and followed up on Cogburn's answers, I thought back to what Caruthers had said. *Was my reputation rubbing off on her?* She and I had known each other for ten years, but we'd only been partners for the last year and a half. We'd been through a lot together. There was no question I'd run to help her through a hail of bullets if she needed me, and she'd do the same for me without question, so now I began to worry that I might be hurting her career somehow by working with her.

"Honest."

I shook my head and focused on Cogburn, who'd turned toward me as though he expected me to corroborate that what he'd just said, whatever it was, was indeed the God's honest truth. Without moving my head, I swiveled my eyes to Casey, hoping she'd realize I didn't have a clue what they'd been talking about.

She jumped right in. "We believe you, Mr. Cogburn. How long ago were you and Carl roping partners?"

"A year ago. He's a hell of a header, and I can pop a loop around a steer's back legs slicker'n snot—uh, pardon me ladies." He ducked his head, believing his words were inappropriate around two women. I hated when that happened. I preferred the times when we spoke with men and they'd forget we were women and focus on the badge, seeing us as police officers first and ladies second.

Casey replied, "No need to apologize, Mr. Cogburn. What happened to break up your friendship?"

Smitty held his black cowboy hat in his lap, fingering the brim whenever Casey asked a question that made him uncomfortable. He fingered it now, running two fingers along the felt edge, moving up and around the curve and then back along the same path. "Well Ma'am, I ain't proud of what I done. But when a man's heart gets involved, well...." He stopped speaking, looking to me as though I'd understand exactly what he meant.

I raised my eyebrows knowingly and nodded. In reality, I'd never dated a married person in my life.

He nodded in return, pleased that someone understood what he'd gone through. "I love Mona, and she loves me. I tried to stay away from her, but something just kept pulling us together."

Yeah, your hormones, you idiot. I nodded sympathetically again, wanting him to keep talking, hoping he'd slip somehow and we'd miraculously find the one clue to where the two kids were.

"Carl and me were at a rodeo in Albuquerque and Mona had driven over to watch us compete. Well, we won the whole thing, $6000 each. Carl had to work the bull riding directly after the roping, so Mona and me went to get some beers and celebrate." He worked the brim of his hat again, rubbing back and forth with small, nervous strokes. "Well, we ended up on the bench seat of my truck. Carl had a break, came looking for us, and well..." He shrugged sheepishly. "You ladies can guess what happened from there."

Casey brought him back to the professional interview instead of allowing him to take the 'you ladies' route. "No, Mr. Cogburn, we can't guess. We deal in facts, not conjecture. Please explain what happened when Carl found you and his wife in your truck."

He glanced at me and I shrugged, wanting him to think that I understood what he'd meant, but he needed to spell it out for Casey. That way, I could remain his friend in case he clammed up and I needed to buddy up to get him to talk again. He shrugged back at me before turning to address her again. "Mona and me... well, we were... well...." He flipped the hat all the way over this time.

I hated when people thought we didn't know the facts of life. *You were screwin' her brains out. Why is that so hard to say?* "Look, Smitty, you won't offend us. It's okay, just say it."

He took a breath and spilled the beans. "We were having sex on the seat." His eyes opened wide as he swiveled his gaze between the two of us, expecting us to faint from surprise or prudish horror. We both raised our eyebrows, silently telling him we weren't impressed, and we'd really appreciate it if he'd just move on with his story.

A kind of disappointment came over his features and he slumped in his chair. The fact that he'd been having sex with Mona was a huge deal to him, a pivotal point in his life, and here he'd just admitted to his great transgression, and we weren't deeply moved by his confession. I wanted to put my head in my hand and rub my eyes from boredom, but I settled for leaning my forearms on my legs, bringing me closer to him as though I sympathized with his problem. I reached out and touched his leg. "Smitty, everyone makes mistakes. What happened when Carl found you with Mona?"

He covered his eyes with his hand, hiding behind it while he told the story. "He pulled me outta the truck and we got into a fight. He was my best friend, but he was a demon. He broke my nose and knocked out these two teeth." He paused, opening his mouth to point at an incisor and a canine on the left side of his head.

Unfortunately, the only question I could come up with was whether his dong had been hanging out during the fight since Carl had pulled him out in the middle of the act. I glanced at Casey, who'd just turned her eyes to meet mine. I knew the question had occurred to both of us simultaneously, and I had to get up and turn around to keep myself from breaking up into fits of laughter. I covered my mouth with my hand while I stood facing the wall, biting my lip hard enough to draw blood.

Smitty misinterpreted my actions. "Aw hell, Detective Wolfe, I didn't mean to upset you none. That happens among cowboys sometimes, and losin' teeth, heck, it's a normal everyday work hazard for us."

I nodded and excused myself from the room before I blew the whole interview. I walked around for a few minutes, marshalling my thoughts before I was able to go back in and take my seat. The two of them had gone on with the interview. Smitty sent me an apologetic look, apparently concerned he had offended me somehow.

Casey brought his attention back to her. "Mr. Cogburn, are you aware that Mona and Carl's two little girls are missing?"

"Yes Ma'am. I knew about it the day they went missing. Mona called me, hysterical, saying Carl had taken the girls and wouldn't tell her where he had them."

"Do you think Carl has them?"

He thought about that a second. "Well, Ma'am, until today I did, but the way he blew up when I saw him made me have second thoughts. Like I said, we was partners for quite a while, and I know him real good. He was real upset today, like he really believed Mona'n me were hiding the girls from *him*. Now I don't know what to think."

"Is it possible Mona might be hiding the girls from him?"

He shook his head, the strength of his convictions evident in the decisive way he flung his head back and forth. "No Ma'am. Mona might have her faults, but that wouldn't be one of 'em. She loves those girls more'n life itself and she wouldn't do nothin' to hurt 'em."

Casey started into the delicate question of the hour. "Mr. Cogburn, is Mona seeing anyone else besides you at the moment?"

"Hell no! She and I are gonna get married in a few months. We just haven't picked a date yet. We love each other, Detective Bowman; that's all there is to it."

Okay, so much for his conviction that Mona couldn't possibly be hiding the kids. He didn't even know about Hondo or the other missing boyfriend. Great. Casey sat up straighter, bracing herself for the next question. "Are you aware there's a man missing whom everyone believes is Mona's current boyfriend?"

Smitty shot to his feet, his hands curled into fists, his lips pulled back from his teeth. "That's a *lie*! Mona loves *me*!" He jammed his thumb into his chest to emphasize his point. "*Me*! You got that?"

Casey and I both automatically stood and took up defensive stances, our left sides to Smitty, gun sides away from him. Since I'd taken the sympathetic role, I put my hand on his chest. "Smitty, relax. She's asking because we've heard different things from different people, and we're trying to get to the truth. Losing your cool isn't gonna get us anywhere."

He brushed my hand away and angrily stared down Casey, who waited patiently for me to get him seated again. I stepped a little bit between the two of them as though I needed to back him down. "Come on, sit down. She probably could have phrased that question a little better." Actually, she'd phrased the question perfectly. An emotional reaction could only work to our benefit since people are more likely to slip up when they're angry or upset.

When he finally broke eye contact with Casey, he walked to the back wall and leaned against it while he stewed over what she'd just said. We waited quietly, knowing people often felt a need to fill the void left open by our silence. He didn't disappoint us. "Mona's a beautiful woman. People think anytime she's with a man, they must be together or somethin'."

Her playing ball tag doesn't help that particular perception either, Buddy. I stepped in front of him and leaned against the wall facing him. "I know what you mean. Maybe you can help us clear up her....." I paused, searching for a more neutral word than 'relationship.' "Her reason for knowing this man who's missing. We really didn't think he was her boyfriend, but we can't figure out how she knows him."

He nodded, then reached over to pull his chair farther back from Casey's. When the distance seemed acceptable to him, he sat.

Casey nonchalantly stepped in front of her chair, reached between her legs and pulled the seat toward him as she lowered herself into it.

Without him realizing it, they were now exactly the same distance apart as when she'd begun the interview.

I made a show of taking my chair by the back of the seat, moving it close to Smitty, and sitting more on his side of the room than on Casey's.

He began speaking to me, as though she wasn't right in front of him. "You're talking about Kenny Finch. I heard he was missing. He's a guy she used a couple times to watch the girls when me and her went out on dates."

Casey nodded. "When was the last time you remember him watching them while you two were out?"

Smitty turned sideways in his chair so his shoulder faced Casey and he sat square to me. "I was in town two weeks ago. We went out then."

"Did he come to Mona's house, or did she take the kids to his house?"

He didn't answer, so the three of us sat in silence. I took a stab at what was bothering him about the question. "My guess is, Mona wouldn't want him coming to her house, right? So she probably took the kids to him?"

The black cloud that had fallen over him descended even more. "Mona never takes men to her place. She knows what's decent."

Casey pushed a little. "She took *you* there, didn't she?"

His jaw muscles rippled, but he remained seated this time. "Of course she did. She's my girlfriend. I already told you we're gonna get married."

I shifted in my seat because I knew she intended to push a little more. She did. "Didn't she take you there when she was still married to Carl?"

The blood rushed to his face and the cadence of his breathing shifted from short, angry breaths to deep, chest-expanding inhalations.

Casey sat back, deceptively unconcerned. She trusted me to keep him from her if he should explode. Her pen tapped a slow rhythm on her knee. "I'm wondering... maybe she had him over one day and you surprised her by coming over when she didn't expect it. She seems to enjoy getting caught in compromising positions."

I anticipated his explosive reaction a fraction of a second before it happened and was on my feet and taking him to the floor before he knew what had happened. He screamed at Casey on the way down. "You fuckin' bitch! You fuckin' bitch!" Casey'd followed us to the floor, wrapping his free arm up around his back close to the one I held twisted behind him.

The two paramedics rushed into the room when they heard him yelling. They stood to the side, waiting to see whether we needed any help.

Smitty kept screaming, spittle forming at the sides of his mouth as he writhed under us. "She loved *me*! She loved *me* and he shouldn't have been there! She loves *me*!" We waited to see whether he'd say anymore, but unfortunately he went silent. With that utterance, he'd become a suspect in Kenny's disappearance, so we couldn't ask him any more questions without reading him his rights.

I recited them to him, hoping that maybe my former connection with him would overcome the warning to remain silent until he spoke to an attorney. It didn't.

"Fuck you! Fuck both of you!"

Years of rodeo competition had made him stronger than the average guy, and neither of us could free one of our hands to reach back for our handcuffs. Firemen have a policy; they can't help us arrest someone unless one of us is getting hurt. I turned to Michael, who knew Kate from some potlucks we'd all been to. "Kate Brannigan was just in the TPD Mobile Command Post. Would you mind asking her to come here real quick?"

He nodded and headed out the door while his partner remained with us. We struggled with Smitty for about five minutes before Kate, Caruthers, and another uniformed officer came into the room. The uniform brought out his handcuffs and the three of us wrestled Smitty into them. When we had him secured, the uniform waited with him while Kate, Caruthers, Casey and I stepped outside.

Casey filled them in on what we had. "We aren't one hundred percent sure, but it looks like he walked in on Mona and Finch at her house doing the dirty deed. When I asked him about it, he went berserk and screamed something about how he, meaning Finch, shouldn't have been there, and that was after he'd told us Finch had never been to Mona's house. We at least have enough to hold him long enough for the homicide dicks to talk to him."

Kate nodded, then turned to Caruthers. "Since this might have just turned into a possible homicide, I'll give Jon Logan a call and see if he wants to send out a couple detectives." Jon was her counterpart in the homicide detail.

Caruthers shook his head importantly. "No, this is better handled at my level. I'll call Lt. Smith and let him know what I've got."

Casey and I both looked at Kate, wondering how she'd handle him taking the credit for possibly solving one of our kidnapping cases.

She didn't blink an eye.

Caruthers pulled out his cell phone and stepped away from us. As he scrolled through the names on his phone, he called over his shoulder. "Nice work, Casey. I'll be sure to mention it was your interviewing skills that gave us this break."

Anything he did to build up Casey scored points in my book. I knew he'd meant to slight me, but I'd started worrying about my influence on her career and wanted her to get all the credit for today. I reached out to squeeze her arm. "You *did* do a great job, Case. I think Cogburn did something to Kenny."

She growled, leveling a malignant stare at Caruthers' back. "*We* did a great job, Alex. Not just me."

Kate caught my eye and winked before turning to join Caruthers a few steps away from us.

Casey growled again. "You may be the first to piss on his grave, Alex, but I'll be a close second."

"It's okay, Case." And it really was okay. I realized that Caruthers had jabbed, and I hadn't reacted. The realization felt good.

When all the arrangements had been made and Smitty had been delivered into the hands of the homicide unit, we all met back at the office to write up our notes on the afternoon's events. Toward the end of the day, Kate walked over to our desks as I tucked my stuff into my briefcase, ready to head for home. "Don't forget the destruction board tomorrow, Alex." When I nodded, she turned to go, then paused and turned back to me. "You did a great job not reacting to his jab this afternoon. Do that again tomorrow and you'll do fine."

I continued to load my briefcase. "How come you didn't even blink when he took credit for possibly solving Kenny's disappearance?"

She put her hands in her pockets while she thought about the question. "One thing I've learned over the years, Alex, is the truth usually comes out. People know his reputation, and they know mine." She raised her eyebrows and smiled slightly, not needing to say anymore.

I understood perfectly. I picked up my briefcase and headed out the door. "Okay, Sarge. I'll be there tomorrow with bells on my toes. See ya, Case." I happened to glance over my shoulder in time to see them exchange amused looks, probably on my behalf. I smiled as the door slowly swung shut behind me.

CHAPTER 16

Instead of heading for home, I swung my car in the direction of the Animal Control Center. I'd promised Shelley I'd go look for Muddy. My head told me my mission was an exercise in futility since it had been several weeks since he'd been brought in, but my heart told me to try anyway. I pulled around to the back of the center where the employees parked their cars. I'd been on the board of the center the year before and knew everyone who worked there. I knocked on the back door and heard the locks click from an automatic unlocking mechanism. The door pulled open easily and I stepped inside to the sounds of big dogs barking, little dogs yipping, and employees clanging gates or helping potential owners.

One of the senior kennel workers recognized me as I walked into the shelter. He hung a short piece of rope onto a kennel gate before walking over to me and holding out his hand. "Alex, good to see you. You haven't been around in a while."

His hand had the grimy discoloration people get when they handle animals all day long. I admired men and women with that type of grime and I shook his hand heartily. "No, I haven't. I hope everything's going well with you." We continued with our small talk, catching up on shelter business, employee changes and whatnot. When the conversation lagged I broached the subject of Muddy. "I'm actually looking for a mutt that came in several weeks ago. I don't know the exact date but I can get it for you if you need it."

The incredulous look he gave me reinforced my belief that, first of all there'd been far too many dogs come through that matched that general description and that second, I'd come about four weeks too late, but I pressed on for Shelley's sake. "He belonged to a homeless woman who died and—"

His face brightened, making my heart leap in my chest. "You mean Muddy! He's still here. We all used to see how loyal he was to that old lady when she walked the streets, so we keep begging for another week's reprieve for him. The problem is, nobody wants to adopt him since he's older middle age and not really that cute."

"Can I have him?"

"Can you have him?" He yelled to anyone who'd listen, "Alex wants Muddy and she wants to know if she can have him!" Cheers went up around the kennels and by the time we walked to Muddy's kennel, the entire staff was clapping. One rather large woman stepped to the side and there he was, happy, healthy and ready to drive Gia crazy. I took his leash and walked him to the front office where I filled out all the paperwork to officially spring Muddy from the hands of these wonderful people who'd saved his life. I couldn't help thinking they might have helped save Shelley's life by their acts of kindness as well.

Muddy walked out of the shelter a free dog. He hopped into the passenger seat of my car, turning to calmly sit on the front seat as though he'd ridden in cars his whole life. We drove to Gia's midtown home in companionable silence. When I rang the doorbell he sat at my feet just as he'd always sat at Anya's whenever she waited for a green light at a busy intersection. Gabe opened the door, his dimple disappearing when he took in Muddy by my side.

I pushed him aside with the back of my hand so Muddy and I could squeeze past him to start on our way back to the library. When I looked back over my shoulder, Gabe was slowly closing the door behind us and covering his eyes with a big meaty hand in anticipation of Gia's reaction. He didn't have long to wait. Shelley must have heard Muddy's toe nails clicking on the tile floor because I heard running footsteps coming from behind the closed library door. When the door burst open, Shelley slid out into the hallway, looking wildly in our direction, hoping against hope that her one connection to the only woman who'd ever loved her had returned.

Her joyful shout told me everything I needed to know. "*Muddy!*" She slid up to him like she was sliding into second base, threw both arms around his neck and burst into heartbreaking sobs that brought tears to my eyes.

On the other hand, the look on Gia's face as she stepped out of the library brought fear to my bowels. Before I lost the initiative—or courage—I backed her into the library where we could speak in private. "She needs him, Gia. Listen to her out there."

The unmitigated anger pouring out of her steely grey eyes unnerved me. She opened her mouth to speak, then changed her mind mid-breath before shutting it again.

Shelley brought Muddy into the library with a determined cast to her own set of steel grey eyes. The two of them stood straight and tall, one a smaller mirror image of the other, and Gia visibly reined in her temper. "Take him outside, Shelley. We'll discuss this later."

Shelley turned her attention to me, shaking her head sadly before gravely informing me, "You are in *deep* shit, Alex."

I watched as she led Muddy down the hallway by his little rope leash that the Animal Care Center had given me. She had to go through the kitchen to get to the back yard, and as she made the turn into the kitchen, she glanced back to give me one more shake of her head.

I stepped back into the library where Gia hadn't moved a muscle. There was no use getting into a staring contest with her, so I walked to the sofa where she'd apparently been reading the *Wall Street Journal* while sipping on a glass of Scotch. I lowered myself into the cushions after I grabbed the glass and drained the contents in one, scared-shit-less gesture of defiance.

Gabe's voice startled me a moment later when he bent down to speak quietly in my ear. "Ms. Angelino requests you leave her home immediately."

I jerked around, expecting to see her standing in the door where I'd left her. The doorway stood empty except for the traces of her very formidable presence. "I want to talk to her. Can you ask her to come back?"

There'd been one other time Gabe hadn't been amused with me. That had been when I'd torn up Gia's second invitation to meet with her. He straightened up, his muscles flexing in his expensive Armani suit. He motioned with his left hand toward the hallway. "I'll see you to the door."

CHAPTER 17

I knew in my heart I'd done the right thing for Shelley and Muddy, but I felt a hole in the pit of my stomach over the loss of a friend. The notepad I usually kept in my car lay open on the front seat. I glanced at it sadly as I backed out of Gia's driveway and caught the name *Chad Caldwell*, written in the childlike scrawl I hadn't improved upon since kindergarten. The scrawl tended to get worse the more rushed I felt at the time, and judging by the looks of this one, I'd been more than a little rushed when I'd taken the note. The problem was, I couldn't remember why I'd written the name or what it referred to.

I picked up the pad as I neared the end of the driveway, flipping back a page to see whether I recognized any other names that might shed light on who exactly Chad Caldwell was. Nothing on that page jogged my memory, so I stopped the car and flipped forward a page. Underlined there I'd written *Randall Bollinger*, which confused me even more. That name at least had a phone number next to it, and since I desperately needed something to counteract my growing depression, I punched the numbers into my cell phone and called Mr. Bollinger to see whether the person who answered could jog my memory.

"Bollinger Research and Avionic Corporation."

That didn't help. "May I speak with Mr. Randall Bollinger please?"

The woman's voice sounded professional, yet friendly. "May I ask who is calling?"

"This is Detective Wolfe from the Tucson Police Department."

"Is he expecting your call?"

"No."

"May I ask what this is about?"

I tapped the steering wheel, not sure how to answer that since I didn't know why I had his name in my pad. "Well, no."

Her curiosity obviously overcame her professionalism, and she lowered her voice to that of a co-conspirator. "This is about Chad, isn't it?"

That surprised me. I decided to play along. "Do you know Chad?"

"Do I *know* Chad? What do you mean, do I know him? Who is this again?"

Suspicion colored her words, so I answered carefully. "This is Detective Wolfe. I'm sorry if I offended you somehow. That wasn't my intention."

I heard her sigh. "That's okay, we're all super upset over the whole thing. I guess I'm a little touchy. Yes, I knew Chad. After all, he worked here for the last ten years. In this company, everyone is like family."

She'd spoken of him in the past tense, so I punted. "Actually, maybe you can help me. I'm following up on some minor details."

"For Detective Langstrom?"

That stopped me in my tracks. Why would Eric be involved in something to do with a name on my notepad? Then the penny dropped. These were the names Roxy had given me while Eric's witness had been howling at me. "Yes, for Detective Langstrom. Is this too painful to speak about over the phone? I know it's getting late, but maybe it would be better if I stopped by your office. Could I get the address? I can come right over."

She recited the address, giving me turn-by-turn directions to an office complex in Midtown. Fifteen minutes later, I was sitting in a conference room with Randall Bollinger, his wife Alice, who was also his receptionist, and two other employees. I had no clue the meeting would turn out to be a community event. "Mr. Bollinger, some of the questions I have are of a sensitive nature. I wonder if we might have a more private interview?" I glanced apologetically to the other employees who agreed readily enough to excuse themselves.

Bollinger rested his hand on his wife's back as she moved past him toward the door. "Wait, Honey." He glanced at me. "Detective, Chad was one of our best friends and I know he wouldn't mind Alice hearing anything you might have to say."

Since I didn't know what I had to say, I couldn't really object. "Of course. Please stay, Ms. Bollinger. I didn't mean to exclude you." When she reseated herself, I plunged right in. "Mr. Bollinger, do you remember a fundraising dinner you attended a few weeks ago?"

Alice popped up in her chair. "You mean the Wild for Wombat gala!"

"Wild for Wombats? You guys raised money for Wombats?"

She laughed. "In a way. The fundraiser was for a wild animal rescue group I volunteer for, and if a wombat ever happens to come in, we'll be ready for him!"

I smiled at her enthusiasm, then turned back to Randall. "Okay... well, do you remember talking to a lady at your table named Roxie Cole? She worked for CPS."

I saw a light bulb flash over Mr. Bollinger's head as he suddenly understood why I'd wanted to speak to him in private. I waited a second to give him time to collect his thoughts. "I can see by your reaction that you remember the conversation. Are you still comfortable discussing the issue with Alice here?"

He nodded and reached for his wife's hand, pulling it into his lap while he spoke. "Yes, Chad was often depressed, and he'd come to either Alice or me or both of us to talk about his life. He blamed all of his problems on his victimization while in foster care." He shook his head sadly. "I just wish he'd come to us that last time."

Alice agreed. "I knew he was feeling down, but I never thought he'd kill himself, Detective Wolfe. He'd just landed a new aerospace patent, and I thought maybe that would pull him out of his depression."

I nodded knowingly. So he had killed himself, and apparently Eric had been assigned the case. Often, if a case is a suicide, the homicide detectives will look into it just to make sure there was no foul play. "Did Chad ever give you the name of the person who molested him? Did he say if it was a man or a woman?"

Alice caught her husband's eyes, apparently asking whether Chad had ever said anything to him about the details. When he shook his head, she brought her attention back to me. "No, he was terrified—or maybe paranoid would be a better word—that people would find out. We asked if the person was still a foster parent, but he didn't know." She retrieved her hand from her husband's lap. "I certainly hope not."

I agreed. "Me too. Mr. Bollinger, you mentioned to Roxie something about the Kindler homicide. Were you just speculating?"

"Absolutely. I only mentioned it because it had been front-page news, and since it had to do with a foster parent, it made me think of Chad. As far as I know, there was absolutely no connection."

It looked like I'd reached a dead end. I closed my notepad and stood up. "Thank you for your time. I'm just trying to tie up some loose ends." We shook hands and I headed out of the office, stopping at a fast food restaurant to pick up dinner before heading home.

CHAPTER 18

My alarm went off way too early the next morning. When I shot my hand out to grab it, I accidently launched it off my end table. It sailed into the closet, still ringing but muffled enough by the clothes tossed haphazardly on the floor to allow me to grab a few more minutes of sleep. I rolled onto my stomach and buried my head under my pillow, pulling the sides around my face to block out the noise. The days of the week shuffled through my mind until Wednesday landed on top of the pile. I relaxed when I couldn't remember any pressing engagements scheduled for the day.

My phone rang loud enough to penetrate the pillow, but not loud enough to disturb my half-slumber. When it stopped ringing I dozed, lazily dreaming about Carl and his jeans. Then the ringing started again, and I picked up the handset and threw it into the closet with my alarm. Pretty soon, my cell phone rang with Casey's distinctive ring. I growled as I crawled halfway out of my bed, walked into the closet on my hands while my feet stayed under the covers on the bed. I grabbed the phone and punched the button. "Yeah?"

The phone continued to ring until I realized I had thrown my house phone, not my cell phone, into the closet. I threw the house phone back into the pile of clothes and pulled myself back up onto the bed just in time for the ringing to stop. I'd just flipped open the cover, intending to hit speed dial to call her back, when the ringing started again. I pushed send and flopped back on my pillow. "Jesus, Case, what's so important that you gotta call me four times?"

"Well, it's seven thirty and I'm at work. Where are you? And is that your alarm I hear in the background?"

I crawled back to the closet, grabbed the alarm and hit the snooze button. "That better?"

"Alex, where are you? You've got the destruction board today. I expected you to be here a little early to make sure you got there on time."

"Shit!" I threw the phone on the bed, grabbed the clothes from the floor of the closet and pulled them on in record time. From my house to the station took exactly twenty-five minutes if I drove the speed limit. I raced to my car, threw it into reverse, and backed a few feet before shoving the gearshift back into park. "Shit!" I left the car idling in the driveway, raced through my house, slid into my bedroom, retrieved my cell phone from under the covers and ran back out to the car. I slid into a parking space at work with two minutes to spare.

The three flights of stairs took me another minute and I slammed into the office door, knocking into a detective who was on her way out. She caught her balance and looked at the clock above the doors, then called out to the general office population. "Eight o'clock! She made it! Who won?"

Nate Drewery scooped up a pile of dollar bills on one of the desks. "I did! You can check! I wrote down eight o'clock sharp on the sheet!" Several detectives clustered around a piece of paper and one of them said, "Yeah, he did. He wins."

Kate came out of her cubicle and grabbed my arm. "Let's go."

I dropped my briefcase on the floor and yelled over my shoulder. "Case!"

She got up from her desk to retrieve it for me. "Got it."

The door shut behind us and I yelled through it as Kate pulled me roughly toward the evidence section, "Thanks!"

Lt. Caruthers waited for us at the front office. For obvious reasons, the security surrounding the evidence storage section is tight, and we all had to sign a visitor's log before being escorted back to the narcotics room. The evidence clerk who accompanied us handed out breathing masks and special, impermeable rubber gloves. This particular clerk and I had been friends for many years and I respected her knowledge and abilities. She was a senior clerk who had a no-nonsense attitude when it came to handling evidence. I always trusted her to do everything exactly according to procedures.

She pointed to the cameras in the area as she pulled on her mask and gloves. "Everything we do will be recorded on several cameras, both inside the room and out. None of us will ever go into the room alone. I realize it's called a Narcotics Destruction Board, but today instead of destroying narcotics, we'll be getting rid of the marijuana that's not needed anymore as evidence. This morning, you'll be weighing every package and double-checking the weights we have recorded on the evidence logs. One of you will also read off the contents of the package while someone else checks to make sure everything matches. Once that's done, we'll work straight through lunch to load the bundles onto the truck and then SWAT will escort us to the destruction site. Any questions?"

Caruthers cleared his throat importantly. "Kate, you and I will handle checking the weights and contents." He looked pointedly at me. "We don't want to have any errors."

I bristled. The first words out of his mouth had been a loosely veiled put-down and I wondered how long I'd last before I decked him.

Kate nodded. "All right."

Edna, the clerk, nodded as well. "Alex, that means I'll hand you the boxes in order. You'll carry them to Sgt. Brannigan, who will weigh the box and read off the contents. Once she's finished, we'll restack and take her another."

Caruthers laughed. "Think you can handle that, Alex?"

Caruthers' gut hung over his belt, and I barely nodded to it with my chin. "Sure, Lieutenant, no problem. I wouldn't want you putting any more strain on your lower back than it already has to contend with."

He closed his eyes partway while Kate remained silent. Edna pulled out a cart and set a desk scale on it. "Let's get started then." We worked two hours straight. Sweat pored down my cheeks as I carried yet another fifty-pound box of marijuana over to Kate and set it on the scale.

Kate read off the weight, then looked at Edna who'd just re-shelved the previous box I'd carried back to her. "Edna, I think we could use a break. What do you think?"

Edna shrugged. "It's up to you guys. Lieutenant, are you ready to stop for a few minutes?"

Caruthers, who'd been sitting the whole time with a clipboard on his lap, sighed heavily. "Well, I'm fine. I'd just as soon get this finished. I'll bet turtles could work faster than you, Alex." He laughed at his own joke, looking to Edna to join in the fun.

She smiled awkwardly at Kate who pulled off her mask while she stretched her arms. "Well, I need a break and some water." She headed out the door, and Caruthers had no choice but to close his book and follow.

Obviously, the break was for my benefit since I was doing the lion's share of the physical labor, and I silently blessed my sergeant. After we'd all filed out of the room, Edna shut and locked the door, then sealed it with evidence tape to prove no one had entered while we were away. I'd missed my morning caffeine, resulting in a slow-building headache I knew would only get worse if I didn't attend to it. "I'm gonna get a soda; anybody else want one?"

Kate and Edna both declined, but Caruthers looked down his nose at me. "Get me one."

No "please," no request—basically an order to get the asshole a drink. Well, I had offered. I moved my chin minutely toward his gut again. "You'll want a diet one, right?"

He glanced at Edna to see whether she'd caught the dig, then smiled dangerously at me. "A regular one is fine."

I tsk'd once at his belly and cocked my head. "All right, but...." I left the sentence hanging while I ambled out into the hallway in search of a soda. The snack machines were in an alcove on the second floor, complete with a microwave and moneychanger. I bought a diet for me and started to push the button for a regular soda when the devil grabbed my finger and made me select the diet button. "Oops."

I carried a can in each hand, shaking one as I walked. I used that can to knock on the door and was admitted back into the evidence section where I had to sign back in. Caruthers was sitting behind a desk in the middle of the room, and I walked over and set the soda in front of him. I flipped the tab on mine; taking a long drink and hoping my headache would go away once the caffeine took affect.

Caruthers picked up his can. "You can't even get drinks without screwing up, can you, Wolfe?" He looked angrily at Kate. "You heard me ask for a regular soda, didn't you?"

I hit my forehead with the palm of my hand. "Oh, shoot, you're right. I'm sorry, L.T. I'm just so used to hitting the diet button, I didn't even think about it."

Edna chuckled. "I know what you mean. I do stuff like that all the time. Old habits are hard to break."

I nodded and took another sip, catching Kate's suspicious glare over the top of my can. I heard a click, then a pffffzzzzz and saw Caruthers shoot out of his chair as the shaken soda exploded onto his shirt and spilled out onto the desk. I covered my face as my soda backed up into my nose. Edna sprang up to grab a towel from a cart next to her, which she deftly threw onto the desk to mop up the liquid spreading out across the surface and down onto the floor.

I couldn't look at either Caruthers or Kate, so I sauntered around behind some filing cabinets to wipe the tears from my eyes. I had an overpowering urge to giggle maniacally, so I pulled a paper towel from a receptacle and covered my face to keep the sounds locked in. When I felt sufficiently under control, I lowered the towel a few inches and came face to face with a pissed off Kate Brannigan. Any leftover urge to giggle vanished. I crossed my arms and tried for my most innocent expression, raising my eyebrows and pulling my shoulders almost up to my ears.

Caruthers barreled around the corner, rage pouring off of him as he bore down on me. Without missing a beat, I offered him the paper towel. "Shoot Lieutenant, I can't believe that happened! Here, I came to get you some more towels." I reached behind me to pull out several more sheets and began rubbing his shirt vigorously.

He slapped my hand away and I marveled at how a red face actually does turn purple, given the right circumstances. There were quite a few witnesses in the room, which seemed to prevent him from pouring out years of accumulated animosity. I thought maybe I could be helpful by offering him a change of clothes. "I have a clean shirt in my locker if you need it." I examined his gut skeptically. "Although...."

Kate grabbed the back of my shirt, practically throwing me out into the hallway.

"Kate! Now I have to sign in again."

"Shut up." She hauled me to an empty interview room, pushed me in and slammed the door behind us.

I shrugged as I held up my hands, palms up. "What?"

"Do you want to work patrol at the Los Reales Land Fill?"

Uh oh. "No Ma'am."

She held one finger inches from my nose and I had to move my head back a little to focus on it. "One more today, Alex... just one more."

"Yes Ma'am."

She reached behind her and pulled open the door. I stepped out into the hall, looking both ways to see if anyone had noticed Kate reaming me again. Then I followed her back to the evidence room where we did, indeed have to sign back in. Caruthers had gone to change shirts, and when he returned, Edna led us back to the drug room. We donned new masks and gloves and she recorded in her book that the tape she'd used to seal the room was still intact. When she broke the tape, we all stepped inside and assumed our previous positions.

Caruthers face had returned to some semblance of his normal, pale, somewhat splotchy appearance. We began the routine once again— Edna handing me a box, me carrying it to Kate, her weighing it, me returning it to Edna and her re-shelving it. Caruthers wrote down the weights and checked off the contents as Kate read them off. As if that wasn't enough to keep his pea brain occupied, he began discussing the problems he'd had over the years with various detectives. "Do you remember that arson detective we had who could never seem to do anything right?"

Kate raised her eyes, her expression non-committal. The detective had actually been a good cop who'd been railroaded into having to quit to avoid being fired.

"I eventually got him fired. He was a worthless work of art, that one. What about the one who embezzled all that money from the narcotics unit? He was mine too." He smiled and ran his finger across his throat. "He's doing time in a federal penitentiary." He watched me carry a box past him. "You remember them, Alex?"

Kate surreptitiously grabbed my hand while she took the box from me and gave it a warning pinch.

I gave a one-word answer. "Yup."

"Did you know I was the one who fired them?"

"Yup."

"That incompetent arson investigator—he trained you, didn't he?" There was the jab.

"Yup."

"You learned well."

I felt the need to defend my friend, who hadn't deserved to be fired. "Do you know what he's doing now?"

Caruthers smiled maliciously. "Working at a convenience store?"

"Nope. He's the top arson investigator for Alcohol, Tobacco, and Firearms. I guess they disagreed with your assessment." I left it at that while I picked up the box from Kate's scales and returned it to Edna, who re-shelved it and stepped down off her ladder. I felt Caruthers' malignant glare boring into my back and hoped Kate would stop him if he pulled his weapon and aimed it my way.

Edna pointed to a rolling cart. "Well, that's the last of them. Now the fun part begins. Alex, would you mind getting that cart? The truck is already at the back ramp. I just need to make a quick call to let the SWAT sergeant know we're going to begin loading." She left the room to make the call.

I wiped the sweat from my eyes with a paper towel. "It's hot in here. I'm gonna step outside for a second." I stepped right outside the narcotics room door, staying within the evidence section itself.

Caruthers apparently thought I meant I was going all the way outside, because he began berating Kate for protecting me from everyone else on the department who, according to him, understood that I should be fired. "Why do you protect that worthless woman, Kate? You were an excellent detective; you should know incompetence when you see it."

"Alex is a lot of things, Henry, but incompetent isn't one of them. She's brash, mouthy, and rude at times, but incompetent? No."

His voice rose several octaves. "How has she pulled the wool over the eyes of one of the best sergeants on the department? You *know* she's a rogue cop, Katy! We need to get rid of her!"

I happened to know Kate hated being called Katy. Her answer was quick and heated. "Leave her alone, Henry. You bait her and then expect her to sit quietly and take it."

"She's a *detective* for Christ's sake! I'm a lieutenant! She *should* sit quietly and take it!"

What she said next shocked me. "And as a lieutenant you should be above baiting my detectives! Leave her alone!" Wow, I didn't think Kate ever spoke to commanders like that. I guess even they respected her enough to take it.

Edna returned, and she and I walked back into the room. Kate and Caruthers stood facing each other, Kate's arms crossed over her chest and Caruthers' hands resting on his hips. When they saw us, they turned away from each other and pretended to check notes or weight scales. I pretended I hadn't overheard their conversation.

Edna directed the loading of the carts. Caruthers continued to bait me, but I'd fallen into a contemplative mood and didn't feel like sparring. I answered any questions he had with a minimal amount of effort and stayed silent the rest of the time. It took about two hours, but we finally loaded the last bale of marijuana into the moving van.

Kate and I sat in the cab of the truck while a SWAT guy climbed behind the wheel and pulled out onto the road. Caruthers and Edna followed in his vehicle. The SWAT guy was an affable young officer I hadn't met before. He and Kate talked about the upcoming detectives' test and I stared out the window, thinking about all the people on the department who agreed with Caruthers. I couldn't help but wonder how the incompetent idiots of the department managed to rise through the ranks and become incompetent lieutenants and captains. Still, they were definitely in the minority. I respected ninety percent of the current bunch of commanders, but the last ten percent made life miserable for ninety-nine percent of the workforce.

We pulled into a walled-in commercial yard that had a huge furnace roaring and ready for our bales of marijuana. Edna, Kate and I shoved all the bales toward the rear door of the van while a man with a forklift transferred them to the furnace under the watchful eyes of the SWAT guys, who were armed with assault rifles. Caruthers sat in the air-conditioned trailer eating the burger and fries he'd stopped to get along the way. We had to stay until the bales were completely consumed, so Edna and I sat on the wall next to the gate while Kate went out to buy us lunch.

She returned after about a half-hour and when I pulled out money to pay her back, she waved it off. "Its on the house, Alex. You did most of the work today and you did an excellent job." She took a bite of her burger. "*And* you kept your mouth shut these last two hours, an even *more* excellent job." She hit me in the arm with her elbow, causing the ketchup on my fry to smear across the top of my nose.

"Hey, watch that elbow, would ya?" We spent the rest of the after-noon talking about our kidnapping cases and plotting strategies for how we were going to locate the two little girls. Both of us believed Mona had something to do with their disappearance, and neither of us felt the case was a legitimate stranger abduction.

Edna wandered over to the trailer to find a bottle of water, and Kate took the opportunity to ask about Shelley's case. "I asked you to brief me on what you're doing with the Kindler case. Have you gotten anything new since we last talked?"

"No. I followed up on a long shot the CPS case worker gave me, but it turned out to be a dead end." I intended to leave it at that, since nothing had come of the information, but Kate persisted.

"Tell me about it."

"Well, Roxy—that's the CPS caseworker—"

Kate interrupted. "I know Roxy very well. Good God, the two of you together... I think I'll stock up on more antacids pills." She sighed. "Sorry to interrupt; go on."

"Roxy talked to a man at a fundraiser who was friends with a man who'd been molested in foster care here in Tucson. The Kindler homicide was front-page news right about then, and he said wouldn't it be funny if Kindler had molested his friend. I followed up, and it's a dead end."

"Why is it a dead end?" I could see why she had the reputation of being a tenacious detective.

"Well, the guy killed himself a little while ago. Committed suicide."

Kate sat quietly a moment. "Alex, do me a favor. See if Roxy can dig up the man's records. Let's take this just one more step to make sure it's a dead end. Find out who his foster parents were. Did you check to see if he left a suicide note?"

I flushed a little. "No Ma'am. I just kinda' thought of it as a dead end. But I'll do some more digging." I didn't like being caught doing something halfway, and those sentiments probably showed on my face.

"It's probably nothing, but let's keep digging, okay?"

"Eric handled the suicide. I can see if he has anything."

She watched the bales burning in the furnace for a while. The smoke alternated between green, red and yellow, the colors mesmerizing if you stared at them long enough. "No, just get Roxie to look into it. No need to bother Eric with it."

I shrugged. "Sure thing." Edna returned with water for all three of us, carefully stepping over the rusted poles and abandoned metal scraps as she made her way back up to our perch on the wall. We chatted about inane topics, trying to keep boredom at bay. The remnants of the bales were still smoldering at five-thirty, but Caruthers finally decided there was no longer anything left that could be recovered and used. We got back to the station at six.

Kate put her arm around my shoulders as we headed for our cars. "Well, for a first lesson, you did... okay. Have you ever seen pictures of people with an angel on one shoulder and a mischievous devil on the other?"

"Yeah."

"Your angel needs a lot of work." She patted my back before sliding into her car and heading out of the garage. Most of the parking spaces were empty since five o'clock had come and gone an hour ago. My footsteps echoed throughout the cement monolith as I made my way to my car. The sound spooked me into looking over my shoulder every few seconds, wondering whether the person who'd thrown me into Gumby's pen might be lurking behind a pillar or post. I smiled at my paranoia as I beeped open the driver's side door and reached for the handle. I froze when I saw what looked like a small bit of hay on the ground next to the door. "Holy shit." I stared at the debris. "He *wouldn't*."

Slowly backing away, I pulled out my cell phone and called Kate. When she answered, my voice shook. "Sarge, can you come back to the garage? I think Caruthers planted some dope in my car."

"What? Alex, first of all, he'd be stupid to plant it the same day we did the destruction board, and second, he knows there are cameras down there. Did you find dope in your car?"

I knelt down to get a closer look at the stuff on the ground. "No, its just there's some kind of hay-like stuff on the ground next to the driver's side door. I thought maybe it was marijuana. Maybe I'm getting paranoid. Never mind." I stood up and was reaching for the handle when Kate stopped me.

"Wait, Alex. I'm almost there. Don't touch anything until you have a witness, just in case."

I sighed in relief. "Okay, thanks."

A minute later, the large bay door swung up and Kate pulled back into the garage. When she walked up, I noticed her scanning every inch of the area around my car as though she were entering a crime scene. She might not have believed Caruthers had planted dope in my car, but she wasn't taking any shortcuts either. She knelt down next to the door, carefully examining the debris on the ground. As she stood up, I heard her knees crack and she shook them out before walking to the trunk of her car and pulling out gloves, evidence envelopes, and a clip board with a property sheet attached.

She handed the clipboard to me and then pulled on the rubber gloves. "Here, you record while I gather. It does look like dope, and we'll treat it as such until we know differently." She pulled out her cell phone, located a stored number and hit send. After a few seconds, she began speaking. "Nate? Do you happen to know the case number from that photo Alex found on her windshield?" She waited a beat. "Sure, I can wait."

I'd retrieved a pen from her car and she plucked it and the clipboard out of my hand to write the case number at the top. When she had it, she thanked Nate, closed her phone and returned the clipboard to me. "Call communications and get a separate case number for this stuff. We'll connect it to Nate's original case." I did as she directed, then began cataloging the items she wanted put into evidence.

As she worked, a thought occurred to me. "Hey Sarge, what if this *is* hay? What if I just assumed Caruthers had planted dope, but this is really from someone from the rodeo who's messing with me, maybe messing with my car?"

She stepped back, obviously thinking. "I think I'm getting paranoid now." Pulling out her cell phone again, she called communications and requested they send two K-9s to the garage—one with expertise in sniffing out bombs and another who could identify dope.

The bomb guy arrived first and after Kate explained what she needed, he released his German shepherd from the back of his vehicle. "Who'd you piss off this time, Alex? You know, if Commo had said I needed to check a detective's car for bombs, yours would've been the first one on the list."

"Very funny, you jerk." I punched him in the arm, momentarily forgetting that his K9 wouldn't appreciate that. The dog swung his head around and eyed me while the handler growled something to him under his breath. The dog immediately lost interest and sat at his master's heels. They circled the car first, checking the wheel wells and seams. When they didn't locate anything on the exterior of the car, he opened the front door so the dog could jump in and sniff around. The handler did a thorough job, popping the hood to check the engine and going into the trunk to check in there. When they didn't find anything, they gave way to the narcotics dog that had arrived while they were completing their search.

The second handler, Buck Paris, unsnapped his leash to let his dog check the car on his own. When the second the dog stepped to the driver's door, he sat and looked expectantly at his master. Buck pulled out a toy and threw it for the dog, who ran happily down the ramp after it. Buck turned to Kate. "You got a hit. That's dope all right. I don't need to go any further unless you want me to see if there's anything on the inside."

Kate's expression turned hard. "Look inside, please." She turned to me. "Now it's time to call Internal Affairs and tell them what we have." Seeing my worried expression, she added, "Don't worry, Alex. You did everything right."

Buck did as Kate requested and directed Bear to search the interior. Bear immediately walked across the seats and alerted on the passenger door. When Buck got him out of the car, Kate opened the door to look in the side pocket. She went back to her trunk, pulled out a large envelope and returned to my car. By the time she'd scooped out a fairly large quantity of marijuana and stuffed it into the envelope, the IAD sergeant and my lieutenant, Jaeme Hawthorne, had made their way down to the garage. Kate handed the envelope to the sergeant. "Hi. You're here late."

As he took the envelope from her, he lifted his chin my way. "Alex again, huh? We had a pretty good stretch going there for a while... three months I think."

I sighed as I went to sit in Kate's car. I didn't mind getting myself in trouble, but when other people jumped on the bandwagon, it bothered me a lot. Kate walked over and knelt by my door. "They're going to dust for fingerprints."

"Oh, man. You know how long it'll take me to clean that black crap off the car?" I fell back onto the bench seat. "Damn it."

"Well, at least you're getting paid overtime for it. C'mon, lets go meet the detective in IA so she can take our statements and we can get out of here for the night."

We walked up the stairs, passing two grinning IA detectives on their way to process my car. One of them, a friend of mine, called up to me after he'd passed us, "Way to go, Alex. I knew I could count on you to give us overtime again! Good job!"

I smiled as I yelled back down the stairwell, "Fuck you, asshole!"

Kate opened the door, waving me through with a bemused look on her face. "Alex, you might not want to cuss out the Internal Affairs detectives who are on their way to investigate marijuana found in your work car."

I shrugged as I followed her into the IA office. The interviews were short and sweet. We were out of there in no time, and when we walked back into the garage, the two IA detectives were standing next to my car, grinning. My blood pressure skyrocketed when I saw what they'd done. I grabbed two traffic cones and hurled them their way as I stormed down the ramp. "You assholes! I'm gonna kick your friggin' butts!" I picked up speed and ran toward them, murder and mayhem the uppermost thoughts in my mind. They knew me well enough to run partway down the parking ramp to give Kate enough time to grab me from behind to stop me.

She sounded amused as she tried to calm me down. "Whoa there! Settle down!"

"Settle down? Look at what those assholes did to my car!" Black fingerprint powder had been literally poured all over the outside of my car. There wasn't an inch of paint that didn't look like it hadn't been driven through an underground coal mine.

The detectives held their sides, laughing hysterically while their sergeant walked up trying to hide a grin. "Look at the bright side, Alex. They wanted to do the interior too, but I told them they couldn't."

Kate let go of me, trying to hide her own grin. "I told you not to cuss them out, Alex. Maybe some day you'll start listening to me."

It was actually a pretty good joke, something I would probably have done myself if given half a chance. I smiled as I looked at my car again. "I hate you guys."

My friend stopped laughing long enough to walk up and put his arm around my shoulder. "Well, we love you, Alex. An opportunity to get back at the department wiseass doesn't come along very often. Thanks!"

I knew this would be all over the department by morning and I loved it. Finally, people could talk about something other than how they thought I'd screwed up or pissed someone off. The IA sergeant tossed me my keys and I took off for the nearest car wash, garnering astonished looks from the gang bangers drying the clean cars as they popped out of the auto wash.

The car actually came out relatively clean since I stood right next to them pointing out black spots and making sure they vacuumed the side pocket in the door where Bear had located the dope. For good measure, I had them double vacuum the entire interior, the inside of the trunk, and every pocket or possible hiding place anywhere on the car. By the time we were done, the manager had come over to see what was taking so long.

I pulled out a twenty and handed it to him. "Here. They did a great job. Can you split this up among the guys?" That shut him up.

It was coming up on eight o'clock and I made a mental note of the time I finally pulled into my driveway so I could give Kate an accurate accounting of my overtime. Newton had obviously been over recently to let the dogs out because neither of them did their business when I opened the door to let them run around the yard. Newt never came out of his house, but every now and then, if I looked real hard, I could see the curtain move just a fraction of an inch.

I saw the telltale movement and walked over to his window where I found him peeking out from behind the heavy curtain. "Hi Newt! Thanks for letting the dogs out. Did you like the apple pie I left on your doorstep the other day?"

His eye crinkled at the edges. I'd known him long enough to realize he'd smiled and I imagined him saying, "Yes, I loved it! Thank you."

"I thought you would. You seem like an apple pie kind of guy." The eye disappeared, although I thought I saw him peeping through the crack in the other side of the curtains. I wondered what the inside of his house looked like. I pictured something dark and dreary with one hundred year old furniture covered with sheets and dust. Some day I wanted to make up an excuse to go in, just to satisfy my morbid curiosity. Maybe he still had the corpse of his dead mother sitting in a rocking chair in her bedroom. Now there was a cheery thought. I waved to the window, then gathered the two dogs back into the house and pulled out Roxy's card.

Late evening didn't seem like a very appropriate time to call anyone about work-related issues, but my days had been pretty full lately and I needed to follow-up on details when I thought about them. Roxy answered in her typically cheery tone. "Hi, Alex! I've got your number programmed into my phone. The little voice on my phone says 'Wolfey calling.' Whaddya think?"

"Wolfey? I'm not a Wolfey. Not even close."

"You are to me. Wolfe sounds mean and serious, and you're sweet and cute."

I took offense to that. "I *am not* sweet and cute. I'm brilliant, quick witted, tough, intense–"

"You're Winnie the Pooh with his bum sticking out of a honey hole."

"*I am not!*"

"Okay."

"I'm *not!*"

"Okay!"

I sighed. "You've only met me twice. You don't even know." My pouty kid took over. *I'm not cute! I'm tough!*

"Ah, but I've heard a lot about you from your friends, my little Wolfey. So to what do I owe the honor of a call at nine o'clock at night?"

"Stop calling me that. Anyway, I wondered if you could dig into the old foster records to see exactly who Chad Caldwell's foster parents were."

"I've already started looking, but it's difficult finding records from that far back. No computers back then, but if I turn up anything, I'll let you know. Anything else?"

It sounded like she was in a hurry to get off the phone. "What's the matter? Am I keeping you from a hot date?"

I heard laughter in her voice. "From what I hear, that's a concept you probably wouldn't understand these last few months. Been in a kind of dry spell from what folks are saying."

First Wolfey, and now this. "Hey Roxy?"

"Yes?"

"Stuff it." I couldn't help giggling as I said it and her laughter rang out loud and clear on the other end. "And get some for me too, okay?"

"Will do. See you." She disconnected. I slowly closed the phone, marveling at the gossip network that linked the police department with the fire department and both of them with the social services. We knew everything there was to know about everyone else, and if you didn't know it, there was no problem getting it. Of course, ninety percent of what you heard was wrong, but we figured that into the equation.

My mind raced through the details of my cases, organizing the next steps I needed to take to further the investigations. Luckily, as I sat in the darkness of my living room drinking a wine cooler, my overcharged brain began to slow as the wine took effect. After fifteen minutes of quiet, I took myself into my bedroom, crawled under my sheets and fell fast asleep.

CHAPTER 19

I work a four-day week, putting in ten-hour days in order to get three days off on the weekends. By the time my first day off arrives on Friday, I'm more than ready to sleep for most of the morning, so when my phone started ringing at 7:00 I turned it off, fully intending to ignore any attempted interruption of my sleep. When my doorbell rang at 7:30, I pulled my pillow over my head and ignored it too. When Megan came running into my bedroom and did a flying leap onto my bed, landing directly on my back, I rolled over on top of her, put my pillow over her face and lay my head back down in the center of it.

A hand snaked out to start counting my ribs, a trick Megan knew would absolutely incapacitate me. If the bad guys ever learned about my one Achilles' heel, I'd have to retire from the police department. I curled up in paroxysms of laughter, grabbing her hand to keep it away from my ribs. Her other hand replaced the first and I jerked sideways, pulling both of us onto the floor where we landed in a heap of bed sheets, pillows and puppy dogs. Tessa and Jynx raced around the two of us, darting in for licks or bites and then racing around the room to set up for another attack. We lay on the floor giggling, completely comfortable in the way our bodies had landed on top of each other.

When I finally caught my breath, I swiveled around and lay my head on her stomach. She stuffed a pillow behind her head and poked me in the shoulder. "So, Lazy Bones, you're too good now to answer the phone when I call?"

"It's my day off, Megs. I wanted to sleep in."

"Well, I want to do something exciting. Let's do something fun." Her stomach gurgled under my ear. The sound started on one side of her belly and rolled completely across to the other side.

"Let me guess—you're hungry and you expect me to buy you break-fast, right?" Megan ate with joyful abandon, only occasionally working her way up to gaining a few extra pounds that amounted to small love handles around her middle. When that happened, she'd drag me to the nearest health club for a month where I'd have to push and cajole her into doing enough exercise to actually lose the extra weight. This month she'd lost three pounds, God knows how, without going to the gym.

"Of course you're gonna buy me breakfast. Then we're gonna get you laid."

"Oh? And how are we gonna do that? I'm not picking up a male hooker."

"I haven't decided yet. I'm sure it'll come to me while we eat."

I nodded, sure Megan would come up with something. Arguing with her never accomplished anything, so I closed my eyes, hoping I'd be able to get back to sleep without her bothering me. She bounced her stomach muscles up and down, jiggling and giggling enough to make me get up and slide into the shower. When this manic mood hits her, I know my only option is to give in and hang on for the ride. I toweled off, and while I got dressed she took the dogs out for a romp in my back yard.

As I started out the door, I grabbed my briefcase, hoping I'd be able to do a little work on Shelley's case sometime that day. I wondered how she and Gia were getting along. The battle lines had been drawn. My money went with Gia since she'd had years to perfect her power and cunning; however, Shelley definitely had the strong, stubborn streak of the Angelino genes. Eric's pushing to have her locked up for the next twenty five years or so had me worried, and I wanted to track down those two girls who'd reported that Kindler had molested them. Eric had unfounded the cases, but I wanted to talk to them myself.

We decided to return to the little Mexican restaurant on the Southside because their food actually tasted like someone from Mexico had prepared it and also because I wanted to ask the waiter whether Mona had been back in the restaurant with anyone since Smitty'd been arrested for Kenny's murder. I hadn't spoken to Ruthanne since they'd interviewed him, so after we ordered our food, I called her to get all the details. She answered on the third ring. "Hey, Alex, what's up?"

"I was just curious to know what happened on the Kenny Finch case. Did Smitty confess?"

"Yeah. He told us everything. In fact we're out in the desert west of town looking for the place he said he buried him. By the way, everyone knows it was you and Casey who broke the case, but Caruthers is trying to steal the credit. What an idiot. Thank God neither of us works for him."

"Did Smitty say anything about the girls?"

"Yeah, he thinks Mona has them hidden away somewhere. Kate has all the details on that and I think she's working on it today.

"Did Mona know about Smitty killing Kenny?"

"They both say no, but we're working that angle too. Right now we don't have anything to hold her on. Hey, I gotta go. The cadaver dog just got here and I have to go with him. Yuck."

"Okay, talk later." I hung up and filled Megan in on what she'd said. She listened with rapt attention, always eager to hear true to life cop stories. When I finished telling her about Kenny and Smitty, I brought her up to date on what I'd come up with on Shelley's case, which pretty much added up to a big zero.

Megan tore off a piece of tortilla and folded it over some refried beans as she listened, then stuffed the whole thing in her mouth. Our young waiter stopped at our table to fill up our iced tea. "Hey, you guys came back! How you doin'?"

I raised my eyebrows at him, silently daring him to mention anything about my sex life or lack thereof. He filled my glass first, then picked up Megan's and set it on his tray. He slowly filled hers to the top and carefully set it back down in front of her again. I could tell he wanted to make a comment, but neither of us gave him the opening he needed. "Can I get you ladies anything else?" He held my gaze, apparently trying to convey manly desire and willingness.

I grabbed some packets of sweetener, and Megan kicked me under the table. I kicked her back. The waiter reluctantly left our table to service the other customers and Megan leaned across the table to hiss at me. "What's the matter with you? We're on a *mission* here! Beggars can't be choosers, you know!"

"I'm not a beggar, and he's young enough to be my son."

"Yeah, if you'd had him when you were ten years old! C'mon, Alex. You're in serious need here!"

"I woulda' been fifteen, and I am *not* in serious need! Eat your damn beans and let me choose my own sex partners, for Pete's sake. God, Megs, give me a break."

She tore off another piece of tortilla, swirling it around in the beans before scooping a pile of rice onto it and stuffing it into her mouth. When Megan had something to say, the fact that she had a mouth full of food never stopped her. "You know—"

I held up my hand. "Stop. Chew first, then swallow; then you may speak to me, not before." She chewed all right, making sure I could see every piece of rice and glob of beans in her mouth. "Megs, please. Are you ever gonna grow up?"

"I will when you do."

I didn't think that was gonna happen anytime soon so I threw some food in my mouth and chewed right back at her as our waiter watched us from across the room. Meg finally swallowed. "Anyway, what I was gonna say before I was so rudely interrupted—I think we should look up those two kids who said Kindler molested them. Maybe it'll give us a lead or something."

"Us? Where did the 'us' come from? And they aren't kids anymore. They were at Kindler's about ten years ago."

"It became 'us' when you dragged me into that ghetto and nearly got me killed, that's when. Besides, maybe it'll lead us on some adventure or something. C'mon, Alex, it'll be fun!"

Fun wasn't exactly how I pictured it, but since I needed to get those interviews out of the way I decided to play along. Our waiter brought us our check. I stopped him before he rushed away to the next table. "Hey, has that lady who plays toe-ball tag come in here with anyone lately?"

He scratched his head, thinking hard as he focused on the booth where they'd been sitting the day Megan and I came in. "Let's see... I think she's been back one time since you guys were here. I've been looking for that guy you asked me about, but he hasn't come in."

That was probably because he was six feet under a cholla cactus somewhere west of town. "Was she here with anybody?"

He nodded. "The cowboy with the limp. They came in and every-thing seemed okay. Then she started screaming at him and dumped a bowl of salsa all over his shirt. She stalked out without paying her bill, but he left a twenty on the table and limped out after her."

The two of them had argued the day we saw them too. "Do you know what they were arguing about?"

He shook his head. "Not really. Something about her girls or... I don't know. Look, I gotta get back to work."

Megan sat back in her seat. "Hmm... her girls. That's interesting. Is the department looking into Hondo as a possible suspect?"

"I'm not sure, but there's one way to find out." I pulled out my cell phone to call Kate. When she answered, I casually broached the subject. "Hey Kate, it's Alex. I was wondering, is anybody following Hondo Forbish? You know, the cowboy who walks with a limp?"

"Why? Is he cute too?"

"Oh I get it. Ha ha. That's a joke, right? You're so funny, Sarge."

Megan leaned in to whisper, "What'd she say?"

Kate asked, "Who's that with you? And why are you asking about Hondo Forbish on your day off? You're not doing anything I'm going to regret later, are you?"

I held the phone at an angle so Megan could listen in. "Of course not. Megan and I are just out for a day of fun. I was just curious about Hondo, that's all. I thought he might have something to do with the kids' disappearance."

Suspicion still colored Kate's response. "Hondo did have something to do with their disappearance. Mona told us all about it when we leaned on her about killing Kenny. She told us Hondo took the girls to his aunt's house in Benson so he and Mona could accuse Carl of kidnapping them. There's a sheriff's deputy on his way to pick them up now." I heard her shuffling some papers. "Right now, we're helping homicide look for Shelley. She's become a priority since she's considered armed and dangerous. I'd hate to see the headlines if we end up shooting her because she pulls a gun on a cop. Anyway, Alex, this is your day off. Stay away from work."

"Sure thing, Boss. See ya later." Armed and dangerous. Things had gotten out of control, and if I couldn't come up with something soon, Eric would get his wish to lock Shelley away for a very long time. I pulled out the notebook I'd brought in with me to look up the numbers for the two women who said Kindler molested them when they were in foster care. When I called, the first one, Maria Santos, said she lived fairly close to where we were having breakfast and we were welcome to stop by to visit. We drove to her house, a one-story square building set in the middle of a large dirt lot.

A small wooden porch covered about five feet in front of the door and served to block out a tiny amount of the early morning sun. The porch leaned to the left, framing the door with a lopsided rectangle that gave the home an almost cartoonish appearance. The wood needed a good sanding and a fresh coat of paint. The porch swayed dangerously as I stepped onto it, straining the one or two nails securing it to the house.

I reached up to ring the doorbell but realized a fraction of a second too late there were bare wires sticking out of the slot where the button should have been. A hammer punched into my chest as I rocked backward off the porch into Megan's arms.

She held me while I got my wits about me again. "Alex! You don't stick your finger onto bare wires! Even I know that!"

They must have crossed their wires somehow because I sure didn't think a doorbell should be able to deliver that hard of a punch. I reached into my mouth to feel my tongue. "I think I bit my tongue. Is it bleeding?" I stuck it out for her to check at the exact minute the door opened.

A young Hispanic woman stepped out onto the porch, a concerned look on her face. "Can I help you?"

I quickly pulled in my tongue, trying to convey a professional demeanor while I felt to see whether any blood had seeped onto my chin. "Ms. Santos? I'm Detective Wolfe, and this is my friend, Megan. I spoke to you on the phone about a half-hour ago." I ran my finger along my chin and lips, hoping to wipe away any evidence that I might have drooled red saliva.

She bounced a baby on her hips, studying me closely. "You don't look like a police. Neither does she."

I pulled my badge and I.D. card out of my pocket and handed them to her. Before she had a chance to check it out, the baby grabbed the wallet and stuck it in his drooly, toothless mouth. I grabbed for it, then pulled my hand back, not wanting to offend Ms. Santos by frightening the little shit. I bent down to bring my face level with his and put on my best kid persona. "Hey, Buddy, that's real leather, and I'd appreciate it if you didn't put it in your mouth, okay?"

He stared at me while he sucked on the corner. His mother tried to pry his baby hands away from it but only succeeded in making him more determined to hang on harder with his slobbery gums. She finally wrested it away from him, but not before slime covered a large portion of the leather. His eyes opened wide until they resembled two huge marbles sticking out of his eye sockets. We all waited expectantly while he gathered every ounce of indignation he could muster. I could tell this wasn't going to be pretty and when he pulled in more air than I thought could fit into his little lungs, he began a keening wail that morphed into an impressive, ear-splitting roar.

Megan jammed her fingers in her ears. "Way to go, Wolfe."

I wiped off my wallet and stuck it back in my pocket. The woman bounced the kid on her hip, shoving different toys into his face to make a stab at conciliation. He grabbed every toy she handed him and threw them at me, his fury escalating each time a rattle or a teething ring hit me.

Megan shouted at me over the din. "Give him back the wallet, Alex!"

I ducked a large set of plastic keys he'd just hurled my way. "No! It's leather and he'll ruin it! *You* give him something."

Ms. Santos retreated back into her house, apparently not impressed with the Tucson Police Department. As Megan and I walked in, she handed the baby to an older woman, who glared at me before taking the kid into another room. When Maria turned to face us again, I wondered at the hurt that passed across her features. The instant I looked into her eyes I went from being irritated at the baby to feeling sympathy for this young woman. Emotional pain is hard to disguise, and as a detective I've had to deal with too many hurting people—enough to recognize a troubled soul when I saw one. She lowered her eyes, suddenly aware that I'd seen more than she felt comfortable showing me. "How can I help you, Detective?"

I waited a beat, hoping she'd meet my eyes again. She wouldn't, so I turned on my tape recorder in my briefcase and began the interview. "Could we sit down? I'd feel more comfortable asking you questions if we were seated. And just so you know, I've turned on a tape recorder because I have a lousy memory."

She didn't move except to fold her hands in front of her, her fingers clasping and re-clasping in an agitated outlet for her emotions. I walked to the couch and sat, motioning for Megan to do the same. She came over to sit next to me, uncomfortable with this woman who refused even to look at us. I knew if I had any hope of getting her to answer my questions, we needed to be physically lower than her to give her the confidence she needed to speak.

"Ms. Santos, I'm here to ask you about—"

She whispered the name. "Kindler."

I spoke very quietly, not wanting to sound even a little threatening. "Yes. You must have heard the news accounts of what happened to him."

She nodded slightly. Her shoulders pulled inward and she ducked her chin almost down to her chest.

I didn't want to lead her into giving answers I expected to hear, so I began asking very open-ended questions. "Did you know Mr. Kindler?"

The malignant look she flashed my way answered that question. She immediately caught herself and lowered her eyes again.

"Did you live with them?"

No answer.

I felt bad dredging up something that had obviously traumatized her, but Shelley's life was at stake. I tried again. "Are you glad he's dead?"

She turned her head to look at me out of the corner of her eye. A little girl spoke where a woman had spoken before. "You left me with him. The police left me to him."

The anguish in her voice broke my heart. "What do you mean? How did we leave you?"

She began to cry quietly, raising a trembling hand to her eyes to stem the tears. She looked so alone that, without thinking, I stood up put my arm around her shoulders while I held Megan's gaze. Megan walked over to us and put her head very close to the woman's ear. "I'm so sorry. We should have protected you. The police should have protected you."

I had to strain to hear her response. "They said I lied, but I didn't lie. He touched me and he hurt me and he put—" She sobbed into my shoulder. "He put himself in me and you left me there. Why? Why did you leave me there?"

I didn't have an answer for her, and I refused to give any kind of hypocritical excuse. "I don't know, Sweetheart. I don't know, but I'm going to find out. I'm sorry we left you. I'm very, very sorry."

The baby had stopped crying in the other room. The old woman tiptoed out as though she didn't want to wake a sleeping child. She walked over to us and gathered the woman to her chest before locking her eyes on mine. "You need to leave now. Please."

Megan and I walked out of the sad little house, quietly pulling the door shut behind us. As we drove away, I glanced back at the door with the lopsided porch and didn't think it looked so comical anymore.

CHAPTER 20

Megan and I drove around quietly for a while, thinking our own private thoughts. She finally broke the silence by asking the obvious question. "How many kids do what they're told to do, report the abuse, then have nobody believe them? I can't believe they left her there after she made the report."

I sighed. "We've gotten a whole lot better at our investigations these days. We've educated teachers and parents about listening to the kids and we have laws that make it mandatory to report accusations to the police."

Her anger at the police flashed at me. "Somebody *did* call the police! The police *left* her there, Alex! *They left her!*"

I didn't want to make excuses for Eric. "Yes they did—*we* did. I pray to God I never make that kind of mistake where someone suffers because of it." I pulled into an empty parking lot and pulled out my notebook. "I want to see if we can talk to the other woman today too. You realize that just because these women tell us he molested them doesn't constitute proof in the eyes of the law. It only helps corroborate Shelley's story, although I'm not sure that's the big issue anymore. She shot at a cop after stabbing a man to death. The courts will see her as a danger to society and lock her away. Damn it."

I punched in the woman's number and waited for her to answer. A loud voice came on the line. "Nora McLennan here."

"Ms. McLennan, this is Detective Wolfe from the Tucson Police Department. I was wondering—"

I had to move my hand away from my ear as she shouted into the phone. "I know what you want. You want to talk to me because you screwed up ten years ago! Well you know what? Fuck you! You're ten years too late!"

Once again I refused to give excuses. "Yes, I am. And I apologize for what you went through, but—"

She interrupted me again. "No buts! You blew it! I'm glad he's dead and I've cheered on that little girl ever since she killed the bastard."

"The little girl is the reason I need to talk to you. She—"

"You're trying to prove she killed him in cold blood! I read the papers! I know what you're doing and I think it's disgusting!"

Her constant interruptions grated on my nerves. "Would you listen to me a minute? Yes, some detectives are trying to prove that, but I'm not. I'm trying to corroborate her story that she was molested and I hoped you could help me." I spoke rapidly, hoping I could finish my sentence before she interrupted again.

No one spoke for a second, so I pushed my advantage. "If you read the papers, then you know Detective Langstrom ran an ad asking anyone who'd been molested by Kindler to contact him. Why didn't you come forward?"

She snorted into the phone. "You just answered your own question, Detective. What happened the first time I told Langstrom that Kindler was molesting me?"

I had to concede the point. "Okay, touché. But I want to hear your side of the story. Langstrom doesn't know I'm talking to you. Please, let me come speak to you."

Her voice took on a suspicious edge. "What do you mean he doesn't know you're talking to me? You work for the same department, right?"

Oh boy, I was about to stick my head in a noose if I was reading her wrong. "Yeah, we do. But I believe Shelley, and I believe you. I'm kind of unofficially investigating what happened to Kindler. I'm making sure all the I's are dotted and the T's are crossed this time."

She didn't hesitate this time. "Fine. I'll be here another forty minutes. If you aren't here by the time I leave, too bad." She rattled off her address too quickly for me to find a pad and paper. I repeated it to Megan, who had a much better memory for things like that than I did. Ms. McLennan hung up before I'd finished rattling off the address.

Megan rooted around in the console for a pen and then grabbed my notebook off my lap. "Here, give that to me. You'll remember it wrong and we'll end up in Timbuktu." She scribbled the address while I made a u-turn to head back to Interstate 10. McLennan lived on the other side of town and I knew I'd have to break a few laws to get there before she left. Once I got on the freeway, I gunned the engine and flew past slower-moving cars, one of which, unfortunately happened to be an undercover DPS traffic cop who pulled in behind me and activated the emergency lights hidden in his grill.

"Shoot! I don't have time for this!" I pulled to the side of the road, jumped out of my Jeep and headed back to the patrol car. Not a good move, since cops generally take that as an aggressive threat and draw down on you, which is exactly what this one did. Since this was my day off, I hadn't worn my badge and gun. I slowed and raised my hands. "Whoa, I'm a cop. Sorry I scared you."

I recognized him as the officer I'd helped on the traffic stop several days ago. When his brain put together the fact that I was a cop with a face he recognized, he put his gun away, shaking his head while he did it. "Jesus, Alex, don't do that! You scared the heck out of me!"

"Sorry. Look, I have a critical witness I have to interview in the next forty minutes in Rita Ranch, and if I don't get there in time, she'll leave and my guess is I won't be able to convince her to talk to me again. That's why I was speeding."

A grin slowly spread across his face. "Hey, you helped me, now I'm gonna help you. Follow me."

"Cool!" I jumped into the Jeep and motioned for Megan to tighten her seat belt. "Hang on, Darlin'!" The patrolman pulled out into traffic, gunned his engine, left his lights on, flipped on his siren, and took off with me right on his tail. I didn't know my little Jeep could hit ninety-five, but here it was, giving me everything it had. Every loose piece of metal rattled, the chassis felt like it was going to fall apart, and Megan screamed as though she were on a ride at an amusement park.

"*Faster*, Alex! You're *losing* him! Yeeee hawwww! Floor it!" She gripped the dashboard with both hands, letting go only to pound on it as though it were a horse that needed to be whipped into action. At the Rita Road exit, we slowed enough to take the curve without flying off the bank and the patrolman pulled off to the side and rolled down his window. I pulled up next to him and shouted across Megan. "Hey, thanks! That was awesome!"

"Don't mention it. And I called ahead to a sheriff's deputy friend of mine who patrols this sector. He's watching for you and will do the same thing if he can catch you! Good luck." Both Megan and I waved as I floored the accelerator and pulled out onto Rita Rd. We passed the deputy going about eighty in a forty-five. He turned on his lights and siren, caught up and passed us, then led us to the edge of the city limits where he had to peel off. We both waved again and laughed when he chirped his siren back at us.

Megan shouted over the wind billowing around us. "This is fantastic! Just the kind of excitement I wanted when I pounced on you this morning! Woohoo!"

The area of Rita Road we'd been traveling on had nothing but desert for miles in both directions. As we began to reach civilization, I slowed to a safer speed. We jogged up to Nora's front door with fifteen minutes to spare. She opened the door before I had a chance to electrocute myself on her doorbell, although I didn't see any loose wires sticking out of this one.

She spoke just as loudly as she had on the phone. "Come on in. I'll have you know you're the first cop I've *ever* let into my private domain. I hate *all* cops. You're all worthless. Sit down over there." She pointed to a heavy kitchen table that didn't fit in with her southwestern décor. The scrollwork on the legs spoke of old world elegance while the dark mahogany top had wear marks from years of family gatherings. Megan and I pulled out two chairs that matched the table and sat.

I let the cop insult slide since I needed her to talk to me, and in reality, she had every reason to despise the organization that had left her in the hands of a child molester. "Ms. McLennan—"

"Nora. Not because I like you. Mrs. McLennan was my mother and I despised her too. I don't let anyone call me by that name."

"Why don't you change you're last name?"

"Because that gives her too much control over me. This way, *I* control what people call me, not her." She stood over us, legs wider than shoulder width apart, fists digging into her hips. "Well? I don't have all day. Ask your questions and get out."

I reached into my briefcase and pulled out my recorder. "Do you mind if I record this?"

"Yes."

I stopped with the recorder halfway out and paused a second before returning it to the case. "Okay then, no recorder." I stood up, uncomfortable with this woman towering over me. "Nora, I haven't read the transcripts from Detective Langstrom's investigation. Could you fill me in on what happened to you when you were in foster care at the Kindlers' home?"

She leaned into me, her eyes boring a hole into mine. "He raped me! People call it molest, but that's too pretty of a word. If a girl or a woman doesn't want it, it's rape, pure and simple!"

"Do you think Mrs. Kindler knew what he was doing?"

"*Knew* about it? Hell! *She videotaped it!* I told that worthless detective that, and did he even search the house? Hell no! He said with my record, a judge would know I was lying and wouldn't grant a search warrant. He probably had a point. I was in and out of detention right up until the day I turned eighteen. By then I knew what women's prisons are like, so I went straight."

I stared at her, incredulous. Of course a judge would grant a warrant for something like that. She must have misinterpreted my stunned silence because she smirked. "What? I was a juvenile delinquent so now I'm an unreliable witness? Well fuck you!"

I came out of my momentary trance, glancing over at Megan while I collected my thoughts. What kind of investigation had Eric conducted where he wouldn't get a warrant to search for solid evidence? I slowly refocused on Nora. "Nora, do you remember if Detective Langstrom recorded his interview with you?"

"Hell no! He barely spoke to me. He listened to what I had to say, called me a liar, and said I'd better not lie about Kindler again or he'd arrest me for lying to a cop. He was a real asshole."

"How old were you at the time?"

"Eleven."

"Did you ever see Kindler with any other girls?"

"No. They had a special room where they'd take us." Her eyes unfocused a second as she tried to remember something. "It wasn't exactly a room... more of a shed out back. It was connected to the house, but they'd put a bed in there and lights. I hated that room." She shook her head to clear it of the memories and spoke quietly for the first time that day. "I *hated* that room...."

I took a card out of my wallet and wrote my cell number on it before I handed it to her. "Thank you for talking to us, Nora. I know it's too little too late, but I believe you, and I'm sorry for what you had to go through."

She stared at my card a second, then reached out and took it from my hand. "Would you let me know what happens to that little girl? I mean the truth, not what I read in the papers."

"Of course I will." I held out my hand, not knowing exactly why it was so important to me that she take it. The way she recoiled spoke volumes. I lowered my hand to my side in a small gesture of defeat. As I looked at her, I pictured the eleven-year-old child she'd been when Eric had abandoned her. As I turned to go to my car, I said quietly, more to myself than to her, "I'm so sorry."

Meg and I climbed back into the Jeep, driving slower as we made our way back to my house. When Megan realized where we were headed, she grabbed the gearshift and said, "Stop the car, Alex."

I hit her hand off the gearshift since I knew she intended to jam it into park if I didn't pull over. "Shit, Megs, why can't you just ask me politely to stop like any other passenger would?"

She glowered at me. "Because I know you won't listen to what I have to say and you need to know I mean business. Now stop the damn Jeep."

I pulled into a parking space outside a business complex and threw the car into park before turning to glare at her. "There! Are you satisfied? What's up with you, anyway?"

"We need to get those tapes out of that shed."

"Ha! Not only no, *fuck* no! *We* are not going to break into a shed to get tapes and no judge in his right mind would grant a search warrant after ten years have passed since our witness claims she was molested."

She reached over and grabbed a hunk of my hair. "Listen to me carefully, Wolfe. I know you. I know you well enough to know that when I leave you'll head over to Kindler's house and break into that shed. I'm going with you. Period."

She let go of her death grip with a shove and sat back in her seat with a look I knew meant I had no hope of changing her mind. I rubbed my head where she'd just about pulled out a huge chunk of hair. "Fine, you want to get saddled with a felony, come along then. See if I care. But we're gonna eat dinner first 'cause I need it to be dark when I commit a burglary." I threw the Jeep in gear and spun out of the lot, wishing I could commit just one small infraction without everybody knowing I was going to do it before I did.

We ordered hamburgers at a fast food place and everyone who worked there spoke Spanish as their primary language. While we ate, I pulled out my cell phone and called Kate. "Hey, Sarge."

She answered suspiciously, probably wondering why I'd called her in the evening on my day off. "Alex."

"Um, can you just listen a minute and not hit the roof right away?"

The expected sigh sounded long and drawn out. "Okay, I'm listening."

I decided to leave out the fact that Megan had accompanied me again on an unofficial investigation. "I spoke to two women Eric investigated ten years ago when he was in the Child Sex Crimes Unit. There's no question in my mind he made a mistake. Kindler molested them all right."

Her one-word answer surprised me. "Shit."

She sounded so dejected I didn't know what to say. "Sarge?" When she didn't answer, I aired my frustration and asked what had been on my mind since we'd first spoken to Maria Santos. "It pisses me off that his sergeant didn't catch it at the time. Who the heck was his supervisor back then?"

She sighed again. "I was, Alex."

I blinked. "*You* were?"

"Those two cases have haunted me for the last ten years. My gut instinct told me they were telling the truth, but I was a new sergeant, and even back then Eric was considered a star detective. I trusted his judgment over mine, and those two little girls and countless others paid for my error."

"We've got to help Shelley, Sarge. We've got to do something."

"I'm afraid she's dug herself a pretty deep hole, Alex. There's not much we can do even if we do prove Kindler was trying to rape her. She shot at a cop and escaped from custody. She's pretty well cooked." I remained silent, still shocked at the fact that she'd been Eric's sergeant when he'd messed up so horribly. She must have felt she needed to say more. "Alex, why do you think I asked you to keep me up to date on what you find on Shelley's case?"

I thought back to what she'd just told me and began to put two and two together. "Because you want to make sure Eric does everything correctly this time. That's why when I asked if you knew what was happening in Shelley's case, you said you did. You were already watching the case."

"Because I knew it involved Kindler again and something just didn't feel right. Call it gut instinct, or call it twenty-five years of investigative experience, my alarm bells started ringing and they haven't stopped."

I didn't want her to know about the tapes yet so I played with the catsup on my paper wrapper a minute. "Okay, Sarge. I'll talk to you later." I closed the phone slowly, knowing that what she'd said about Shelley's case was true. Even if Megan and I did find the tapes, it would be too little too late. Besides, they couldn't be used in court since I'd obtained them illegally. "Meg, there's no need for us to break into the shed. It's not gonna help."

"We need those tapes, Alex. Kindler's wife at least needs to pay for what she's done."

"If we break in and steal them, they're not admissible in court. It's that simple."

"Fine, if you won't go with me, I'll go by myself. Take me back to your house." Megan crumpled her hamburger wrapper and threw it on the floor of the Jeep.

I stared at the steering wheel a minute, collecting my thoughts. A smile slowly spread across my face. "You're bound and determined to get me fired, aren't you?"

"And...." She held up a finger. "We're gonna share the same jail cell together."

I laughed as I pulled out of the lot and headed for Kindler's house. We parked one street down, not knowing whether Ms. Kindler still lived in the house where her husband had been killed. The sliver of the moon barely gave off enough light to see where we were stepping.

Megan whispered, "I thought you said the darkness was our friend. I can't see anything!"

"There was a full moon that night. Just step carefully and don't let anyone see you tiptoeing like that. It looks suspicious."

Megan straightened up from her hunched over granny walk, trying to convey the impression that she belonged in this alley at nine o'clock at night. When we reached Kindler's back yard I peeked over the top of the fence to scope things out. Sure enough, a shed had been erected right up close to the back sliding glass door. Unfortunately, the shed door faced the glass and there couldn't have been more than twenty feet between the two. I lowered myself back down to where Megan waited. "Okay, you wait here. I'll be back in a little while."

I slipped through the back gate, keeping to the edge of the fence while I made my way up to the shed. When I stopped to make sure no one inside the house could see me, Megan bumped into me from behind. I hissed, "Megan! I told you to stay!"

She hissed back. "No!"

I growled as I got down on my belly to crawl over the open ground to the shed. Megan got down and pulled herself right behind me. I crawled along one side, looking for a way to get in without using the front door. Nothing. I turned back and had to crawl around Megan, who apparently wasn't about to let me out of her sight. I ran my hand along the back wall, feeling for any loose panels. My fingers brushed over a screw sticking partially out of its hole. Testing its strength, I slowly turned it counterclockwise until it slipped completely free. Megan saw what I'd done so she quickly grabbed a screw next to her and turned. As she unscrewed it, she whispered, "Righty tighty, lefty loosey."

"Shhhh." I couldn't believe she didn't understand the gravity of the situation. We were committing a felony and she was reciting nursery rhythms. We managed to pull out enough screws to allow me to wiggle under the panel and scoot inside. I held the panel out while she squirmed in. "I'm caught! My shirt's caught!"

"Tear it and get in here!"

"It's an expensive shirt, Alex!"

I grabbed the offending shirttail and pulled. A ripping sound echoed throughout the shed. Megan slid the rest of the way in before she hauled off and hit me on the arm. "You're paying for that, you moron!"

"Shhhh!" We stood silently while I pulled out my Mini-Mag flashlight. The room hadn't changed much from when Nora had been there. An unmade twin bed had been pushed up against one side wall, but what really caught our attention were the floor-to-ceiling cabinets on the other side of the small room. Tiny flip latches kept the doors locked shut, although it didn't take much jimmying to open them. Thirty or forty tapes lined the shelves, all labeled and dated with the victim's name and a year.

"God, Alex, these go back to the 1960s! Look at this! Here's one from 1965!"

The ones from 1997 interested me more, and I ran my finger along the tapes looking for two particular names. "Bingo!" I pulled out the tapes and stuffed them into a bag I'd brought with me.

"What?"

"Nora and Maria. Let's go. I've seen enough." I closed all the cupboards before I pushed out the back panel so I could slide back out into the yard. I expected Megan to follow immediately but several minutes passed before she finally slid out to join me. "What took you so long?"

She shrugged. "Nothing, just looking around, that's all."

We needed to get out of there, so I didn't have time to quiz her on exactly what "just looking around" meant. We made it back to the Jeep without any mishaps. I threw the bag into the back, climbed in and gunned it toward home. When I parked in my driveway, Megan surprised me by walking straight to her car. I called after her. "Hey, where you goin'? Don't you want to see what's on the tapes?"

She scrunched up her nose. "No. Do you?"

I'd seen child pornography before, but the idea of watching yet another sick tape turned my stomach. "No. I'll let you know what I find, okay?" Tessa and Jynx greeted me as I walked into the house. "Hey guys! You need to go outside?" They didn't, which told me Newt had come over to let them out. At this rate, they were going to be more bonded to him than to me.

I reached into the bag and found not two, but three tapes nestled down in the bottom of the fabric. The first two read Nora M, 1995 and Maria S, 1996. I didn't have a clue where the third tape had come from and as I turned it over to read the name, my cell phone rang. The phone I.D. read G. Angelino. I quickly hit send while I stared at the tape.

"Hi Gia. You still mad?"

"Alex, Shelley's missing. You have to find her. I've had people out looking for her all afternoon and evening."

When I didn't answer right away, she continued. "Look, I'm sorry I became so angry with you, but you have to help me. I can't lose her, not now."

"What happened? Did she leave or did someone take her?"

"I had Gabe take Muddy back to the pound, and Shelley threw a fit and ran away. Please, Alex. I'm begging you."

I sat stunned. Gia had once told me she'd never beg for anything ever again after she'd unsuccessfully begged for her brother's life. "Gia, you don't have to beg. Of course I'll find her. That wasn't why I didn't answer you. I just put two and two together, and Shelley's in big danger if we don't find her before the police do. Look, I gotta go. I'll keep in touch."

I hit autodial and called Megan's cell phone. "Megs, how did this tape get in my bag?"

"Well, when you turned off the flashlight, I was scanning the old tapes and the name Eric L caught my eye. Is it him?"

"I don't know and I don't have time to look. Shelley's missing. I'm gonna leave this tape here. You have to come and get it and take it to Kate while I try to find Shelley."

"I'm on my way. Leave her address and phone number on the tape."

I quickly scribbled the information on a piece of scrap paper, then set the tape and the paper on the coffee table. My badge and gun were on the top shelf of my closet, and I grabbed them along with my radio before I headed out to the Jeep. I took a second to thread my belt through my holster and clip on my badge. My mind raced through all the clues I'd missed during the last few weeks: Eric falsely closing two excellent molest cases; one molest victim allegedly committing suicide and Eric investigating the case; Shelley insisting she'd never shot at Eric; Jared Scone insisting Shelley had run out the front door instead of out the back. She'd been trying to get away from Eric. My guess was, Eric had actually shot at her, not the other way around. He'd been making sure no one ever found out he'd been molested, and I was positive he was panicked someone would find the videotape of him and Kindler. In his mind, in order to keep his secret, he had to prove Kindler had never molested anyone.

I had no clue where to look for Shelley. I drove aimlessly for a while, putting together everything in my head. Right now it was all just conjecture because I had no real proof. I flipped on my radio, hoping the familiar chatter would push my brain into gear.

What I heard next shoved it into overdrive. Eric was directing SWAT to the location of a barricaded subject who'd already fired at officers and was considered armed and dangerous. I spun the Jeep one hundred and eighty degrees at a thirty-five mile an hour clip, hoping the Jeep's tendency to flip had been exaggerated by their competition.

I listened to the responding units checking in at the scene and my heart sank when Lt. Caruthers came on the radio and assumed Incident Command. I had to know for sure who the barricaded subject was. I keyed my radio. "9 David 72. Do we have an identity on the subject?"

Eric responded. "It's Shelley Greer. She shot at me again. She's completely whacked out this time!"

Lt. Caruthers came on the radio. "4 Lincoln 6 to 9 David 72. You are not needed at the scene. Code 4 your response."

He'd just ordered me not to respond to the scene. I threw the radio on the seat beside me and muttered, "Not this time, Asshole."

The scene appeared to the untrained eye to be a chaotic jumble of bodies and vehicles, when in reality all the players knew their roles and hurried to assume their assigned positions. I ran to the makeshift command post where Eric was briefing Lt. Caruthers and the SWAT Commander. They were getting ready to storm the house since Shelley hadn't answered any of their hails. I overheard Eric tell them, "She's armed and she'll shoot at your team when they enter. Make sure they all know that even though she's a kid, she won't hesitate to kill them."

When Caruthers saw me walk up, a triumphant expression flashed across his face. "Detective Wolfe, you are disobeying a direct order to stay away from this scene."

I couldn't take the time to explain myself. "You have to listen to me. It's Eric! He wants her dead! She can prove Kindler *did* molest kids. That Kindler molested *him!*"

I pointed to Eric, who laughed away my accusations. "You've finally gone over the edge, Alex."

Caruthers motioned to a SWAT officer. "Get her out of here." Caruthers then turned to the SWAT commander. "Let's get on with this."

The SWAT guy grabbed my arm in a loose grip, expecting me to go quietly. I jerked out of his grasp and grabbed Caruthers. "You *have* to listen!"

Caruthers grabbed me, intending to turn me over to the SWAT officer again. Ruthanne stood five feet away watching us. I frantically called out to her. "Ruthanne, you have to believe me!"

She stepped forward and looked at Lt. Caruthers. "She's not crazy, Lieutenant! Hear her out!" Caruthers ignored her and jerked me toward the waiting officer. Ruthanne threw her body between the

SWAT guy and me just as Caruthers released his hold. I took advantage of the momentary freedom and raced toward the house where Shelley had barricaded herself.

Eric yelled, "Cover her! Lay down cover fire!" Shots rang out. A hammer tore through my back and I watched in slow motion as a bullet exited the right side of my chest. Time slowed to a crawl, bringing a clarity of mind I'd only experienced one other time in my life. As I fell I knew without a shadow of a doubt Eric had fired the shot that hit me. When I hit the front porch, someone yelled, "Hold your fire! Hold your fire!"

Breathing became agony as I pulled myself by my left arm up to the door. "Shelley... It's Alex... I'm coming in... Please don't shoot me."

Caruthers yelled, "Wolfe, she'll kill you! Stay there! I'm sending people to come get you!"

I reached up to turn the doorknob but I couldn't reach high enough. I pulled my body up so I could lean against the door, turned the knob and fell in when the door slid open. Every movement caused a blinding pain to shoot through my chest, but I knew I had to crawl inside before they came for me. I inched my way in, then pushed the door shut with my foot. "Shelley?" I pulled in a strangled breath. "Are you here?"

I heard a whimper behind the couch that told me the brave little girl I'd met one night in a pitch-black back yard was terrified. I painfully edged over to her. "It's okay, Honey." Blood seeped from my chest, leaving a thick red streak on the floor as I pulled myself along.

She pushed a .22 pistol over to me. I expected panic, but when I could finally see her, I saw gritty determination on her tear-streaked face. She pushed the gun closer to me. "He found me when I left Gia's and he took my knife. He brought me here and left this. He said he'd kill me if I came out of the house."

Caruthers called in. "Wolfe! We're coming in after you!"

I gathered all my strength and yelled back. "I'll shoot anyone... who comes through... that door!" Black spots floated in front of my eyes, but I pulled in another breath. "Shelley's innocent... Eric's... the murderer. He wants... her dead." I pointed to the jacket Shelley had on.

"Honey." A strange wheezing came from my mouth and lungs. "Can you... stop the bleeding? Front... and back?"

Shelley slid over to me and whispered, "Anya taught me." She took off her jacket and pushed the fabric hard into my chest and into my back. The black spots appeared again and I lay down on the floor, the material bunched up under the entry wound, her little hand pressing into my chest. My cell phone rang and I motioned to it with a weak flick of my finger. Shelley opened it and held it to my ear.

Kate's blessed voice came on the line. "Alex. I'm coming in, okay?"

My voice barely rose above a whisper. "It's... Eric, Kate. Don't let him... kill her."

Kate's voice broke. "I know, Hon. I'm coming in."

"Kate." The wheezing kept me from getting enough breath. "If I die... promise me... she'll be okay." The door opened just as I heard "I promise." And everything faded to black.

CHAPTER 21

I heard a hissing sound that confused me. My mind fought to focus, to pull through a muddy reality where nothing existed. I had to know where the hissing came from. I had to protect someone but I didn't know who I had to protect. Without realizing my body had opened its eyes, I stared vacantly, unsure of where the pictures in my mind were coming from. After some time, I realized the pictures were people sleeping in reclining chairs placed haphazardly around my bed. Consciousness inched into my brain, and although my eyes were heavy, I managed to move them from Kate's sleeping form to Megan's to Casey's and last of all to Gia, who was the only other person awake in the room.

She started forward when she realized I'd regained consciousness. Tears immediately formed in her beautiful eyes and I tried to raise my hand to comfort her. She came over and gently held my head while she laid her cheek on mine. She whispered, "Cara Mia... We thought we'd lost you." She kissed my cheek, then said quietly. "Sleep, little one. We're watching over you."

I let my eyes fall closed again.

I must have slept the rest of the night because the next thing I knew, I heard Maddie's voice from somewhere on the other side of a tunnel. "Can you open your eyes, Alex?"

Several times my mind winked out, leaving me confused as to what I needed to do. Someone had told me to do something. A hand gently squeezed my arm. "Come on, Hon... open your eyes for us." *That's it. Someone wants me to open my eyes.* My eyelids refused to cooperate with my brain. I focused all my energy on that one task and heard someone say, "Look, her blood pressure's moving up!"

Is that good?

I focused again, wrestling with my body, forcing it to obey. I felt my eyelid move and someone said, "There!" I wrestled my eyes open, confused when five smiling faces loomed over me.

Gia exclaimed to the excited group, "I told you she'd awoken!"

Kate's exhausted face came into focus as she wiped a tear from her cheek. She laughed when she realized I was watching her. "Don't think this is for you, Alex. I still need to yell at you for a whole bunch of things." Her voice caught on her last words as several more tears found their way down her cheeks.

Megan sat on the bed, gently taking my hand in hers. "They told us you wouldn't make it, but we told them you would. We've only left your side the last week to shower and change." She looked over her shoulder. "Gia brought in doctors from New York. She made them give you the best room in the hospital, and she made them give us these chairs."

My lips and throat were dry, but I managed to get out. "Shelley?"

Gia answered for everyone. "She's mine now." Her brows came together, but her laughing eyes belied the stern look she tried to send me. "And so is Muddy."

I smiled sleepily and closed my eyes as everyone sank back into their chairs to wait.

As the days turned into a week my strength increased, allowing my guardian angels to take turns watching over me while the others returned to their families or went back to work. This particular morning, Kate sat with me, talking about how her husband had fallen apart without her taking care of all the household duties while she stayed at the hospital. I listened half-heartedly. No one had told me what had happened with Eric. Even Ruthanne avoided the subject when she sat with me. My mind wandered to his twin boys, who might some day play in the major leagues. Had their father's dreams for them been shattered?

Kate smiled sadly when she noticed my pensive mood. As usual she guessed exactly what was on my mind. She rose from her recliner to come sit on the side of my bed. "There's so much to tell you. We didn't want to overwhelm you immediately, but I can see you'll spend all your energy worrying about it instead of waiting patiently while you heal."

She took my hand and held it in her lap. "I'm not sure where to begin." She chuckled. "I have to tell you Megan is not especially good in an emergency. She flew up to my house in her convertible and just about drove through my front door. When she shoved the tape into my hands, she babbled on about you and Shelley and Eric while she dragged me to my television and demanded I look at the tape." She held my gaze a second. "A tape she says *she* obtained by breaking into the Kindler's shed."

I raised my eyebrows in a fair imitation of surprise.

She shook her head. "Anyway, the second the tape started, I recognized Eric, even though he was only about twelve in the film, and everything fell into place." Her eyebrows rose. "I imagine that's what happened with you... that's why you knew you had to find Shelley before Eric did, right?"

I nodded sadly and she squeezed my hand. "Like you, I heard the barricaded subject call and flew to the scene, but not in time to keep Eric from shooting you." She paused, working her jaw to keep the tears locked in. "Or himself."

I blinked. A wave of grief enveloped me, poured out of me because I didn't have the strength to hold it in. The wound on my chest re-opened as I pulled myself into Kate's shoulder, my blood staining her shirt as I grabbed her to me, needed her to hold me, to tell me everything was going to be all right. I couldn't hold in the sobs that wracked my chest, sending blinding pain throughout my body.

Her arms enfolded me as best they could, hampered by the bandages covering the wound on my back. She laid me back on the bed, holding me while I cried out my grief. I felt her tears running down my neck as she spoke quietly in my ear. "Let it all out, Alex. We'll make it through this together; I promise." Her comforting voice failed to soothe me as I began to choke on my overwhelming heartache. Soon, a familiar haze settled over my consciousness as a nurse added something to my I.V. I fell asleep in Kate's arms, the grief so sharp I never wanted to awaken again.

Kate didn't relinquish her watch when Casey came to relieve her so both of them were with me when I awoke. My chest had a new bandage on it while Kate had obviously changed into a fresh shirt. No one spoke for a while. Depression settled over all of us. Too much had happened over the last few weeks for any of us to avoid it. I had to know the rest of the story because there were so many unanswered questions floating through my mind. "Did he kill Chad Caldwell?"

Kate sighed. "We think so. Eric's phone records show Chad contacted him when the department put out the notice for anyone who'd been molested by Kindler to contact us. Eric called him back the same day Chad died. They're exhuming the body tomorrow to take another look."

Casey sat forward in her chair, resting her arms on her thighs. "Nate's pretty sure he can prove it was Eric who threw you in with Gumby and left the picture and the dope in your car."

I lay my head back on the pillow. "But why? Why did he have to destroy so many lives?"

Kate blew out a breath of air. "That's a question we'll never know the answer to."

The drugs must have weakened my control because I couldn't stop the tears from starting all over again. I thought of all the lives the Kindlers had destroyed over the years. Kate sat on the bed, holding my hand. I covered my face with my other hand while my tears turned into sobs again and Kate leaned down to hold me. "You helped end part of the destruction, Alex. You saved one little girl's life. You are so very special. Please, don't ever change who you are."

I realized Casey sat on my other side, running her hand through my hair as her tears fell onto the bed. Exhaustion overcame me and I fell asleep mourning for all the lives I hadn't been able to save.

CHAPTER 22

Three weeks later, I sat at the Rillito Racetrack in Gia's private lounge overlooking the grandstands. I still hadn't recovered my strength, but Gia felt I should get out of the house to try to shake the melancholy that had settled over me. Shelley and Muddy brought me a diet soda on a tray laden with every meat and cheese and pastry known to man. Gia and Shelley thought I'd lost too much weight in the last month between the shooting and the depression, so they'd been sending food to my house on a daily basis.

Megan reached over to take a piece of chocolate cake off the tray.

I sat on a sofa, leaning up against Gia since I still couldn't put weight on my back for any length of time.

Shelley held the tray in front of me while I decided what I wanted. She put her foot on the sofa and rested the tray on her knee. "Take some of everything, Alex. You gotta eat."

I picked up the diet soda, sighing as I set it on the end table next to me and grumbled to Gia, "I don't see why I can't have a Scotch. It's not like I'm a little kid. If I want a Scotch I should be able to have a Scotch."

Gia took a petit four off the tray. "You're still on too much medication. Here, eat this." She handed me the pastry, then picked up a plate and filled it with a little of everything. When she'd finished, Shelley set the tray on the coffee table, then got an excited look in her eye. "We've got a surprise for you!"

Over the loudspeaker, the announcer began his rundown for the sixth race.

I smiled at Shelley, who could barely contain her excitement. "What do you mean you have a surprise for me? I think you guys have done enough already."

The horses paraded past the stands and I wondered why the announcer had changed the format for this particular race. Usually he only gave the horses names, but for this race, he was giving the names of both the horses and their owners. When he came to a striking, muscular black gelding, Shelley's face lit up and she bounced up and down on her toes.

The announcer continued the introduction. "Entry number thirty-two, six-year-old Credo's Legacy, owned by S. Greer and A. Wolfe."

Megan stood up and screamed. "Alex! Oh my God! He's *yours*! You and Shelley own a racehorse!"

I sat forward, not believing my ears. Shelley and Megan stood with their noses pressed to the huge glass window that bordered the front of the lounge. I looked at Gia, who raised her glass to me in a toast. I tried to stand so I could watch the race from the window, but Gia put her hand on my shoulder to keep me down. "You'll see it all from here, Alex. You're not supposed to walk around too much, remember?"

"I can't *believe* you! How can I own a racehorse? He's gorgeous!" The starting bell sounded and Credo's Legacy took the lead right out of the starting gate. Megan and Shelley bounced from one end of the huge window to the other, screaming and cheering as Legacy pulled ahead by three lengths. He raced effortlessly, his ears forward, running for the pure pleasure of doing exactly what he'd been bred to do. He crossed the finish line a good four lengths ahead of the number two horse, and Megan and Shelley went absolutely wild.

I would have been right with them if I could, but I had to settle for celebrating there in my seat next to Gia. Gabe brought over my wheel chair, but I refused to ride in it. "Thanks Gabe, but if I'm goin' to the winner's circle, I'm goin' on my own two feet." It took about fifteen minutes for me to make my way to the winners circle, but they waited for me. Credo's Legacy was just like Gia's other horses, calm with a kind eye and an eager disposition.

Shelley and I accepted the winner's cup and posed together for the winner's photo. Gia stood off to the side, her cigar held casually next to her face. When I looked up, she caught my eye and smiled. In that moment, the black cloud that had followed me around for so long lifted, and I started to believe that maybe, just maybe, life could somehow begin to be a fun ride again.

NEWSLETTER SIGNUP!

Be one of the first to read about my latest releases by signing up for my newsletter HERE.

I put out my newsletter once a month and in it you'll find information about new releases, upcoming novels, and I even have a section where you can find free or radically discounted books. Give it a try! I'd love to see your name among my subscribers!

ABOUT THE AUTHOR

"If you don't like to read, you haven't found the right book." – J. K. Rowling

Alison, who grew up listening to her parents reading her the most wonderful books full of adventure, heroes, ducks and puppy dogs, promotes reading wherever she goes and believes literacy is the key to changing the world for the better.

In her writing, she follows Heinlein's Rules, the first rule being *You Must Write.* To that end, she writes in several genres simply because she enjoys the great variety of characters and settings her over-active fantasy life creates. There's nothing better for her then when a character looks over their shoulder, crooks a finger for her to follow and heads off on an adventure. From medieval castles to a horse farm in Virginia to the police beat in Tucson, Arizona, her characters live exciting lives and she's happy enough to follow them around and report on what she sees.

She has published nine fiction novels and one screenplay. Her first novel, The Door at the Top of the Stairs, is a psychological suspense, which she's also adapted as a screenplay. The Screenplay advanced to the Second Round of the Austin Film Festival Screenplay & Teleplay Competition, making it to the top 15% of the 6,764 entries. The screenplay also made the quarter finalist list in the Cynosure Screenwriting awards.

Alison's previous life as a cop gave her a bizarre sense of humor, a realistic look at life, and an insatiable desire to live life to the fullest. She loves all horses & hounds and some humans...

For more information:
https://alisonholtbooks.com

For More Information
www.Alisonholtbooks.com
ANHolt@Denabipublishing.com

ALSO BY ALISON NAOMI HOLT

Mystery

Credo's Hope - Alex Wolfe Mysteries Book 1

Credo's Legacy – Alex Wolfe Mysteries Book 2

Credo's Fire – Alex Wolfe Mysteries Book 3

Credo's Bones - Alex Wolfe Mysteries Book 4

Credo's Betrayal - Alex Wolfe Mysteries Book 5

Credo's Honor - Alex Wolfe Mysteries Book 6

Fantasy Fiction

The Spirit Child – The Seven Realms of Ar'rothi Bk 1

Duchess Rising – The Seven Realms of Ar'rothi Bk 2

Duchess Rampant- The Seven Realms of Ar'rothi Bk 3

Spyder's Web - The Seven Realms of Ar'rothi Bk 4

Mage of Merigor

Psychological Thriller

The Door at the Top of the Stairs

ACKNOWLEDGMENTS

Editor: Harvey Stanbrough
   http://harveystanbrough.com

Cover Art: Kat McGee
   Cover Design Creations